THE LAST GUARDIANS

Books by R.S. Veira

Turner Street: Where the Monsters in the Closet are Real

Turner Street: The Cain Seed

Turner Street: Anomalies

Dream With Me: A Dreamer's Ramblings on Life, Love, God, and Achieving the Dream

THE LAST GUARDIANS

Tales of Aela Book One

R.S. Veira

RSV Ink
An Imprint of Dream With Me Productions

The Last Guardians

RSV Ink 2nd Edition 2021

Copyright © 2018 by R.S. Veira

Published by RSV Ink
Los Angeles, California

Cover design by Laurie Wright
https://www.fiverr.com/lauria

Map design by Dylan Bocanegra
http://www.dylanbocanegra.com

Edited by Vince Font (Glass Spider Publishing)
https://www.glassspiderpublishing.com

RSV Ink books may be purchased for educational, business, or sales promotional use. For information please e-mail RSV Ink at RSVInkbooks@dwmprod.com

Dream With Me Productions Website: https://www.dwmprod.com

FIRST RSV INK PAPERBACK EDITION PUBLISHED IN 2021

Library of Congress Control Number: 2021910181

ISBN 978-1-7369742-6-1

EPUB ISBN 978-1-7369742-7-8

For the dreamers

Table of Contents

Map of Aela

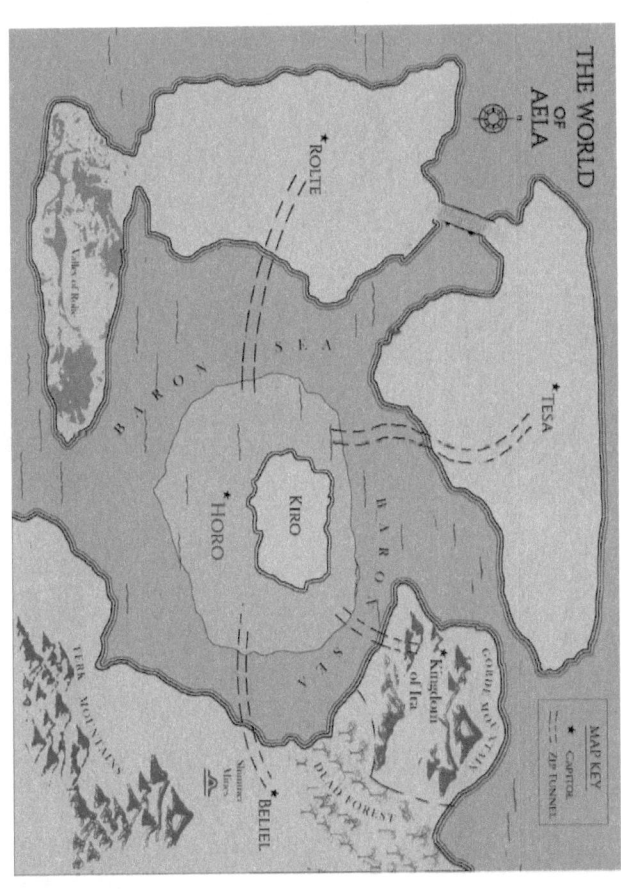

REUEL (I)

"The Guardians are dead!" the pale man gloated.

His words shattered the nightmare in which Reuel found himself like a sledgehammer against a sheet of glass. Convulsing, Reuel fell from his bed. The cold stone floor caught his flailing limbs and bare back. It was enough of a shock to assure him he was no longer dreaming. He was no longer in danger. While his mind was aware of this fact, his body had yet to catch up. The floor was sodden from his sweat. His eyes darted from side to side, and his heart thundered in his chest.

He had once again dreamt of the pale man with the dragon tattoo. The dragon's head was etched into the base of the pale man's skull, and its body snaked down the ridges of his sculpted back. The pale man, and the reoccurring nightmare in which he lived, were the only constants Reuel knew since his parents had uprooted him from their home of the past fourteen years.

Reuel held his hands tightly against his mouth so his heavy breathing wouldn't wake his parents. His room was only separated from the rest of his family's home by a thin curtain. As his breathing slowed, his mind tentatively began to replay the events of the nightmare.

He had been stumbling through a dark, dense forest with trees so tall and thick they blotted out any trace of light. Its absolute darkness was suffocating.

He stretched out his arms and used his hands as his eyes. The close proximity of the trees allowed him to use their trunks as a natural wall, and he inched along. Reuel figured moving anywhere was better than standing still in such darkness. Eventually, he caught sight of an orange beacon in the distance. He was wary of the orange glow, but after a few moments of consideration, as always, he decided to continue on.

As he drew closer to the eerie, orange glow, waves of dread and panic suddenly flooded his system. He pleaded with himself to wake, but his cries went unheeded.

His feet continued to trudge forward like moths drawn to the light. Once close enough, he saw it was a fire emitting the ambient glow. It sat in the middle of a large clearing. The fire was small, too small to be visible from where he had originally seen it on a normal night, under normal conditions, and in a normal forest. But there was nothing normal about the woods in which he stood.

He had been staggering through the Dead Forest, a place his parents had stressed, nearly begged him, to never enter. However, their warnings were unnecessary. He had no plans to ever venture there. A dark, wooded area referred to as the Dead Forest failed to arouse any sense of adventure within him.

Kneeling by the fire was the clearing's lone inhabitant, the pale man. The firelight did little to improve his ghastly appearance. The pale man's dragon tattoo now appeared to be more of a horrific scar than anything else.

Reuel's eyes were drawn to the man's hands. The pale man always held them close to his face while his head moved slightly back and forth as if eating a cob of corn.

A strange scent rose to Reuel's nostrils. He imagined it was the same odor a mouse released when cornered by a cat. His fear was pungent.

Suddenly, taking his chances in the Dead Forest was a far more appealing option than spending any more time in his presence. Yet Reuel's feet again betrayed him and carried him even closer. He stopped just behind the pale man and groaned. Lying in the

3

pale man's palms were the remains of a half-eaten heart.

Realizing he had a visitor, the pale man turned and smiled, revealing his ruddy teeth.

"The Guardians are dead!" he laughed and seized Reuel's neck, forcing him to awaken at last.

Reuel's left hand lightly massaged the base of his neck as the nightmare drifted deeper into his subconscious.

That's enough, he thought. It's only a dream, only a dream. At least that was what his father continually told him, and that was good enough. It had to be.

There was no telling what inspired this reoccurring nightmare. It very well could have been the child of Reuel's loneliness and depression. He was no closer to making an acquaintance, let alone a friend, since his family had moved to the Kingdom of Ira. His heart craved companionship beyond that of his parents. A teenager can only reasonably spend so much time solely in his parents' company before snapping. He had never been a social butterfly, but there was a fundamental difference between choosing to be a loner and being forced to be one.

He sat up, took a deep breath, and got to his feet. His hair lightly brushed against the ceiling of his room. He was only fourteen, his birthday only days ago, but he was rather tall—even for a Windwalker.

His people were famous for their height, among other things. Understandably, he was still getting used to life at this new altitude. It seemed to him as if one day he woke up and suddenly every room was smaller.

However, his recent birthday was significant for a variety of reasons other than shrinking rooms. He was finally of age, and his inherent Windwalker abilities, such as his astonishing speed, quickness, and agility were maturing. He tapped into and harnessed these gifts when he glazed, and his eyes gleamed a bright and beautiful green.

The fastest and most durable Windwalkers were classified as Elites and Premiers. They ran at speeds that caused the world around them to slow to a near halt. But, interestingly enough, the Windwalker name was derived from the lowly Auxiliaries.

The Auxiliaries lacked both the endurance of the Elite Windwalkers and the speed of the Premier Windwalkers. Yet they moved just fast enough that when they were seen using their abilities, they looked as if they were walking on air.

Reuel stretched and put on his harem pants. He ran his long fingers through his shaggy silver hair, and sorrow pricked his heart. He missed how long his hair used to be. In its prime, it hung between his shoulder blades. Back in Tesa, his birthplace and the Windwalker capital city, he had worn it in a ponytail with two gold rings at the bottom that signified his royal status, and because of that, his parents had it cut off when they moved to Ira. They justified their decision by claiming his hair would draw too much attention. Why that suddenly mattered was anyone's guess.

Ira was unlike Tesa. In Tesa, the majority of the citizens were tall, lanky Windwalkers. In Ira, Windwalkers were just one of many races that walked the streets, but they stood head and shoulders above the rest. After his growth spurt, Reuel stood taller than most of them.

Regardless of how long his hair was, there was no hiding for Reuel. Despite his parents' sudden yearning for him to blend in, he seemed cursed to stand out. He ran his hands through his hair once more then pushed aside the curtain and walked into the living room.

His eyes traveled across the room, scanning for the baskets of goods his mother had bought from the market the day before. He remembered she'd paid a young Grindbler two gold coins to carry the burdensome containers home. The boy's name escaped him, but he never forgot a face. He made a mental note to thank the boy the next time their paths crossed.

Finally, Reuel's eyes landed on four baskets that were resting by the front door. After a few long strides, he towered over them. He was delighted to find one of the baskets full of plump red apples, his favorite. He helped himself to one and walked through the curtain that separated his home from the outside world.

Hopping on the ground at Reuel's feet was a small bird, and resting a short distance behind it was a plump beetle. The bird suddenly turned around, as if seeing the beetle through Reuel's eyes. Its abrupt action caused the beetle to scurry away.

The bird gave chase and pecked feverishly at its prey. One of the bird's pecks hit its mark, and it was rewarded with one of the beetle's legs. The bird took a moment to eat its prize, but the beetle continued to crawl and managed to squeeze under a nearby rock. The bird, realizing its mistake, chirped anxiously while it tirelessly attacked the beetle's hiding place.

Reuel watched silently, thoroughly entertained by the spectacle. He admired the beetle's resilience. Even with a missing leg, it had still managed to escape. For that, it deserved to see another day.

He broke off a piece of his apple and tossed it to the bird. The bird stopped chirping and inspected the piece of fruit. Then it looked back at the rock and finally faced Reuel. For a brief moment, they locked eyes, and Reuel believed they had an understanding.

The bird fluttered on top of the apple. It took hold with its talons and flew off with the peace offering.

Reuel looked to the rock where the beetle had hidden just in time to see it scamper off. He thought about what other adventures it might get itself into later, and he allowed himself to follow this train of frivolous thought and eventually lost himself in it. He mindlessly bit into his apple and gazed out at the Kingdom of Ira.

Ira was nearly silent in these early hours, but by sunrise, this silent kingdom would give birth to a teeming metropolis. For now, the only sound was the soft hum of rushing water through the underground aqueducts. These aqueducts transported water from the lake behind the mountain down to the city's fountain.

The Kingdom of Ira was the biggest, most densely populated city on planet Aela and home to the Angelics. It had been built into the base of the Gorde Mountain, which formed a semicircle around it, protecting it on all sides. At the mouth of the kingdom was an enormous stone wall and iron gate that completed the semicircle. Initially, no such wall and gate existed, but they were erected due to the deaths and disappearances attributed to the animals residing in the Dead Forest, which stood just outside the kingdom.

Aela was home to five distinct races, four of which—Windwalkers, Grindblers, Aquatis, and Shimmers—were said to have been created by a deity known as Zuriel and were thus commonly referred to as Zurielians. The fifth race, Angelics, were said to have been the children of his brother, Gideon. Embossed on the iron gate doors of Ira were the five emblems of those five races.

On the top of the east door was the emblem of the Windwalkers, a Giant Hawk with its wings spread wide. On the top of the west door was the emblem of the Grindblers, which consisted of two crossed war hammers. On the bottom of the east door was the Aquatis' emblem. It depicted two outstretched hands with fruit in one and various other indistinguishable goods in the other. The bottom of the west door was the Shimmers' emblem, the profile of a wolf. Finally, in the middle of the two doors, half on each door, was the new Angelics emblem. It was a five-pointed star that represented the unity amongst the five races.

After the Civil War, where the Guardians quelled the Angelics uprising almost fifty years ago, the Angelics were ordered to replace their old emblem if they wished to be accepted back among the races. Their original emblem, a dragon, had come to represent oppression, tyranny, and death. The Angelics not only redesigned their emblem but went a step further and stamped the emblems of the other races on their iron gates. By doing so, Ira became the melting pot of Aela.

A long, wide road known as Darius's Way started

at the iron gates and ran through the middle of the entire kingdom. It was tradition that the road was named after the current King of Ira. It stretched from the gate to the base of the Gorde Mountain.

Ira could more accurately be described as two cities in one. Old and New Ira, respectively. Each city consisted of fifty side streets that branched off Darius's Way. The first fifty streets, one through fifty, started at the base of the mountain and ended at the king's palace, which stood in the middle of the kingdom. This was known as Old Ira.

After the Civil War, there was an influx of Zurielians moving into Old Ira, which caused the majority of the Angelics to migrate from Old Ira and into a previously deserted part of the kingdom, the land between the palace and the gate.

Before the wall and gate were constructed, the land had served as a buffer between the animals of the Dead Forest and Ira. However, with the gate's construction, the land was now safe and hospitable. The Angelics developed it for themselves, and it came to be known as New Ira. It occupied streets fifty-one to one hundred.

Old Ira was home to the largest market space in all of Aela. It was run by Elite and Premier Zurielians, and the Angelic or Zurielian Auxiliaries lucky enough to own their own stands. For the most part, Angelic and Zurielian Auxiliaries maintained the public bath-houses, lit the candles in the street light posts at night, and tended to the scrab sheds, where the public disposed of their bodily waste.

New Ira, on the other hand, produced more specialized goods and was run by the Elite and Premier Angelics. Jewelers, bakers, blacksmiths, and the like thrived there, allowing the Angelic patrons to live lavishly.

Directly in-between the two cities sat King Darius's Palace and the Ira Institute of Glazing Mastery. The Institute was a gargantuan oval building made out of rock bricks. Its dragon-skin dome roof was not only durable but removable.

The Institute shared an immaculate courtyard with the king's palace that rested a couple of yards to the east of it. The entrance of the palace was held up by beautiful marble columns. The palace's looming watchtowers dwarfed the Institute, but the palace itself was a smaller building. The walls that used to surround the palace had been torn down after the Civil War in an attempt to make the king more accessible to the newly diverse citizens of Ira. Without the walls, the watchtowers seemed naked.

At the end of Darius's Way, at the base of the Gorde Mountain, was a large set of stairs that led up to the mountain living quarters. They were mainly occupied by visitors and those who couldn't afford housing in the city. Every dozen stairs, there was a large landing that stretched a mile either way. On each landing were dozens of homes that had been carved into the mountain.

Reuel was standing on one such landing. He finished his apple and, for no particular reason, a small smile spread across his face. The nightmare that had troubled him earlier that morning had now faded from his mind.

A woman's voice came from inside. "Reuel," she called.

Reuel turned his back to the city and walked inside. To his left was his mother, looking into one of the food baskets. Her long silver hair fell over her face as she bent over.

"I'm going to need you to go to the fountain and get some water before you go to Instruction today." She stood up with a head of cabbage in her hand.

"Oh, yeah," he mumbled. "Instruction."

At the beginning of early summer, all fourteen-year-olds from every race were required to attend Instruction at the Institute. This was where they learned how to master their various abilities.

Reuel sat down at a square wooden table in the middle of the living room. His mother walked over, her light-green skin meshed beautifully with her white gown. The candle in the middle of the table reflected off the gold chain around her neck, which signified her Elite status. She sat down to Reuel's left with a bowl, which held a chunk of salted meat, a head of cabbage, and an apple.

"I'll make you breakfast before you go fetch the water," his mother said. She picked up a knife and began to chop up the items that lay before her. Her eyes started to shine a vibrant green. She was glazing.

Reuel watched as her hands danced at an astonishing pace. Her hands were green blurs as she sliced the head of cabbage, diced the meat, and then scrapped both piles into the bowl and slid it over to Reuel. The entire process took no more than a few moments.

"You're getting a little slow, Abigail," a masculine voice said playfully. "When we first met, I couldn't see your hands at all."

"Hazael, that was a long time ago," Abigail said with a shy smile. She got up, walked to her husband, and greeted him with a kiss. His long arms wrapped around her waist and held her tightly.

Reuel averted his gaze and aimlessly picked at his food with his fork. He admired that his parents cared for each other so deeply, but that didn't make it any less uncomfortable when they expressed such feelings around him. However, there was a part of him, a more mature part, that quietly hoped one day he would have what they shared.

"Son, are you ready for your first day of Instruction?" Hazael asked.

Reuel glanced up. He hadn't noticed that his father had come over to the table, but there he was, looking down at him. Reuel gave an uneasy smile and nodded. He and his father shared the same dark-green complexion, strong features, straight nose, and gentle eyes. He was a mirror image of his father's younger self.

Reuel glanced past his father in time to see his mother give Hazael a concerned look and then retire to their bedroom. His father played with his short silver beard and sat down across from him.

"Reuel, look at me," Hazael said with a gentle smile.

Reuel stared into his father's eyes and basked in the unconditional love they carried. He couldn't help but grin, and he couldn't help but idolize him. Like most sons, all he really wanted was to be like his father: kind, just, and strong.

"My son, there is no need to be worried," Hazael said.

Reuel broke eye contact and squirmed uneasily in his chair. "It's not that I'm worried, Father, it's just I don't feel like I need to go. I mean, you can teach me everything I need to know. You already trained me some in Tesa—and what if I'm an Auxiliary?" Reuel stole a glance at his father's gold chain. "I don't want to be an Auxiliary. I don't want to embarrass you and Mother."

Hazael tugged his chain. "Reuel, this doesn't make me who I am. Yes, I am an Elite, but I would be the same man if I had been classified as an Auxiliary. Your status as an Elite, Premier, or Auxiliary is simply a measurement of your abilities, not of your character. No matter what you are classified as today, you will still be my son, and your mother and I will love you regardless."

Reuel nodded and smiled. It was an answer fit for a king.

Hazael reached over and ruffled Reuel's hair. "You are greater than you give yourself credit for, my son. One day, you'll see what I see."

DANIEL (I)

Daniel could no longer deny the gravity of the situation. He had to face the fact that it was time to assemble the new generation of Guardians. He was an older man, in his seventies. His face was covered with a thick graying beard that matched his unkempt hair. His body was lean and wiry like a man many years his junior, but his eyes confirmed his age. They were those of a man who had seen far too much.

His light-teal skin gave away his Aquati heritage, and the silver chain around his neck certified his Premier status. Like all Aquatis, regardless of class, he was capable of telepathic communication and could live the entirety of his life underwater. However, what made him a Premier Aquati was his ability to heal himself of nearly all wounds and illnesses—but unlike Elite Aquatis, he was unable to heal others.

Decades ago, Daniel had constructed a personal telepathic link with each of the Guardians. When he created a personal link, it not only allowed him to talk to an individual privately but he was able to broadcast their messages to others he shared a personal link with, as a group or individually. All Daniel needed to construct such a personal link was physical contact; most times, it was a handshake. However, this personal link was not necessary when broadcasting a message to a crowd or a large group of people who were in close proximity to the Aquati broadcasting. The broadcast's scope was dependent on the strength of the Aquati. Broadcasting in this way was similar to raising one's voice.

His link with Uri, the Windwalker Guardian, had been silent for almost a year now. The only conclusion Daniel could come to was that he had been unsuccessful in stopping Abaddon and that it was time for him to prepare for the dark days ahead. Daniel had avoided such a conclusion for months, but there was no more denying it. There wasn't any more time to mourn the loss of the four individuals he had come to consider his family. Every day he continued to do nothing meant that more innocent blood would be spilled.

Under such tremendous pressure, Daniel couldn't steady his thoughts long enough to conceive a viable plan. His head throbbed, but it was almost pleasant compared to his agonizing heartache. He pined for times when his heart was not wrapped in the chains of despair and burdened by the immeasurable weight of sorrow.

In the midst of his grief, a calm voice drifted into his head and quieted his chaotic thoughts. It came in on a link that had been silent for nearly fifty years.

"Daniel, my child," the voice said.

"Zuriel?" Daniel replied. *"Where are you...we...I need you."*

"You must return to Horo and retrieve Azriel, son of Joanna," the voice answered.

"What? Joanna's youngest son?"

"Listen, Daniel. You must go and bring Azriel to the others. Without him, they have no chance."

"What about the rest of the family?" Daniel asked.

"The queen and her family will not follow you to Ira," the voice explained. *"Regardless, you must retrieve Azriel,"* the voice repeated.

"My Lord, then what?"

There was no answer. Daniel cupped his head in his hands. It was again abuzz with thoughts. The fact that Zuriel was alive was reason to rejoice, but if he felt it necessary to get involved after all this time, then the situation was far worse than Daniel had originally thought, and that sent a chill up his spine.

Daniel had long believed Zuriel to be dead. He

hadn't heard as much as a peep from him in decades.

I should have known better, he thought. *If Zuriel wanted to disappear, he is more than capable of doing so.*

Daniel sighed, and at last he began to steady himself. Zuriel had been clear on what his next move needed to be, and he could take solace in that it would be the correct one. Even though the reasons were less than ideal, Daniel couldn't resist looking forward to returning home to Horo. The Aquati capital city was an immense underwater utopia whose beauty was unrivaled. After the Civil War, he had left and settled in Beliel, the Shimmer capital.

Until just moments ago, he'd had no need to return to Horo. He had built a new life amongst the Shimmers. He had learned a lot from his dealings with them, but the trade he developed and held most dear was blacksmithing. He spent years as an apprentice to the best blacksmith in Beliel, Isle Spherelik, and absorbed as much from him as he possibly could.

When Isle passed, Daniel opened his own shop in Beliel and made a name for himself. As the years evaporated, he became the foremost blacksmith in the city, and at one time was considered the best blacksmith on Aela. He was highly sought after for his excellent craftsmanship when it came to weaponry and armor, but like all good things in Daniel's life, it came to an abrupt end. He'd closed the doors to his shop and moved miles outside of Beliel, where he built a cabin on the hillside.

Daniel dropped his hands from his face and leaned back in his chair. The chair fell against his cabin's wall, allowing him to sit at a slant. His eyes moved around his wooden abode as he took a mental inventory of everything he would need to pack. It didn't take long. Daniel lived quite modestly. Besides the chair he was sitting in, there were only two pieces of furniture in the cabin: the table that sat in front of him, and his cot in the corner. Yet there were a few very unique amenities in Daniel's cabin.

On the wall adjacent to his cot hung hammers, tongs, files, and hacksaws, all of which he used when forging. In the middle of the cabin was a large circular forge. It had smooth stone walls and a steel roof. Sitting to the right of the forge was a large anvil that he used to help shape the hot metal he withdrew.

The Guardians had built him the forge just a few years ago. It was the last time he had seen them all together. He remembered it vividly as if it had occurred yesterday. They had stopped by to pay him a visit after he'd closed his shop in Beliel and moved to the hillside. As Daniel stared at the forge, he allowed himself to be swept away by a current of memories.

"Daniel, as a token of our appreciation for everything you have done for us—" Uri said.

"And in memory of your sister," Maria interjected.

"Yes, of course," Uri continued. "We have decided to present you with a gift."

Daniel had rarely thought of Phoebe since her death. This was on purpose, of course. The thought of his sister brought nothing but pain, and seeing the Guardians caused the memories of her to come rushing back. Uri, Cyrus, Maria, and Asa stood in the middle of his cabin, smiling, unaware of how heartwrenching their presence was to him.

Uri was their leader. He was tall and slim but radiated an immense strength. His face was long and drawn, and his skin was a dark green. He wore a gold sash across his chest and black harem pants.

To Uri's left was a large, sandy-skinned man, Cyrus, the Grindbler Guardian. He had no hair on his body except for his eyebrows. Although he stood relaxed, his muscles seemed to bulge as if flexed. Cyrus's skin was renowned for its durability. He had famously worn no armor during the Civil War, and to Daniel's knowledge, very few things could pierce it or leave even the faintest scratch. He was an intimidating presence but ironically was a jolly and caring man. He wore only black harem pants, leaving his upper body completely bare. This was a popular style for men on Aela.

He had a strong nose to go along with a bald head that reflected the sun's rays coming in through the single window in the cabin.

"Yeah, I think you're really going to like it, Danny," Cyrus said with a wide grin.

Daniel shifted in his chair excitedly, shielding his eyes from Cyrus's gleaming dome.

"Well, what is it?" Daniel asked.

Uri smiled and nodded at Cyrus. "Give Cyrus some space," Uri ordered, taking a step back himself.

With that, Asa and Maria backed up to the doorway so that Cyrus was alone in the middle of the cabin. Daniel was leaning forward in his chair expectantly when a soothing voice entered his head.

"You should back up too, Daniel," the voice said. He recognized it instantly. A voice so beautiful could only belong to Maria, the Shimmer Guardian. He shot her a quick glance and nodded. She flashed him a smile, and his heart nearly burst.

He considered all of them close friends, but he had always been fonder of Maria. His love for her was nearly tangible. While he was moving his table and chair against the far wall, he stole one more glance. She was standing to the right of Uri. A long, white gown covered her body, leaving her shoulders bare, and her lengthy black hair rested on them, framing her face perfectly. She had a large, radiant smile that complemented her bright, black eyes. Her cherry-red skin only amplified her features.

Her body was covered in intricate markings and tattoos, but only those on her shoulders and arms were visible to Daniel. It was a Shimmer tradition to extravagantly mark their leaders, symbolizing their strength. As far as Daniel was concerned, she was the embodiment of grace and elegance. In terms of sheer power and ability, she was perfect.

Like the other Guardians, she had the ability to generate, control, or manipulate the element her people were said to have been born from. In her case, it was fire.

Each Guardian possessed the abilities of the Elites, Premiers, and Auxiliaries of their respected races, but their own abilities far surpassed those. Unlike other Shimmers, Maria was not confined to either the physical or invisible plane when it came to projection. She could freely move between both. Her powers were thought to be unlimited.

Numerous times during the war, Daniel witnessed her project multiple versions of herself on the physical plane without fatigue. He had watched her fight side by side with *herself*, but when it came to her abilities on the invisible plane, he had no personal experience. He had only heard stories of her influencing the actions and thoughts of others.

23

Daniel settled into his chair just in time to watch Cyrus begin his work. He stood perfectly still, his body at ease and his eyes focused on the wall directly above Daniel. But Daniel knew that he was staring far past the wall, far past everything.

In one fluid motion, Cyrus spread his legs shoulder-width apart, extended his arms to each side, and pointed his hands to the ground. He then began to glaze. His eyes shone a dull yellow. The ground at Cyrus's feet splintered and cracked. Daniel watched in awe as the ground around Cyrus sank. He could hear the earth ripping violently as it descended. At first, it dropped slowly, but steadily it gathered speed. It was descending so quickly that Daniel could faintly hear a sucking noise he assumed was the air rushing to fill the empty space.

In a matter of moments, Daniel no longer saw anything beneath Cyrus. Just a black hole. It was a perfect circle. Cyrus stood in the middle of the hole on a small dirt platform attached to the outer rim by a narrow pathway. There was nothing substantial that Daniel saw supporting the platform and pathway to prevent it from tumbling into the hole. How such a small piece of earth could support Cyrus's weight was lost on him. He was again taken aback by the astonishing feats the Guardians were capable of.

After a little while, Daniel could no longer hear the

hole being dug. The Guardian was finished. Cyrus then backtracked until he had completely crossed the narrow pathway. Once both of his feet were on solid ground, the pathway and the platform broke apart and fell into the hole. Cyrus's eyes returned to normal.

Daniel stood up and approached the hole's edge. He leaned over and cautiously peered in. There was only darkness. The light from the window allowed him to see only a couple of feet down, so he picked up a pebble and tossed it in. He listened closely to hear when it reached the bottom, but no indication ever came. Daniel looked across the hole at Cyrus, puzzled.

"Well…Thank you for the hole, Cyrus. I'll try and put it to good use," Daniel mumbled.

"Patience, Danny," Cyrus responded. "We're just warming up. Sunshine, it's your turn."

Maria stepped forward so that she was standing next to Cyrus. "Cyrus, we're not children anymore. Why do you still call me that?"

"'Cause you're the light of my world," Cyrus said with a goofy grin.

Maria rolled her eyes and sighed. "I'm not sure which is worse, your attempts at humor, or the fact that you actually find yourself amusing."

Cyrus took a few overly dramatic steps backward, wildly grasping at his heart. "Ouch…that hurt!" he exclaimed.

"Enough!" Uri boomed. Maria and Cyrus were immediately silent. "Let's finish what we came here to do."

Without another word, Maria gracefully waved her arms in front of her as if trying to catch a whiff of some delicious aroma. Her eyes glazed a dark red.

Streams of sweat raced down Daniel's face. Maria's body was generating absurd amounts of heat. It seemed logical that she would spontaneously combust at any moment, but she remained intact. She was mesmerizing, and Daniel couldn't take his eyes off her. His heartbeat steadily quickened as he watched her move so effortlessly, and he was hard-pressed to think of anything he had ever seen that was more beautiful than what lay before him.

She didn't look a single day older than when they had fought side by side over forty years ago. He, on the other hand, had aged greatly in that time. If his arithmetic was correct, the Guardians aged about ten times slower than all other Zurielians.

Daniel was only able to pry his eyes away when he noticed that there was a light coming from the hole. He looked down and instinctively leapt backward. Liquid magma was rushing up to the surface. Daniel stared blankly at Maria and shook his head. It was embarrassing that after all these years, he was still unable to fathom the power of the Guardians.

The magma stopped rising about ten feet from the surface. Maria's arms were still and stretched out in front of her as if holding the magma in place. She turned her head and nodded at Cyrus; his eyes were already glazing brightly. He clapped his hands, and Daniel heard the earth smash together but was unable to locate the origin of the sound.

Maria's eyes returned to normal, but the magma she had raised was still resting near the surface. The gears in Daniel's brain churned as he tried to piece together this puzzle. He was perplexed by the fact that although Maria was no longer glazing, the magma had not fallen back down the tunnel. Then it dawned on him: Cyrus had sealed the hole.

He made the hole a basin, Daniel thought.

Cyrus, still glazing, slowly raised his hands to the ceiling as if giving an offering to some supreme being. Daniel felt the ground shake again as smooth stone walls were erected around the basin. As his eyes returned to their natural black color, Cyrus turned his head to the door.

"If you wouldn't mind, Asa, would you bring the lid inside for me?" Cyrus asked.

"Of course," Asa broadcasted to them all telepathically.

Asa walked outside and returned a few seconds later with a large, round steel plate. Asa was of slight build and average Aquati height; his head came up to

Uri's chest. He was the Aquati Guardian and the least physically intimidating of them all. He had dark-teal skin and, like Daniel, he too had messy black hair. He wore nothing but hufflud skin shorts, which acted like a second skin.

Huffluds, a fascinating combination of a lizard and an eel, resided in the deepest parts of the Baron Sea. Due to their speed, the Aquatis often kept them as companions. The Aquatis were a modest people and believed in covering their bodies, even underwater. So they used hufflud skin. Even though it was body-hugging, it still allowed the wearer's skin to breathe, and because it was both light and durable, it was the only attire appropriate for anyone who lived in the underwater city of Horo. Seawater eventually eroded all other types of clothing.

Since Aquatis mainly resided at the bottom of the Baron Sea, they rarely communicated verbally. Such communication was quite ineffective underwater, and because of this, Aquatis regularly conversed telepathically. As a Guardian, Asa's telepathic abilities were unrivaled, dwarfing Daniel's. He was able to maintain personal telepathic links with as many people as he wished, and over vast distances; he did not require physical contact to construct these personal links. He was not only linked to all Aquatis on Aela but was also connected to the Guardians and their families simultaneously. Daniel and other Aquatis had to make physical contact to create personal links, and there were limits to how far those links could stretch before communication ceased.

Despite his diminutive stature, Asa was powerful in his own right. He had complete dominion over water and was even rumored to be able to pull it out of the very air. He approached the middle of the cabin and placed the steel lid on top of the forge, completing it.

"Well, Daniel. It is finished," Uri said.

Daniel was speechless. He stepped forward to inspect it and found no faults. He grinned from ear to ear. The immense heat the magma provided would allow him to melt and forge anything, even Absolium.

Daniel scratched his head. *But how do I keep the magma from cooling?*

As if reading Daniel's mind, Cyrus spoke up.

"Danny, you're probably going to want to make a rod of some sort to stir the magma every once in a while to make sure it doesn't solidify."

"Great idea, Cyrus. I'm thinking an Absolium rod would work perfectly. What do you think, Daniel?" Uri asked with a smirk.

"That would be great—but where would I get that much Absolium?" Daniel asked.

A chuckle escaped Cyrus's lips. "Danny, by now I

would hope that you would know we would provide it for you. Just look outside."

Daniel moved toward the only window in his cabin and stared out. His mouth dropped. Sitting roughly twenty feet from his window was a large black mound. It was Absolium, the rarest metal on Aela. It could only be found in the desolate Terk Mountains, which themselves were located in a faraway and isolated part of Aela. The location of Absolium was no mystery, but very few dared to travel there since the mountains were claimed by the dragons, and dragons proved to be a powerful deterrent. The fear of dragons was widespread since the Angelics had used them to devastating effect during the Civil War.

The dragons also did not take kindly to the harvesting of their precious resource. They protected the Absolium ferociously, as it was an integral part of their diet. Dragons tended to eat anything and everything they pleased, and because of this, they were susceptible to all kinds of dietary problems, most notably indigestion and poisoning.

In order to cure both problems, dragons consumed Absolium, which would absorb the poisons and calm their stomachs. The mineral was such a rarity that the average citizen of Aela knew very little about it besides its whereabouts. Many believed it held mystical properties, but Daniel was not one of them. According to him, the only indisputable fact about Absolium besides its location was that it was nearly indestructible once it was melted down and refined. This made it priceless when forging weapons and armor.

Although he would not say it aloud, Daniel believed that an Absolium weapon would be strong enough to pierce even Cyrus's skin. It would be more than sturdy enough to withstand the heat of the magma.

Daniel's eyes were still fixed on the Absolium. "Honestly, I don't know what to say…"

"Say nothing, my friend. After everything you and your sister did for us, this is the least we could do," Asa answered.

Two hands lightly gripped Daniel's shoulders and turned him around. It was Maria. Tears were pouring down Daniel's face. He desperately tried to avert his eyes from hers. It wasn't the tears he was ashamed of but his wrinkling skin and graying hair. Ever since he'd begun to noticeably age, he had become increasingly more insecure about their relationship. Maria, however, showed no reservations. She continued to stare at him until his eyes finally met hers.

"This is the greatest thing anyone has ever done for me. Ever." Daniel choked.

She leaned in and gave him a light kiss on the cheek. His whole body tingled. He felt as if a cloud had come down and swept him away. He was floating. After decades together, her touch still had this effect on him.

She embraced him and whispered into his ear. "I love you, Daniel, and will always, until the end of my days."

"And I you," he responded.

She pulled away. "I'm sorry I made you leave Beliel."

"It was for the best." Daniel took her hands and held them between his.

She kissed him once more and then rejoined the other Guardians by the cabin door. Daniel remained silent and still. He was still floating.

"Well, Daniel, we will leave you to your work. I'm sure you can't wait to get started," Uri said. "Let's go."

Daniel could finally feel the ground again, and he managed to utter a single "thank you" as the Guardians left his cabin.

"You're welcome, Danny, be careful," Cyrus said over his shoulder.

When Daniel regained all of his wits, he sent Uri a quick telepathic message. *"Do you need me to make any Absolium weapons for you or the others?"*

"You know we don't use weapons. But I will let you know if we need anything. I'll see you again soon," Uri responded.

Daniel's cheeks were wet with tears when he finally tore himself away from his memories. He never did see Uri again—none of them, actually, except for Maria. She continued to visit, but the visits had stopped about a year ago. Around the same time, Uri had surprised him with a request to forge Absolium weapons for the Guardians to wield, and Daniel quickly did what he was told. However, it was now clear to him that Uri had requested the weapons be forged for the new Guardians.

He packed up the weapons, a few days' worth of food, and then took one last look around his cabin before he was out the door. There was no more time to waste. He was heading home to retrieve Azriel, the new Aquati Guardian.

REUEL (II)

Reuel finished his food, put on his sandals, and prepared to leave for Instruction.

"Don't forget about the water!" Abigail called from her bedroom.

"I won't!" Reuel yelled back, though he already had.

Reuel walked out into the scorching morning-light sun, and beads of sweat instantly dotted his face. He wasn't surprised it had gotten hot so fast. It was summer in Ira, after all. The city was known for its notoriously blistering summers. There were four seasons on Aela: early summer, late summer, early winter, and late winter. Early summer had always been Reuel's favorite.

Reuel wiped the sweat from his face and headed toward the stairs. Days were divided into six parts on Aela: sunrise, morning-light, midday, high-day, evening-light, and night. During morning-light and midday, the stairs were always the busiest. Morning-

34

light had just begun, and as expected, the stairs were crowded and nearly overflowing with people.

While he waited for a chance to squeeze onto the steps, he observed the people around him beginning their daily rituals. There were women carrying empty baskets to the market, men heading to their jobs in the city, and a few children around his age who he assumed were also heading to their first day of Instruction.

Reuel finally saw a slight opening and maneuvered his way onto the stairs. Unfortunately, it was not long before his descent was halted. The stairs had become so crowded that all movement ceased. He found himself squashed between a Windwalker woman and a rather fat Shimmer man. He fought to keep his ground as the man behind him continued to push him into the woman ahead of him. His face was planted into her sweaty back, and with each breath, he inhaled nothing but damp hair.

Reuel quickly turned his head to the right in search of fresh air. He was on the edge of the stairs, and only an empty landing and a row of doorways were in his sight. He closed his eyes and inhaled deeply, savoring the feeling of fresh, unobstructed air rushing into his lungs.

He opened his eyes to see two young Shimmers, a boy and a girl, playing along the previously empty landing. Both children had cherry-red skin and were wearing white tunics that stopped just below their knees.

As Reuel paid closer attention, he realized that "children" was not the most accurate description. The girl was much older than the boy, maybe fifteen or sixteen, and a silver chain hung from her neck. The boy couldn't have been any older than seven.

The girl sprinted along the landing toward Reuel, followed closely by the boy. For no particular reason, she suddenly stopped running, turned, and stuck her tongue out at the boy, taunting him. The boy dove at her and flew right through her. He skidded on the ground until he was just a few feet from Reuel. Reuel couldn't stifle his laugher, nor could those around him.

"She's a clever one!" the woman ahead of Reuel shouted.

"I don't know about clever, but it's a cute trick," the man behind Reuel responded.

Reuel caught a glimpse of the same girl farther down the landing. She was walking out of one of the doorways maybe a hundred feet away.

Projection, Reuel thought.

The girl yelled something that Reuel couldn't quite make out to the little boy. The boy got up slowly and brushed off his knees. He gazed up at Reuel, his eyes glistening. The sight tugged at Reuel's heart, and his laughter ceased. He felt obligated to say something. His brain raced frantically to produce anything uplifting. Nothing came.

The boy wiped his eyes and mumbled, "She's not as mean as she seems." He turned around and raced back toward the girl.

After what seemed like an eternity, Reuel finally reached Darius's Way. The street was exceptionally wide; twenty people could walk it comfortably side by side. The side streets were clearly labeled. A tall pole with a wooden sign displaying the street number stood at each corner. The even-numbered streets were on the west side of the city, and the odd were on the east. Each street was lined with stoned buildings of various sizes that served as homes.

Darius's Way was booming. Citizens scurried about, trying to complete whatever tasks they had for the day. To Reuel's left and right were rows upon rows of stands. In order for anyone to get to streets behind them, they would have to pass through at least two or three rows. Horse-drawn carts rolled up and down the street, carrying goods to the stand owners. The owners unloaded their carts and mingled as they set up for the midday rush.

There were stands that sold fruits such as apples, pears, cherries, bananas, and strawberries. Most fruits were flown in from Tesa by the Tesa Air Service through the use of the Windwalkers' prized Giant Hawks. Other stands sold fresh fish and purified water that was imported from Horo. Farther down the road, Reuel could make out a few stands that were selling corn, wheat, and other grains from the Grindbler capital, Rolte.

As Reuel continued on his way toward the city fountain, a stand near 11th Street caught his eye. Why? He did not know. There was nothing spectacular about it, but the longer he stared, the more it drew him. The first thing he saw when he reached the stand was a bald young man setting up fruits for sale. His back was to him, but Reuel recognized him immediately. It was the Grindbler who had helped his mother the previous day.

Reuel cleared his throat. "Excuse me, my name is Reuel. I wanted to thank you for helping my mother yesterday."

The Grindbler turned around. He was only a year or two older than Reuel, but he had the muscles of a grown man. Reuel was easily five to six inches taller than the boy, but the Grindbler's girth made Reuel feel much smaller. The Grindbler was handsome, with caramel skin.

"No problem. You guys just moved to Ira in late winter, right?" the boy asked.

"Yeah, my dad said it was time for me to experience other places besides Tesa."

"Tesa?" the young man said with a slight grin. "You guys traveled a long way, pal. The city life is probably a little different than what you're used to, huh?"

"Whole different world," Reuel said. "But I was going to have to come here eventually for Instruction, anyway. So what's your name?"

The young man's grin widened. "I'm sorry, my name is Elon. A word of advice. The first day is the worst, you should prepare yourself."

Reuel wrinkled his brow. "What do you mean?"

"Calm down, my friend. I didn't mean to worry you. It's just that since today is the first day of sessions, all new pupils will be classified. You will be put on your life track."

Reuel stood silently while he absorbed this information.

Life track? he thought. He suddenly had the urge to reveal to Elon that he was a prince and that his life track was to be King of Tesa, but his parents had made it very clear when they moved to Ira that no one was to know that. He was supposed to be a regular citizen, just another Windwalker. Apparently, the truth would draw too much attention.

"How long have you lived here?" Reuel asked.

"About a year now. We moved here from Rolte."

39

"Rolte? That's the Grindbler capital, right?"

"Yeah. My family and I traveled a long way as well." Elon bent down, picked up a crate, and glazed. His expression was stern, and his eyes shined a dull yellow. He effortlessly pulled off the lid though it had been nailed shut. His eyes returned to normal, and he proceeded to unpack the fruit inside.

"What's it like?" Reuel prodded.

Elon stopped unpacking the fruit, and the corners of his mouth turned up a bit. "Well, innovation is really important there, so there's always some new invention around town. Everyone wants to invent the next world-changing device. There's a laboratory or factory of some sort on nearly every corner."

"Sounds incredible, you must miss it."

"I do. My parents are like yours, they wanted me to experience new places. So here I am, managing their fruit stand." He waved his hand at the assortment of fruits.

"Don't forget the cabbages." Reuel pointed at the lone pile of cabbages sitting at the edge of the stand. The boys glanced at each other and broke out into raucous laughter.

When their laughter finally died down, Reuel continued. "Well, what were you classified as?"

Elon stopped unpacking the crate and took a deep breath. "I thought it was obvious. My neck is bare. I'm an Auxiliary."

"Oh, I'm sorry…" Reuel had not even noticed Elon wasn't wearing a necklace. "But how are you working a stand? I thought only Elites and Premiers owned stands."

"Some Auxiliaries do, too—but my parents own this one, they're Elites."

"Mine are too," Reuel said meekly.

An awkward silence fell between them, and the noise of the bustling crowd only seemed to amplify it. Reuel's eyes roamed around anxiously, trying to avoid eye contact, but it was pointless, and his eyes eventually met Elon's.

Reuel couldn't understand why he was drawn to Elon. They had only formally met moments ago. Yet he wanted to share everything with him. Reuel lacked the wisdom to put what he was feeling into words. The best he could come up with was that it was fate. He and this Grindbler were meant to meet at this moment. There was a bond here, deeper than anything he had ever experienced in his young life. It was more profound than the love he had even for his parents. It was a bond of obligation, of duty, of destiny.

And then for a moment, Reuel understood why he had been drawn to *that* stand, why he had to meet Elon, but just as fast as it came, the revelation was gone. The boys finally broke eye contact.

"Hopefully, your classification goes better than

mine. You might even end up being an Elite or Premier. I mean, you could be a great warrior, leader, own a shop, join the Tesa Air Service, the possibilities are endless," Elon said.

"Or I could end up an Auxiliary like you, stacking vegetables at the stand next door. You sell the apples, and I'll sell the cabbages," Reuel responded.

Elon chuckled but was soon bent over in laughter. Reuel suffered a similar fate. Tears rolled down both boys' cheeks as they screeched with laughter, and in that laughter, their friendship was cemented.

Reuel offered to help unload the rest of the goods before he went to Instruction. His exceptional speed and dexterity made the time-consuming chore short. While they unpacked the crates, Elon explained his daily routine. Every morning, he woke up and collected the new shipment of goods from the loading docks. His great strength made it so he only had to make one trip. He would singlehandedly load as many as ten crates full of an assortment of fruits onto his family's cart and bring them back to the stand. By the time he unloaded all of the crates, it was usually the end of morning-light and almost midday, prime selling time. Reuel had caught him right around that time.

"I appreciate the help, my little brother was sick this morning," Elon said.

"You're welcome, but I have to go. You want to meet after Instruction?"

"Sure, I'll probably just be cleaning up anyway."

"Great, see you then," Reuel said over his shoulder as he walked away. He walked with a little more pep in his step, and he beamed while he replayed his inter-action with Elon. He was the first friend he had made since leaving Tesa. His parents had confined him to their mountain home since they had arrived. He had left only a handful of times to fetch water for his mother.

The water! Reuel thought anxiously.

The fountain that supplied all of Ira with drinking water was located between 14th and 15th Street, and Reuel was already crossing 18th. He had been so pre-occupied with finally making a friend that he had walked right past the fountain. He needed to be at the Institute by midday, and that time was nearing. He decided that today, his mother would have to do with-out the water. He felt a tinge of guilt, but it was quickly overwhelmed by his jubilant vibes. It was liberating to be out of his parents' sight for an extended period.

In Tesa, he had been free to do whatever he wished. He had been able to roam its vast meadows without even a hint of supervision. But since they moved, his parents had been acting differently, more on edge. He often caught his father staring alertly out at the city as if expecting something to happen. To be free of all that tension was a relief, and to be on his own for a while would be nice.

Reuel not only felt freer mentally but physically. He was no longer bumping into people with every step. Darius's Way was still crowded, but not nearly as much as before. This was most likely due to the fact he had left the market behind and was now passing 30th Street, and from here to the Institute were only residential buildings. Reuel also noticed that he was walking in the middle of a group of youngsters his own age. How this occurred, he was unsure. He assumed he had probably been walking with them since he left Elon's stand and hadn't noticed them until the traffic thinned.

All races were represented in the group. He saw Angelics, Grindblers, a single Aquati, and some Shimmers sprinkled all around. There were also a few silver-haired heads bobbing above the crowd, and he was pleased to know he was not going to be the only Windwalker. Of course, that was if they were actually all headed to the same place.

Reuel felt something tap his back, and naturally, he glanced over his shoulder. It was an Angelic girl. Once she noticed she had his attention, she picked up her pace so that they were walking side by side. This was no simple feat since Reuel took very long strides. She worked hard to keep pace.

Between heavy breaths, she spoke. "My name is Ruth. Yours?"

Before he answered, Reuel took a good look at her. His cheeks promptly caught fire. Ruth was beautiful. She had long blonde hair that reached the small of her back. Its golden sheen brought out her beautiful black eyes. Her face was round and her features soft. She had thin lips that were pressed tightly together in a vain attempt to hide her growing fatigue. She took deep breaths through her nose. Her skin was pasty like all Angelics, but her slight tan indicated she spent a majority of her time outside. Angelic skin was notorious for its inability to gain any color.

She was possibly the most beautiful girl he had ever laid eyes on. Reuel cursed himself. She was actually the second most beautiful. He firmly believed that his mother held the crown, but he quickly decided that such a comparison was unfair since his mother was a woman and Ruth was just a girl. At last, he shook the initial shock of Ruth's beauty and responded.

"Reuel," he answered.

A small grin spread across Ruth's face. "Excuse me?"

Reuel turned his head forward to regain his nerve. "Reuel."

Through his peripherals, he saw Ruth smiling from ear to ear, showcasing all of her white teeth.

"I'm sorry, I'm not sure what you're saying," Ruth said.

"My name is Reuel!" he shouted and watched in horror as everyone turned their heads and stared. A few laughed while others looked at him strangely then continued on their way.

Ruth, on the other hand, was beside herself, letting loose wave after wave of uncontrollable laughter. Reuel's cheeks burned with embarrassment. Every time he thought her laughter was dying down, she started anew. He picked up his pace to get away from this strange girl, but she followed close behind and was now jogging to keep up.

"I'm sorry, I heard you the first time," she said between gasps for air. "I could tell you were a little flustered, and I wanted to break the tension, but it went a little further than I planned." She broke out into a fresh wave of laughter and fell behind.

She again raced up beside him. "I really am sorry, though. Can you slow down a little bit?"

Reuel eased his pace and settled back into his naturally brisk walk.

"I guess it was a little funny," he chuckled as he thought of how foolish he must have looked. "So, are you heading to the Institute too?"

"Yes, I'm pretty sure we all are," Ruth answered.

A silence fell between them. "So, was there a reason you tapped my back?"

"Yes. I saw you, and I thought you were cute," Ruth said.

Her bluntness caught him completely off guard, so much so that his brain and body fell out of sync for a moment. While his brain tried desperately to comprehend exactly what was going on, his body was in complete chaos. His ears had apparently stopped receiving outside stimuli. He was only able to hear two things: himself taking obnoxiously loud breaths, and a ridiculously loud beating drum he figured was his heart. The burning sensation in his cheeks was now so intense that if he didn't know better, he would've sworn they had actually caught fire.

After what felt like an eternity, his brain and body were in sync once again. He cleared his throat, but before he could begin, Ruth was already talking.

"My twin brother is supposed to meet me at the Institute." She shrugged. "I couldn't wait for him this morning because I had to go to the jeweler before he opened for the day."

Reuel caught a glimpse of a gold bracelet wrapped around her left wrist. It was a dragon. The dragon's body wrapped around her wrist, and the clasp was its jaws biting down on its own tail.

"Looks expensive," he said.

"Yeah, it would have been, but it was a gift."

"You have very nice friends."

"My father has very nice friends," she said.

"Isn't the jeweler in New Ira?"

"Yes. Why?"

"Then why are you coming from Old Ira?"

"Good question," Ruth laughed. "After I went to the shop, I went to the fountain. I like to people-watch in the morning."

He gave her an odd stare. "Sounds…fun, I guess."

"It is. You should join me sometime."

"Maybe—"

"Look!" Ruth interrupted. "We're here."

Reuel was still staring at her and almost ran into the person in front of him. The group had come to a standstill. In front of them were a couple of hundred more of their peers. He and Ruth stood near the back of the crowd. Evidently, they had already walked twenty streets and had entered the heart of the city.

They stood in a beautiful courtyard roughly fifty feet from the Institute. The Institute was a large oval building that reached two stories high with a dome top made out of white dragon skin. A massive arch doorway draped in a red curtain stood before them. There were no other visible entrances or exits, and there were no windows anywhere on the building. The Institute sat on a landing surrounded by steps, and the mass of children waited at its base.

The sun was directly over them. Midday had arrived. The red curtain in front of the doorway slowly retracted to either side. At first, nothing happened, and Reuel could feel the anticipation building in the crowd. The entrance was cast in shadows, which made it difficult for him to make out anything. However, he could detect movement and the vague outline of three shapes approaching the doorway. Three figures ambled from the Institute and into the bright sun. They stood in a straight line and looked out at the crowd of children.

The three individuals were draped in beautifully woven navy robes. Two wore gold chains around their necks while the other wore silver. Reuel sized each of them up. The man in the middle was one of the two wearing a gold chain. He was an Elite Angelic. He had short blond hair and typically pasty skin.

To the Angelic's right was the other who wore a gold chain, an Elite Grindbler. He was large to Reuel, but by Grindbler standards, he was small. Reuel figured Elon was bigger, and he was only an Auxiliary, which went to show that size was no indicator of strength. The Elite Grindbler's vast strength came along with armor-like skin. Elon's Auxiliary-level strength and durability were intimidating to other

49

races, but laughable compared to his own.

The Grindbler was the same height as the Angelic but a bit thicker. He was also part of the select few of his race who were able to grow hair of any kind, and he was taking advantage of it. He had a full, curly black beard to go with a head of short, curly black hair, both of which complemented his dark-brown skin.

Finally, to the left of the Angelic was a woman who wore a silver chain, an elderly Premier Shimmer. She was a head shorter than the other two. She had dark-red skin and straight gray hair tied up into a neat bun. Her entire face was exposed, and the drawings on the sides of her face were visible. They started at the base of her ears then traveled down her jawline and spiraled down her neck. He assumed they continued and spread across the rest of her body.

All three of them shared the same serious expressions, their brows wrinkled and their mouths turned downward forming disapproving frowns. They scanned the crowd, expressions unchanging. Eventually, the Angelic stepped forward and addressed the crowd of youngsters.

"Welcome, children, to the Ira Institute of Glazing Mastery," he boomed. "You may refer to me as Captain Jadon, and I am the director of the Institute." The captain paused as if to let them take that in.

"Traitor!" an Angelic boy suddenly yelled. Reuel

couldn't see the boy, but the outburst had come from the front of the crowd.

"Traitor?" Reuel whispered to Ruth.

"Yeah, he was a captain during the Civil War. But near the end, he gave up Gideon's location in order to receive mercy from the Guardians," Ruth whispered back.

The captain smirked and descended the steps. He reached the front of the crowd and stood there. The children who were standing between him and the Angelic boy immediately parted and left the boy alone to his fate.

Reuel stood on his toes to get a better view. The captain bent down and spoke into the boy's ear. Reuel watched the captain's lips move and the boy quiver more and more furiously. When the captain was finished, he straightened up and walked back to the top of the steps. The boy's head fell into his hands, and his shoulders moved up and down as he sobbed. The children who had left him alone retook their original positions. Nobody comforted him. Reuel quickly took a deep breath. He hadn't realized he was holding his breath during the whole ordeal.

The captain regained his original expression of dissatisfaction and continued with his address. "Allow me to make this clear. I will not stand for insolence nor disobedience. And while you are here, you will respect me and my team. We are here for one reason, and one reason only: to prepare you for the rest of your lives. Make no mistake, today is your first day of adulthood. You can think of today as your rite of passage. For the last fourteen years of your lives, you have all been relatively identical, except for your exterior appearances, of course. Today, all that changes. For fourteen years, you all have had access to the Auxiliary-level glazing abilities of your races. Now that you are of age, your abilities have matured, and you are now able to realize your potential."

The children giggled excitedly.

"This is great news for some of you," the captain continued. "Over the next season, you will be trained to fully comprehend and control your gifts. We will help you ascend and usher you into the ranks of the Premiers and Elites on Aela. Unfortunately for some of you, this will be your last day. Auxiliaries won't require extensive training, since you have been using your abilities since childhood. Those classified as Auxiliaries will ascend, achieve your limited potential, and be on your way."

The captain then beckoned the Grindbler to his side.

"This is Micah. He will be in charge of developing the…" Before the captain could finish, he burst into a coughing fit. The Grindbler delivered a couple of firm slaps to his back. The captain cleared his throat and said nothing, but his eyes glazed a deep blue. Reuel jumped. He could now hear the captain's voice in his head.

"My voice is not what it used to be, and because of that, for the rest of the time we are together, I will address you telepathically." The captain then leaned over to Micah and whispered into his ear.

Shaken by the fact the captain was conversing in his head, Reuel looked to Ruth for answers. "You don't know much about anything, do you?" she whispered playfully.

"Well, I know a little," Reuel replied, staring at the ground.

Ruth shook her head in amazement. "Well, first off, the captain is nearly ninety years old. You try yelling at a crowd when you're that age. I'm surprised he was able to say all that clearly. After all those years of barking orders, I can understand why his voice is strained."

"Ninety!" Reuel gasped. "I didn't know you aged that slowly."

Ruth shook her head again, this time in disbelief. "We age slowly once we turn fourteen. The captain, for example, is an Elite, so he ages about five times slower than a Zurielian, while a Premier Angelic would age only three times as slow, and an Auxiliary twice as slowly. Physically, he's probably about thirty years old."

"Okay…but that doesn't explain the telepathy."

"Look at his eyes."

"Yeah, they're blue."

"He's guilty of one of the most heinous crimes committed during the war. He permanently absorbed an Aquati."

Reuel had heard of permanent absorption from one of the older Windwalkers in Tesa but was unsure of the specifics. He tried to hide his uncertainty from Ruth; it was pointless. She slapped her forehead.

"How have you manage' to survive so long?" said a new voice to his left. It was followed by a series of giggles.

A Shimmer girl stood next to him. She had a thin face, high cheekbones, and large, almond-shaped eyes. She was a little taller than Ruth and almost reached Reuel's shoulder. Her skin was a beautiful light ruby and tattoo-free. Some of her hair rested just above her eyebrows, covering her forehead, while the rest of it lightly bounced against her shoulders when she giggled.

"Excuse me," Reuel glared.

"I' sorry, but y'all conversation was much more entertainin' than what's goin' on up there," she responded, displaying her smooth Shimmerian dialect.

Shimmers were the last race to adapt to the Common Language, and they modified it to their own liking. They adopted it grudgingly, and in an act of rebellion added their own words like "y'all" and "ain't" and dropped letters as they pleased, mainly at the end of words. Reuel took pride in the fact he actually knew why she talked that way.

"That doesn't mean you can join in," Reuel answered.

"It' not my fault you' an ignorant Walker with no idea how anythin' works outside of your precious Tesa," she sneered.

"My parents said I didn't need to worry about anything beyond Tesa until I was older." Reuel turned to face her. "I learned a little on my own, but clearly not enough."

"Well, I' sorry to hear that." The Shimmer girl paused. "Let me give you this little tidbit. Permanent absorption is when an Angelic *eats* the heart of their victim. That' why the captain can speak to us telepathically. Now, I' say this slowly. Do not confuse permanent absorption with temporary absorption. Temporary absorption is still allow' nowadays. With it, Angelics can mimic your abilities for a short time by touchin' you."

Reuel nodded. "I see."

"Haven' you noticed that there ain't many Aquatis

here?" the girl continued.

He looked around and counted maybe five blue-skinned individuals in the entire crowd.

"Most Aquatis refuse to sen' their children here since Jadon is the director. He kille' one of their own, and they take that very seriously."

"I don't understand. If he permanently absorbed an Aquati, then he should be able to heal his vocal cords, shouldn't he?" Reuel asked.

"Sure, if he absorb' an Elite or Premier. But Auxiliary Aquatis can only heal others. And since no self-respectin' Aquati healer woul' heal *him*, I' assumin' he absorb' an Auxiliary," the girl responded.

Ruth reached across Reuel and extended her hand to the girl. "Finally, someone who knows something about Aela. My name is Ruth, and this is Reuel."

The Shimmer smiled. "The name is Eve Demas."

"I apologize for before," Reuel grumbled.

"It' okay, your ignorance isn't entirely your fault," Eve smirked.

The two girls giggled wildly at this and clasped their hands over their mouths to smother their laughter. Reuel again felt his cheeks begin to kindle with embarrassment. It was becoming a far too familiar feeling. Before his ego was forced to take any more hits, the captain's voice was again in his head.

"Micah and I will be in charge of training the Elites

and Premiers. Sophia will take care of the Auxiliaries."
The captain pointed to the elderly Shimmer. She raised her hand and gave a polite wave. *"Shortly, you will all march into the Institute. Micah and Sophia will lead you through classification. You will receive further instructions after."*

The captain did an about-face and disappeared into the Institute. Micah sidestepped to where the captain had just been and gave his own set of instructions.

"You will enter the Institute in a single-file line and then line up according to your race. You will then be called one by one to be classified by Sophia. Now, move!"

DANIEL (II)

Daniel had taken no more than ten steps from his front door when a large shadow fell over him. He jerked his head up, expecting the worst but was pleasantly surprised to see Gale floating down to him. The Giant Hawk glided effortlessly, swooping side to side as it approached the ground. Its red feathers shone brightly in the sun, so much so that Daniel had to shield his eyes. The bird landed in front of him, cocked its head to the side, and let out a loud shriek.

"It's nice to see you, too, Gale," Daniel said and rubbed his ears.

He wrapped his arms around Gale's neck and embraced her. She lowered her head and rested it on Daniel's shoulder.

"I'm going to miss Uri, too." Tears ran down Daniel's cheeks and pelted the bird's feathers. Daniel released her and quickly wiped his eyes.

"Zuriel must have sent you, huh?"

Gale let out another loud shriek. Daniel smiled.

"I'll take that as a yes. Well, we have a lot to do, girl. First, I need you to take me to the zip tunnel in Beliel."

Daniel attached his bag of supplies to Gale's harness and mounted the giant bird. He placed his feet in the holsters, laid flat on her back, and tapped her sides lightly with his feet. Gale spread her wings and flapped. Her wings moved slowly, but they steadily began to pick up speed. She bent her legs, pushed off the earth, and sent them into the air. They rose effortlessly, and once they had ascended a few hundred feet, Gale tucked her wings and dove toward the ground.

Daniel's eyes widened in horror and his heart nearly leapt from his chest as they raced toward certain death. Just before impact, Gale spread her wings and soared into the sky.

"Ahhhhh!" Daniel roared, smiling wide.

They sailed through the open sky, and Daniel watched as the hilly terrain faded and became farmlands, then transformed into small villages. They rocketed past the Beliel mining village, the cornerstone of Shimmer civilization, indicating they were closing in on the city. Within moments of passing the mining village, they were flying over Beliel's city limits.

Beliel was an expansive city. It covered the majority

of the countryside. There was no real order to the city's layout. Everything just seemed to radiate from the Beliel zip tunnel that lay in the middle of the city. Shops and homes intertwined, lacking any kind of organization.

Compared to the rest of Aela, Shimmers lived quite humbly. They were a tribal community. They didn't believe in luxury, and all citizens lived relatively the same. They lived in small- to medium-sized huts, and no one Shimmer lived beyond their means. Even the king and queen lived plainly. Shimmers were a tight-knit race that believed in self-sufficiency, and for countless generations, they had lived in solitude.

This changed when Maria became a Guardian and ruled over Beliel. She spearheaded the effort to bring Shimmer society out of isolation and dedicated years of her life to transitioning Shimmer civilization to the Common Language, outlawing Shimmerian, the native tongue.

Since their creation, Shimmers believed themselves to be a race of warriors, putting more stock in physical and mental fitness than technological innovations. The first Shimmers to live on Aela quickly realized that their ability to project physical copies of themselves gave them a distinct advantage. It allowed them to substantially increase their numbers and become the first race to build any kind of civilization. They were able to triple their numbers through projection on the physical plane and create a massive labor force.

They were also able to influence the thoughts of others through projection on the invisible plane. This ability helped them convince the Windwalkers, who had originally inhabited the area, that the meadows across the sea would be a better fit for them.

It was clear to early Shimmer leaders that if they could only teach themselves to fight and master their abilities, they could rule Aela by sheer numbers and force of will. Thus, a warrior race was born.

From an early age, young Shimmer minds were trained in the art of war. Male children were raised to be smart, efficient, and brutal warriors and would join the Imperial Guard after Instruction.

Female children were raised to be more than capable fighters but were specially trained to be excellent tacticians. The Shimmer women formed a group known as The Link, which controlled all Shimmer military actions. However, before the Shimmers could go on the offensive, Zuriel intervened.

As Gale came in for a landing, Daniel spotted the famous Beliel training grounds on the outskirts of the city. It was there where Shimmers spent the majority of their time honing their skills. Their abilities called for careful attention and focus.

The key to any Shimmer's training was mastering

the art of projection. Elite Shimmers had to perfect their use of the invisible plane. Their ability to influence thought made them formidable, but while projecting on that plane, their physical body was left vulnerable. It was not the best ability when in the midst of combat. Because of this, many Elites served in The Link. Interestingly enough, a disproportionate amount of these Elites were women.

Premier Shimmers focused on mastering the art of projecting on the physical plane. They could produce up to three copies of themselves, which had obvious advantages in combat—however, if a Premier's copy was killed, the Shimmer would be severely fatigued, and if all three were killed, the projector could be pushed to the brink of death. The Imperial Guard consisted mainly of Premiers.

Auxiliary Shimmers had neither of the projection abilities. They were trained to be soldiers and serve their nation in any way they could. The brightest female Auxiliaries were given a spot in The Link. The rest, along with the male Auxiliaries, were sent to the mines.

Gale landed near the Beliel zip tunnel. A small crowd of Shimmers gathered around the Giant Hawk, admiring its beauty. Beliel was littered with huts, many serving as homes while others were shops of all sorts.

From atop Gale, Daniel was able to see his old blacksmith shop, and it looked as if someone had picked up where he'd left off. Smoke billowed from the chimney, and the poignant smell of melting metal was in the air. In the distance, he saw a large box of a building that was The Link's headquarters.

From the small crowd, a man with a distinct limp stepped forward and waddled toward Daniel and Gale. He reached for Daniel's bag, causing Gale to jump back and begin screeching.

"It's okay, girl, he's a friend." Daniel patted and soothed the bird. He leapt from Gale and extended his hand to the crippled man. "How's it going, John?"

"Okay, sir. The leg still givin' me some trouble, and the mines ain't helpin', but I' alive."

"I thought you would be out of the mines by now. It's been what, ten years?" Daniel asked, taking his bag off of Gale.

"Yes, sir," John responded. "But I' doin' all my years. I have another twenty years of service before I retire."

"I'm guessing this is your season off, then?"

"Yes, sir."

Daniel threw his bag over his shoulder and looked at his old friend. John had aged considerably since their last meeting. Even though Daniel was almost ten years older, John looked as if he was his senior.

Daniel's eyes traced the deep wrinkles carved into

the man's face, the large bags that hung under his eyes, and the gray hair that had spread across his head. The last ten years had not been merciful. The mines of Beliel had that effect.

Daniel shouldered the guilt for the fate of his former assistant, warranted or not. If he had not left Beliel, John would not have joined the mining crews. Before Maria, the other races were not welcome in Beliel. Shimmers did not take kindly to strangers, but she had allowed Daniel to settle in the city. She wanted him close by, and Daniel wanted a fresh start after the war.

At first, he faced hostility from the native Shimmers, but as Daniel refined his forging abilities under the tutelage of Isle Spherelik, his reputation grew and he gained their respect. When Isle passed, Daniel was allowed to take on an assistant.

His search for a suitable assistant overlapped with the return of the children that had been sent to Instruction that year. The children arrived in carriages pulled by Northern Aelan Wolves—large muscular beasts. Serendipitously, when the carriages pulled into Beliel, they happened to stop in front of Daniel's shop just as he was coming out of the door.

He had not planned to stop—he had many things to accomplish that day—but he stood spellbound in his doorway and watched the children disembark.

It was a scrawny, awkward-looking child clumsily jumping from his carriage that caught his eye. Daniel watched the boy walk aimlessly, certain he had no idea where he was going. So he called him over.

"Ah, you, come here!" Daniel shouted, pointing at the awkward boy.

The boy turned and looked at him curiously. Daniel was the only Aquati in Beliel, after all, but after a moment's hesitation, the boy strode over.

"Sir?" the boy asked.

"What was your classification?"

"Auxiliary, sir. It' the mines for me."

"You don't have to call me sir, my name is Daniel. You seem to be a little lost?"

The boy sized him up before he answered. "No, everythin' is fine, sir. I was just tryin' to figure out what I was goin' to do before my service starts in the mornin'. No disrespect, sir, but I can see that you are a Premier." He pointed at the silver chain around Daniel's neck. "It is my duty to show you that respect."

Daniel nodded. "You should spend the time with your family. You won't see them too often once your tour begins."

"I woul', but they die' in the war."

"I'm sorry to hear that. I lost family as well." They stood silently. "Do you really want to work the mines?" Daniel asked.

The boy's mouth formed into a nasty sneer. "Of course, sir, it' my duty as an Auxiliary. It' my duty as a Shimmer and as a servant of our great Queen Maria."

Daniel nodded. He liked the kid. "What if I could offer you an opportunity to work for me instead? It will be hard work, but at least you won't be in those dark, narrow caverns."

The boy was silent as he considered the offer. He dropped his head and started to shake it side to side. He muttered the same phrase repeatedly: *"Acree Lati...Acree Lati...Acree Lati."*

Daniel was taken aback. He had never heard anyone but Maria speak authentic Shimmerian, and Maria had only spoken it to him telepathically. It had been outlawed for years. From what he knew, which was very little, *"Acree Lati"* meant "My queen."

"She's fine with it. The job is yours if you want it," Daniel said.

The boy raised his head and looked Daniel dead in his eyes. "I' at your service, sir, my name is John."

Looking at John after all these years, Daniel still admired his loyalty. John, ever dutiful, felt obligated to fulfill his time in the mines and did so after Daniel had moved away. From his years in Beliel, Daniel knew one thing for sure: the life of an Auxiliary Shimmer was not glamorous, but they were the backbone of Shimmer civilization.

For thirty years, they worked the mines, mining coal, diamonds, rubies, and other gems. The mines were home to an assortment of valuable jewels, an embarrassment of riches. However, the mines did not willingly give up their fruit. It took days to gather enough jewels to make any kind of profit, but when they did gather enough, they were traded throughout Aela, providing Beliel with a consistent stream of gold.

The Auxiliaries worked from sunrise to the dark of night. Their lives were the mines. They spent three of the four seasons working at the mining camp, and in their fourth season were allowed to return to Beliel to do as they pleased. Some gave up the dream of having a family and instead married the only thing they really knew, the mines. Yet, if asked if it was worth it, none would hesitate to answer in the affirmative. That was the depth of their loyalty. It was a testament to their wholehearted belief that the success of the nation was greater than their own individual happiness.

However, mining for such a long period of time was not particularly beneficial to the health of the Auxiliaries. Many died during their service. Cave-ins were commonplace, and it was not unheard of for miners to get lost in the labyrinth. John's leg was a causality of such a cave-in. He had been trapped for five days. By the time help had arrived, there was nothing that could be done to save the leg.

After hearing of the accident, Daniel begged Maria to do all she could to help John. However, Maria claimed that amputation was the only logical option. It was customary in these injuries. Ultimately, she couldn't deny Daniel anything, and she turned to fellow Guardian Asa, the greatest healer on Aela, for help. He, too, concluded that amputation was the only option. The injury was too old.

Upon hearing this, Daniel went to work and created an Absolium leg for his former assistant, the first of its kind. Even with only one real leg, John went back to work because he had yet to "finish his duty."

John again reached for the bag. Daniel waved his hand away. "You don't have to carry anything, John, you're not my assistant anymore."

"Sir, I' on duty until I can no longer do the job to my fullest ability. I tol' you I was your assistant almost forty years ago, and nothin' has change'."

Daniel reluctantly handed the bag over to John. He turned back to Gale and gave her a hug.

"Meet me in Ira," he said and released his grip.

Gale let out a loud screech, spread her powerful wings, and flapped until she was airborne. Within moments, she was out of sight and on her way. The crowd dispersed and went back to their usual routines. Daniel started to walk toward the zip tunnel, followed closely by John.

"Where are you goin', sir?"

"Horo. I have some business with the queen and her son. Things are going to get bad soon. I advise that you enjoy this time."

John smiled. "Sir, I' a Shimmer, we live for the bad times. I' surprise' you ain't see the queen before you left."

"Maria? I thought you knew..."

"Of course, sir, the queen has been gone for more than a year now. We have accept' that the worst has happen'. We're still in mournin'. But I was talkin' about her daughter, Candace. She has taken her rightful place. She ain't nearly as powerful as her mother but has her courage and wit."

Daniel chuckled. The last time he had laid eyes on Candace, she had been a young woman. "Candace. It's been a long time since I've seen her. She's almost fifty now."

"Then why don' you? You can stay the night and see her in the mornin'. It' the least you can do, sir. She' love to see you."

"I can't. I have to get to Horo as soon as possible. How's Eve?"

"From what I hear', she left for Instruction some time ago."

"Good, at least she is safe."

For the next few seconds, they walked in silence.

When they reached the steps of the zip tunnel, and before Daniel could take one, John grabbed his arm.

"Sir, have you tol' them?"

Daniel took a deep breath. "No."

"I know it' not my place, sir, but Candace already lost her mother and the man she *thought* was her father. She and Eve deserve to know who their real parents are."

Daniel knew there was truth in John's words. John was the only living person who knew that Candace and Eve were his daughters. It was frowned upon to mix between races. Each was to stick to their own. Even though it was difficult to tell when the deed had been done since the children were born resembling one race or the other.

Luckily, both Candace and Eve were born resembling Shimmers, and because of this were able to live in Beliel under their mother's watchful eye, but Candace was luckier than Eve. Maria gave birth to Candace shortly after the war and was able to claim Candace was her late husband's child; he had died in the war's final days and couldn't say different. Eve, on the other hand, was conceived when Maria had no husband, an issue Shimmers took very seriously.

Maria knew she wouldn't be allowed to care for Eve as her own child, not without revealing who her father was, so she left Beliel for the duration of the pregnancy under the guise of "Guardian Duties." She returned shortly after Eve was born and gave her up to an old friend, a Shimmer named Abel Demas, who knew nothing of Maria and Daniel's relationship, and who promised to raise Eve as his own.

Although Daniel kept his distance, Candace and Eve found their way to him. As fate would have it, they both had an affinity for weapons and spent a lot of time around his shop, but they knew him simply as a talented blacksmith and not their father.

Eventually, the burden of the truth was too much. Her inability to tell Candace who her real father was when he lived just down the road, and the guilt of giving up Eve, forced Maria to ask Daniel to close his shop and leave Beliel. The pain of watching his children grow from afar had already worn Daniel thin, and he was ready to leave when she asked.

"I can't, not yet."

"Sir, I can' say that I agree, but I' trust your judgment." John handed Daniel his bag. "Be safe, sir. Hopefully, the next time I see you it will be under better circumstances." John stretched out his arm.

Daniel grabbed his forearm, a typical greeting on Aela, and shook it firmly.

"Thank you, and I hope so, too." Daniel watched John limp away before he ascended the zip tunnel steps.

REUEL (III)

A Shimmer boy was the first to walk up the steps of the Institute. He was immediately followed by one of the five Aquati youth, then another Shimmer. It took a while for the line to finally reach Reuel and the girls. Reuel was in line behind one of the other five Aquati, and Eve and Ruth were in line behind him.

"Showtime," Eve said eagerly into Reuel's ear.

"I guess so," Reuel responded.

"My dad says I'm sure to be an Elite, it's in my blood," Ruth began. "So I'm thinking of following in my mother's footsteps and joining Ira's Trauma Services. There are still a lot of people who are trying to recover from the war, you know. Or maybe I could be the first woman to be named a Wisdom Keeper in Ira's Scroll Repository. Did you know it has the largest collection of scrolls in the realm?"

Reuel shook his head. "No, I didn't."

"I' gonna join The Link in Beliel after Instruction," Eve stated. "They only take Elite Shimmers, so if I' a Premier, I' just join the Imperial Guar'. I' sure to be one of those. What do you wanna be, Slim?"

"My *name* is Reuel," Reuel shot over his shoulder.

"Okay, *Reuel*, you ain't answer my question."

"An Elite, like my father." He straightened up a bit.

That, however, was not entirely accurate. Reuel did want to be an Elite like his father, but in his heart of hearts, he truly wanted to be like Uri. He had only met the Guardian once, which was more than most people. Uri had made semi-regular visits to Tesa to see his father. This wasn't strange to Reuel. He figured that since his father was the King of Tesa and Uri was the Windwalker Guardian, it only made sense that they would communicate regularly.

Reuel remembered one visit in particular. It was years before his family moved to Ira. Reuel had been walking past his father's chamber and heading to the meadow when he ran into Uri. As he passed the chamber, the doors opened and a tall, slender green man walked out. He had on harem pants held up by a wide gold band around his waist. He wore a cloth sash across his chest that was held up by his left shoulder.

Reuel froze as the Guardian approached him. Uri's presence was paralyzing.

Uri knelt down in front of him and plainly asked,

73

"Have you ever flown, little one?"

"Yes," Reuel responded promptly. "Everyone in Tesa has flown on the back of a Giant Hawk. I've flown my father's many times."

Uri chuckled. "Have you flown without a hawk?"

Reuel said nothing, but his bewildered expression said everything. Uri laughed.

"Reuel, would you like to fly?"

Reuel was stunned the Guardian knew his name. His lips groped for an answer but produced nothing. Uri again laughed.

At last, Reuel found his voice. "Yes!" he exclaimed, a bit too loud.

Uri's eyes glazed, and Reuel felt the air start to pick up speed around him. Before he knew what was happening, he was off the ground. Uri smiled widely as he waved his right hand back and forth, and Reuel's body followed suit.

Reuel floated gracefully through the air and then returned safely to the ground. He was momentarily stunned by the experience. The freedom was unexplainable. For those few seconds, no rules or restrictions had applied to him. Even nature's fundamental law of gravity was powerless.

Reuel stared at his feet as he rocked back and forth. He stumbled a little bit as he got used to the feeling of solid ground again. He now saw his feet as lead blocks weighing him down, unwilling to let him soar. Reuel looked up at Uri. He caught him staring back lovingly.

Uri quickly shifted his gaze. He stood up, ruffled Reuel's hair, and walked out of the palace without saying anything more. Reuel remembered standing like a statue for a while before he was able to finally dislodge himself.

He knew he could never be a Guardian—there had only been four in the history of Aela—but he still allowed himself to dream.

"Reuel. Reuel! Are you just going to stand there?" Ruth asked.

Reuel snapped back and heard the kids behind him complaining.

"I don't understand how you people can be so fast and walk so slow!" someone shouted behind him.

"Sorry," Reuel mumbled.

"Yeah, we' been standin' here for two days waitin' for you to move," Eve added.

The Aquati ahead of him was already at the top of the stairs, Reuel took two long steps and closed the gap.

"No gaps in the line!" Micah shouted, staring directly at Reuel.

"It won't happen again, sir," Reuel said.

"I know it won't."

The line funneled through the entrance of the

Institute and into an enormous room. It was so massive that even with the four to five hundred pupils spread out in five separate lines, there was still more than enough room for a couple hundred more. The room was made up of four walls that formed a large rectangle, with a doorway in the middle of each wall and two in the wall straight ahead of them. Six statues stood against that same wall. Reuel recognized four of the statues as the Guardians.

The statue to the far left he did not recognize, but he assumed it was an Angelic since all the Angelic children had lined up in front of it. The next statue was Uri, then Cyrus, then a second statue that Reuel did not recognize. Then there was a gap, much bigger than the ones between the other statues—as if a statue was missing. The next statue after the abnormal gap was Maria, and the last one was Asa.

One of the two doorways was between the statues of the unknown Angelic and Uri. The other doorway was between Maria and Asa. The room had an unusually high ceiling to accommodate the larger-than-life statues, and from it hung candle lamps that showered light down on the pupils. The majority of the light in the room, however, came from the torches that littered the walls. The marble floor gleamed in the firelight.

Reuel, Ruth, and Eve were now with their respective races. Reuel had settled in near the back of the

Windwalker line. He guessed that there were around fifty or sixty others ahead of him, and another thirty behind him. The Aquati line was by far the smallest, and Reuel saw that there were actually ten of them instead of five. The Angelics outnumbered them all, with about a hundred and fifty pupils. Reuel estimated that the Grindblers were the second largest, with around a hundred. The Windwalkers and Shimmers had about eighty each.

Sophia stood in front of them all with her hands crossed behind her back, Micah stood several feet behind her.

"This room is known as Assembly Hall!" she proclaimed. "Most likely, many of you have been here before. This is where patrons receive their tickets for the annual Ascension Ceremony in late summer. The ceremony is also where the Elites and Premiers among you will receive your gold and silver chains, respectively, signifying that you have ascended."

Reuel noticed that Sophia didn't speak using Shimmerian dialect, but she had fully acclimated to the Common Language.

Sophia then pointed at the statues behind her. "These statues are of the original members of the High Council, known by most of you simply as the Guardians. To the far left is the Angelic Nahor Rukist, who was actually an Elite and the only one not a

Guardian or Creator. He was the first King of Ira after the Civil War. For his pivotal role in the war, this was his reward—"

Sophia was interrupted by cheering from the Angelic line.

She smiled and raised her hands. The cheering ceased. "Next in line is Uri the Wise, the Windwalker Guardian!" she roared.

The Windwalkers shouted and clapped in response. Reuel clapped excitedly.

"Then Cyrus the Courageous, the Grindbler Guardian!" Sophia yelled, and the Grindblers screamed gleefully. "Followed by Zuriel, who is said to have created Windwalkers, Grindblers, Shimmers, and Aquatis!"

The four races applauded.

"His brother, Gideon, whose statue used to stand right next to Zuriel's, is said to have created the Angelics."

The room was silent except for a few claps from the Angelic line.

"Zuriel and Gideon were the first statues built and were the only ones in the hall until after the war. For obvious reasons, Gideon's statue has been torn down. The final two are of Maria the Fierce, the Shimmer Guardian!"

The Shimmers erupted.

"And Asa the Patient, the Aquati Guardian!"

The ten Aquatis clapped politely.

"It is tradition that before classification, I share the story of Aela's Creators."

Reuel smiled. He loved this story, at least the version his mother told him. It had been one of his favorites as a child.

"Legend has it," Sophia began, "that in the beginning, there were two brothers of unparalleled power: Zuriel and Gideon. They existed alone in the emptiness of eternity. To occupy their time, they crafted brilliant gaseous and rocky bodies that became the stars, planets, and galaxies. However, the two brothers soon grew weary of their desolate planets and lonely stars, and in their boredom, they sought to create life. Each brother ventured to his own part of the universe and labored to create beings in his own image.

"The brothers soon realized that creating life was far more complex than the planets and stars. After innumerable failed attempts, they reunited and together began working on a planet like no other. They called her Aela. Despite their combined effort, their new creations mirrored their failed attempts and were nothing more than mindless drones.

"The brothers were devastated, but all was not lost. Zuriel was struck with an epiphany. He offered that they forgo their immorality and gift part of their souls to their creations. Gideon agreed, and the people of Aela truly came to life. The brothers were pleased, but only for a short time. They loved their creations so completely that they could not stand to be out of their presence. So they abandoned their life amongst the stars and made Aela their home."

The room erupted in applause at the conclusion of her story. Reuel frowned. His mother had never mentioned the stars or the part about life on other planets. She only talked of how Zuriel and Gideon together created Aela. He knew little of the stars and planets anyway; he was no Angelic astrologist. Regardless, he enjoyed Sophia's take on the story.

"I will now classify each one of you one at a time," Sophia said. "Starting with the Angelics and ending with the Aquati. After your classification, I will send you through one of the two doorways behind me." She paused for a moment, then yelled, "Snaretooth!"

Reuel heard rumbling coming from one of the doorways—he wasn't sure which. As the noise drew closer, an eerie scraping sound became apparent. His mind went wild contemplating what would come through the door.

A very unsettling image entered his head. He envisioned the pale man from his nightmares walking toward the doorway, dragging a bloodied body behind him. The body was that of his father, and the pale man was coming to claim him next.

Reuel's heart jumped into his throat. His hands moistened with sweat, and his head was becoming increasingly lighter. The noise was very close, and whatever was creating it was about to come into view. A deathly silence fell over the pupils as they anxiously waited to see what was coming.

"Please, not him, please, not him," Reuel whispered.

The first thing to emerge from the darkness of the doorway—between Nahor and Uri—was a large paw connected to a great, muscular leg. A wolf walked into the room, dragging a cart carrying two large scrolls.

The Shimmers broke out into a chorus of excited chatter at the sight. The reactions from the rest of the children were mixed. Some talked in hushed whispers. as if in reverence. Others, like Reuel, stood speechless in complete awe of the animal.

The wolf was jet black with one long white streak across its back. As it strolled across the room, its long, bushy tail swung from side to side. It stopped beside Sophia; it was slightly taller than her. It bent its head down and rubbed it against Sophia's shoulder. It then rested at her feet.

The wolf glanced around and then opened its mouth to let out a long yawn, putting its two rows of incredibly sharp teeth on full display. Its tongue hung from its mouth while it panted. Sophia patted its head affectionately.

"Allow me to introduce, Snaretooth," Sophia said. "He is a North Aelan Wolf, one of the few that are still living today. As the Shimmers in attendance know, they are faithful companions to our people. For those of you who do not know, the North Aelan Wolf is said to be one of the first species of animals to inhabit Aela, along with the Giant Hawks of Tesa."

Reuel was vaguely listening to Sophia. His attention had not left the wolf since it had entered the room. Snaretooth, on the other hand, didn't seem at all interested in the children. He barely acknowledged their presence. His head rested on his outstretched paws as he stared off into the distance.

A wave of anger washed over Reuel. His lack of worldly knowledge was starting to bother him greatly. The wolf was just another example of the mysteries and wonders of Aela that he knew nothing about. He couldn't help but wonder what else was out there besides Ira and Tesa. What else was there that his parents had neglected to tell him?

Sophia walked to the back of the cart, which held two large scrolls, and spoke as she walked. "Written on these scrolls are the names of all the children age fourteen on Aela. The yearly census gives us the names of potential pupils. *Most* of the names on these scrolls are standing here in the room."

She glanced at the Aquati line. Then she grabbed one of the scrolls from the cart and handed it to Micah. He took the scroll and pulled out what looked like a yellow bird feather from his waistband.

Reuel immediately recognized it as a lobit feather. He had harvested multiple lobit feathers himself back in Tesa. Lobits were small, colorful birds that inhabited all parts of Aela. They were fat, flightless birds that struggled to catch their prey, and to combat this, nature had endowed them with a black, sticky liquid they fired from their mouths. Upon contact, the liquid caused instant paralysis that could last up to three hours. When a lobit hunted, it would stalk its victim, spray it, and drag the animal back to its nest to feast. The fluid did not cause paralysis in people; it only stung momentarily.

As the story of the lobit feather went, a Windwalker man had once hunted and killed a lobit and planned to eat it for dinner. But before the man pruned it, he decided to hang it upside down while he prepared the rest of the meal.

After the man finished his preparations, he began to prune the bird, and as he removed the feathers, he threw them onto his table. After a while, he noticed that his table was covered in the bird's sticky black fluid. He wasn't sure where it had come from, but it soon occurred to him that since the bird had been hanging upside down, the fluid had seeped through the body and into the bird's feathers. When the tip of the feather was pressed down onto the surface of his table, it released the fluid.

The application of this was immediately apparent to the man, and the lobit feather soon became the fundamental writing instrument on Aela. Reuel stood up a little straighter after remembering the story—he did know something.

Sophia ambled from behind the cart, stopped in front of Snaretooth, and motioned for the Angelic boy in the front of his line to come forward.

"I will start with the Angelics. This is a simple process. The first person in line will walk to me and state their name, and Micah will cross it off the list. I will then classify you and direct you to one of the doors. That's it."

The Angelic boy slowly shuffled forward until he reached Sophia. Reuel was pretty sure it was the same boy the captain had addressed earlier. The boy stood in front of Sophia. All eyes in the room were glued to him. He was trembling slightly.

"What's your name?" she asked gently. The boy opened his mouth to answer, but nothing came out. "It's alright. There is no reason to be afraid."

The boy took a couple of rushed breaths and blurted out "Isaac Lunkin!" The room erupted in laughter.

"Got it," Micah said.

"Quiet!" Sophia shouted. "Now, relax, Isaac." Her eyes started glazing a vibrant red. She reached out and grabbed both of Isaac's shoulders. His head fell backward, his eyes shining bright silver.

Isaac's whole body looked as if it had gone completely limp, and the only thing that seemed to be holding him up was Sophia's hands on his shoulders. Reuel watched in stunned silence, his mind working hard to keep up. He knew Sophia was glazing, but was Isaac glazing too?

A few moments passed before Sophia's eyes returned to their normal black color, and so did Isaac's. His head came forward and he stood up straight, looking Sophia directly in the eye.

"Premier!" she shouted. "First door on the left Isaac." Isaac turned around and faced the rest of the children, grinning from ear to ear. He practically skipped to the door. Micah scribbled and waited.

The next person in the Angelic line came forward. It was a girl. She stated that her name was "Bethany Potsin." The same process occurred, and Sophia shouted "Auxiliary" at the end. Then she said, "Go through the second door, sweetie."

This process continued for a while, and the Angelic line steadily withered away. Sophia had announced multiple Premiers and even more Auxiliaries. The first Elite came near the end of the Angelic line. A tall, blond boy confidently strolled toward Sophia. He walked as if the world was owed to him. His blond hair lightly bounced as he strolled. He was a handsome young man with a strong jaw and round black eyes. He had a familiar look to him. He stood in front of Sophia, completely relaxed, confidence radiating from him.

"Asher Rukist," he said proudly.

Once again, the room was alive with chatter. Reuel looked at what was left of the Angelic line to see Ruth beaming, and Reuel knew why the boy looked familiar. He was Ruth's twin.

"What's the big deal?" Reuel asked aloud.

The boy in front of him turned around and stared at him as if he had two heads. Reuel had now become accustomed to these looks.

"You don't have to look at me like that," Reuel snapped. "You can just answer my question."

"Rukist doesn't sound familiar to you? Darius Rukist, the King of Ira, that's his son," the boy responded and turned back around quickly before Reuel could ask any more questions. He clearly didn't want to miss his opportunity to see a prince.

Reuel wanted to slap himself for his idiocy. Of course he knew the Rukists, at least in name. He remembered when they first moved to Ira. He'd overheard his father explaining to his mother how he believed Darius was too weak to rule. Unfortunately, Reuel had been caught eavesdropping before his father had finished explaining why he felt this way.

It now struck Reuel, like lightning striking an open meadow, that Ruth was a princess. His head snapped to his left, his eyes racing to find her again. He stared at her for a while and came to the conclusion that she didn't seem much like a princess, but he then realized he didn't know any princesses in the first place. Now that he thought about it, he had never met any of the other princes or princesses of any of the other races. Ever.

A fresh wave of anger washed over him. His stomach was uneasy from his newest discovery. The magnitude of his isolation in Tesa was now fully dawning on him. As much as he loved and believed in his parents, he hated them for this.

Sophia once again glazed and reached out to grab Asher's shoulders. It looked to Reuel as if he drew back, but Sophia's hands still found their mark. Asher fell to his knees, and his head fell back just like the others. His eyes were glowing metallic silver, and his arms swung limply by his side, barely off the ground.

Sophia suddenly snatched her hands from his shoulders and stumbled a couple of steps backward. The docile Snaretooth was suddenly alert and interested in what was transpiring. He stared intently at the kneeling Asher.

Sophia rubbed her hands and whispered, "It's alright, boy," to the now snarling wolf. Snaretooth laid his head down but did not take his eyes off Asher.

Asher wobbled to his feet, his eyes filled with disgust as if Sophia had violated him. Sophia glared right back at him, but there was a hint of uncertainty in her eyes. She took a breath and exclaimed, "Elite!"

Asher turned around, smiled a handsome smile, and waved his arms happily at the rest of the children. They erupted with applause and adoration at the announcement of the first Elite, as if oblivious to what had just transpired between Asher and Sophia.

Reuel, however, did not clap or cheer. He was unable to describe precisely what he was feeling, but he knew that something was wrong with that boy. Asher disappeared through the doorway, and things proceeded as before.

Ruth was called up next and was declared a "Premier." A rhythm developed, and the proceedings began to pick up speed, and before Reuel knew it, the boy ahead of him was walking toward Sophia. The boy's name turned out to be Joseph Lazarine. He was classified as an Elite and was sent on his way. According to Reuel's count, Joseph was the tenth Elite, and none of their classifications went anything like Asher's.

Reuel's turn had finally come. His hands were clammy, and the saliva in his mouth had all but evaporated. Yet he marched forward, determined to become part of the world that his parents had shielded him from. He reached Sophia, and to his surprise, she smiled at him, but it vanished quickly.

"Name!" Micah shouted.

"Reuel Haldane." Again, to his surprise, no one recognized his name. It had been that way since he had arrived in Ira. He never had to deny his royal lineage because no one even seemed to recall his family's name. As if they had never ruled at all.

Sophia's eyes were already glazing. She reached out and took hold of Reuel's shoulders. His head rolled back and his body went numb, but at the same time, he could feel himself unconsciously glazing.

Energy was rushing to all parts of his body. He had never glazed without also performing some task or activity, like running. Now, for the first time, he was *only* glazing. It was the most perplexing feeling he had ever experienced. The energy bubbling inside of him was about to reach its limit, and if he had been able to run, he would've been going fast enough to glide across bodies of water.

He had never pushed himself further than this point; his father had warned him that if he did, his heart would burst from overexertion. Of course, he had been tempted. He knew he could tap into much more power, but he trusted his father and had never tried.

Sophia was about to push him past this point, but right before she did, she pulled her hands off his shoulders. Reuel felt the controls of his body being returned to him, and he readily accepted them. He consciously stopped glazing and looked at Sophia expectantly.

"Auxiliary!" Sophia exclaimed. "Take the second door, Reuel."

Reuel felt the strength that was returning to his body slip away. His heart sank to the pit of his stomach, and tears stung his eyes. He used every ounce of his will to keep them at bay. He had already disgraced his father enough by failing to be an Elite; he would not embarrass him further.

He dropped his head and slowly moved toward the door. Something wet and rough moved across his leg as he walked. Snaretooth looked up at him, panting heavily. The wolf stood, and all the remaining children's eyes were on Reuel as they watched nervously to see what would unfold. Reuel's heart jumped from the pit of his stomach and back into his chest.

On its four legs, the wolf was as tall as Reuel's chest. Reuel wasn't sure exactly how fast the wolf was, but he was certain that if he got a head start, it wouldn't catch him easily. He was about to glaze when he heard Sophia sharply hiss, "No, boy, sit down."

In his panic, Reuel wasn't sure if she was talking to him or Snaretooth. The wolf, however, understood and began to lie back down. But before Snaretooth laid his head onto his paws, he looked up at Reuel, then at Sophia, and then back at Reuel. Snaretooth tilted his head slightly as if confused.

"Keep it moving, scrab!" Micah shouted.

Reuel was not only caught off guard by Micah's ferociousness but also by the fact he had just been referred to as a scrab. He had heard the word used before by some of the Elites and Premiers in Tesa when describing Auxiliaries. He didn't have to be worldly to know it was a negative term. It referred to the fact that many Auxiliaries spent their days cleaning the scrab sheds, which held the public's bodily waste.

He was a prince. The thought of ever being referred to as a scrab never crossed his mind—not even as a joke. His parents were both Elites, not to mention the King and Queen of Tesa. This should have been impossible, but here he was.

He looked to Sophia, who was no longer paying him any attention and was already beckoning the next pupil to step forward. Reuel bowed his head and sulked toward the door. The truth sank into the fertile soil of his mind. He was officially at the bottom of the Aelan hierarchy.

He passed through the doorway and into a moderately sized circular room. Torches lined the walls, providing the entire room with light. The room was also filled with large stone blocks. In the middle of the room sat the largest block, and from there, the rest radiated out in a circular pattern.

Most of the children who had been classified as Auxiliaries had already settled down on a block of their own. A group of children bucked this trend and congregated near the largest block in the middle of the room. They were leaning on it and talking casually.

Reuel gazed at his feet and teetered. He didn't want to sit by himself, but he didn't recognize anyone in the room, either, so he took a deep breath and approached the group of children in the middle.

The group consisted of three Angelics—two boys and a girl—and two Windwalkers—a boy and a girl. The tall Windwalker girl was talking.

"Before I came here this morning, I heard my parents talking about how strange things were getting. You know, with the children disappearing and all. My father said that nobody has seen the Guardians in at least a year."

"Who cares…we're scrabs…" the lone Angelic girl said in disbelief.

"Of course *you* would say that. The missing children have only been Zurielians," the Windwalker boy shot back.

"My father said if the Guardians don't come back soon, we're going to leave Ira," the Windwalker girl said.

"What do you think is happening to the kids?" a chubby Angelic boy asked.

The Windwalker girl paused for a moment, "I—I'm not completely sure, but none of them have been found."

"Am I the only person who cares that we are all scrabs?" the Angelic girl yelled, now on the verge of hysteria.

"Get over it," the Windwalker boy said plainly. "There's nothing you can do about it."

Reuel quietly slipped in and joined the group. "Being a scrab can't be that bad."

All eyes shifted in his direction and glared at him. They all had to look up—he was tall, even for a Windwalker.

"What do you mean 'it's not that bad'?" the Angelic girl said mockingly. "We're scrabs, destined to live the rest of our lives as the dirt of Aela."

"I think you may be blowing this a little bit out of

proportion," Reuel responded. "Sure, we may not have the abilities of the others, but that doesn't mean we're 'the dirt of Aela.' My father said that classification only measures your abilities, not your character."

The Angelic girl shook her head and stared at the ground. The Windwalker boy spoke up for her. "I'm not sure what rock you've been living under, but scrabs don't live great lives. Both my parents are scrabs, and they spend their days cleaning scrab sheds and the bathhouses. They didn't have the endurance and speed to join the Windwalker Gatherers & Exporters Association, and if you're not at least a Premier, you're not even considered for the Tesa Air Service. So they do what most scrabs do: whatever they can to get by. So don't try and tell us that being a scrab isn't so bad." The boy stopped. "You will see for yourself soon enough."

Reuel opened his mouth to respond but couldn't think of anything substantial, so he closed it in defeat. Then a familiar voice came to his rescue.

"Give him a break, there' no reason for all of you to gang up on him. He obviously doesn' know what he' talkin' about." Eve stepped into the group next to Reuel.

"Whatever..." The Windwalker boy was about to say more, but the look in Eve's eyes gave him pause. He turned and walked away. The rest of the kids followed, leaving Eve and Reuel alone in the middle of the room.

"Thanks, Eve."

"You' welcome. Someone here has to look out for you. Since your girlfrien' ain't here, I thought I' step in."

"She's not my girlfriend," Reuel said, turning his head to hide his embarrassment. "We just met today."

Eve grinned widely and playfully punched him in the arm. "I' just playin', Slim."

Reuel rubbed his arm, smiling uneasily. Even though she annoyed him greatly, he was drawn to her, like he was to Elon. In a single day, he had met two complete strangers who he felt he had known his entire life. Reuel was not one to believe in coincidence but was unable to put all these pieces together, so he pushed the thoughts aside.

"I see things didn't go as planned at classification," Reuel said.

"You' one to talk," Eve shot back.

"I didn't mean to offend you. I just didn't expect to see you here."

"I had no plans on bein' here, but I guess that old lady thought different. Anyway, we might wanna take a seat before they' all gone."

Reuel noticed that the room had filled up considerably. All races were represented.

"Let's sit over here," he said, pointing at two empty stone blocks near them. They sat cross-legged atop their own blocks.

Reuel cleared his throat and spoke slowly and lightly. He didn't want anyone overhearing him. "Before you came in, a girl was saying that the Guardians had disappeared. Nobody has seen them."

"An'?" Eve asked.

"Well, what do you think about that?"

Eve didn't say anything. She just sat on her block and stared straight ahead. Then she turned her head and looked at Reuel. From the little time he had spent with her, Reuel had her pegged as opinionated and fearless, but now he could sense her uncertainty. Finally, she spoke.

"I' not too sure, but before I left Beliel, Queen Candace had officially taken over for Maria…She hasn' been seen in almost a year. An' since she' disappear', I—" She fell silent.

"What?" Reuel asked softly.

"For about a year, I' been havin' really strange dreams. They start with me walkin' in the Dead Forest towar' this strange light. I don' wanna go towar' it, but it' like I'm bein' drag'. And when I finally reach the light, I see it' a fire and there'—"

"A pale man eating a heart," Reuel finished.

Eve stared at him. "Yes. The palest Angelic I' ever

seen. How did you know?"

"I've been having the same dream for about a year too. Do you know who it is?"

"I have no idea. But I do know that I first start' havin' these dreams when Maria vanish'."

"You think they could be related?"

Before Eve was able to answer, Sophia entered the chamber and everyone around them fell silent. Eve followed suit. Sophia spoke as she approached the large block in the middle of the room.

"As the captain informed you earlier, today will be your only day of Instruction." She reached the block and climbed on top of it. She stood with her arms folded across her chest. "It is time for you to ascend and reach your full potential as Auxiliaries."

DANIEL (III)

Daniel stood on the platform before a technological marvel. The zip train in front of him was a lengthy, segmented vehicle made up of multiple interchangeable cylinder-shaped cars used for transporting either cargo or passengers. The only two parts of the train that were not interchangeable were the head and caboose. The head of the train had a pointed face—in order to be as aerodynamic as possible—while the caboose housed a coal chamber that fueled the engines that powered the train.

Passenger cars could be identified by their rectangular windows, which were installed to help prevent claustrophobia; there wasn't much to see underground. The cars were magnetically connected to each other, allowing them to be freely interchanged.

This gave the train the ability to have only cargo cars during a busy import season or only passenger cars for a heavy travel season, but most of the time it was a mixture of the two.

There was not much to the station, if it could even be called that. Just like the rest of Beliel, only the necessities were present. There was no building housing the train; it floated on a long, black, magnetic strip in front of a dark tunnel. On the station's platform were a tollbooth and a line of poles with metal chains strung through to prevent anyone from falling under the train.

Daniel approached the small wooden booth with a sign that read "Toll" nailed to its roof. To the right of the booth was a small gate that allowed access to the train.

"I need a seat on the train to Horo," Daniel said.

A slender, cherry-skinned girl stood inside of the booth. "Of course, sir. You do know that this is the last train of this season and you won't be able to leave Horo until late summer?"

"Yes, I am aware. How much for the ticket?"

"Five coins, sir."

Daniel took his bag off his shoulder and riffled through it until he came up with the necessary amount. In his hand were five small gold coins with little hammers etched onto the surface. The emblem of the Grindblers, they forged all the gold coins used on Aela. He handed them over to the girl in the booth.

She took the coins and slipped them in what Daniel recognized as a small safe.

"Sir, you are set to board whenever you're ready."

Daniel nodded and strolled to the small gate next to the tollbooth. He pushed through and briskly walked across the boarding plank. The outside of the train was lined with magnetic strips that were the polar opposite of those that lined the tunnel, allowing the zip train to float when within.

The particular train in front of Daniel had seven cars including the non-interchangeable ones. There were three passenger cars behind the head and two cargo cars following them. He was boarding the second passenger car when something caught his eye: a glint of sunlight reflecting from some metal by the door. He turned his head to see a large embossed Grindbler insignia on the wall of the car.

They never miss an opportunity to sign something, Daniel thought.

The zip train and tunnel were by far the Grindbler's greatest achievements, allowing for easy travel to the otherwise unreachable city of Horo. When the Aquatis first settled in the Baron Sea, it was clear that their city would be rather exclusive. Unless one possessed the ability to breathe, eat, and live underwater, spending any time in the Aquati capital was not feasible. It was located at the bottom of the sea, miles from the surface, and it was impossible to even hold your breath long enough to see the top of their tallest structure.

Like the Shimmers, the Aquati lived in isolation until shortly after the war. Asa believed, as did the rest of the Guardians, that Aela must be united in order to prevent another Civil War from happening. Daniel remembered the transition well. He was just a young man when the construction of the zip tunnels began.

The thought of the construction caused Daniel to reach over his shoulder and rub his back. His fingers ran along three raised lines—there were two sets, a set on each shoulder blade. He had not put his gills to work in a long time. He sometimes sat in the rain and allowed them to open to keep them active, but he had not relied on them for oxygen in decades.

The familiar feeling of his gills and the thought of the zip tunnel gave his mind an opportunity to visit old memories seldom remembered, and it didn't hesitate to capitalize. Daniel's eyes were fixed on the Grindbler insignia while his mind went on a trip of its own.

Daniel had lived in a coral home with his mother and father in the heart of Horo. It was a two-story house with jagged-edged windows and an open doorway. There were no stairs in the house; everything was

101

easily accessible by swimming. They didn't own a single piece of furniture—there was no need. The Aquatis never sat or laid down underwater. They were in constant motion, like sharks. This allowed for their hearts to stay at a brisk pace, which in turn allowed their blood to move quickly through their bodies and keep them warm even in the cold depths of the Baron Sea.

If they were not walking on the sea floor, they were treading water in place. Even when they slept, they treaded water. His parents, like the rest of the residents of this underwater paradise, did not work. Again, there was no need. The Aquatis had no use for money underwater; their community was based on a simple principle that was burned into the mind of every Aquati born in Horo: "An Aquati in need has no need to plead."

This mantra was the heart of life in Horo. The Aquatis' system was not perfect, but it worked. When problems did arise, the parties involved presented their case to the king and queen, who would have the final say.

One particular case Daniel would never forget had involved his friend Emon. Food was plentiful in Horo. Crabs scurried about the streets, and fish freely swam through the city—they even swam through the homes. However, they could be tricky to catch. Because of this, most families in Horo owned a fishing lance or two that was used for hunting. Emon, in need of a lance, stole one from his neighbor, and even though it was returned, King Michal and Queen Joanna had him banished from Horo. He was sent to live the rest of his life on land. Extreme, maybe to the eyes of outsiders, but it was necessary to keep the system running. When goodwill is currency, theft is the ultimate crime.

From birth, Aquati children were taught to speak telepathically. An Aquati only had to think of what to say and then broadcast it to those for whom it was intended.

Communicating on private telepathic links required the establishment of a personal link—one made through physical contact. Predictably, children often struggled with the ability and would unknowingly broadcast their thoughts for all to hear.

Like verbal communication, there is no way to stop someone from speaking to you. Luckily, all children under the age of fourteen only possessed Auxiliary-level abilities, so their broadcasts reached only short distances.

Daniel was twenty the day construction on the zip tunnels began. He had been on a leisurely ride through the city on the back of his pet hufflud, an animal with the head of an eel and the body of a lizard with large, webbed feet.

They had been swimming just above the city's

buildings in an area reserved for Aquatis traveling via animal. Sky Lane, as it was commonly referred to, was faster and more spacious than swimming through the crowded streets.

It was during this time when Daniel heard Asa's voice in his head. He patted his pet on the neck, signaling it to stop and tread instead. Everyone around him followed suit. He saw the movement in the streets below him also come to a halt. Everyone listened as the Guardian spoke.

"My brothers and sisters, a new day is upon us. Today, Horo will join the rest of Aela. We have long lived in seclusion and distanced ourselves from others. If the war has taught us anything, it is that we must stand together or fall alone. I called many of you into service, to fight alongside me in a war that many wondered why we even joined. For that, I thank you. I tell you now, if we had not fought, Horo would be no more.

"We will never forget the loved ones we lost, but we cannot allow our sorrow to stand in the way of our development as a people. Their sacrifice will live on through us. I have recently met with the High Council, and we have decided to construct great machines that will be the first of their kind. In order to build them, I will require the aid of all able men: Auxiliaries, Premiers, and Elites from ages fourteen to

fifty. Construction will begin today. Report to Town Square immediately following the swarm."

Something tugged at Daniel's arm and brought his mind back to the present. A small Aquati boy and an Aquati woman stood behind him. The boy was holding her hand with one arm and gently tugging on Daniel's with the other.

"Mister, are you going inside?" the boy asked telepathically.

Daniel turned and looked at the two of them. There was a hint of red in the woman's cheeks.

"I'm sorry, my son is a little impatient, but he has a point," she added.

Daniel smiled. *"Of course. I'm sorry."*

He entered the passenger car. There was only a handful of passengers, all Aquati—not surprising, since Horo would be underwater for the season. He walked down the aisle in search of a suitable seat. There were two aisles of seats and four per row. He found one in an empty row in the back next to a window. The boy and his mother settled into the row across from him.

BEEEEEEHHH!...BEEEEEEEEHHH!...BEE EEEEEEEEHHHHHH!

"This is my favorite part!" the boy exclaimed to no one and everyone at once.

His mother reached over and pulled down the harness on his seat then proceeded to fasten her own. Daniel did the same and prepared for takeoff.

The train slowly inched forward until the nose was just inside of the tunnel. It then lifted several more feet into the air; the magnetic strips near—and in—the tunnels were much more powerful than the ones at the dock. As the nose of the train crept deeper into the tunnel's entrance, the engines fired and bright orange flames erupted from the thrusters. The train took off, diving underground and moving at a stunning speed.

Daniel was thrown back into his seat. He had forgotten how powerful takeoff was. He chuckled to himself and smiled. He had allowed himself to forget a lot of things outside of his cabin walls.

"Yeahhh!" the boy exclaimed.

Daniel stared out his window. There was only darkness. The train coasted along smoothly, the magnetic strips that lined the tunnel keeping the train gliding through its middle. The ride wouldn't be long, at most a quarter of a day.

His smile faded as he remembered why he was heading home. When he arrived, there would be no time for a joyous reunion, only business. He leaned his head back, still staring out of the window, and allowed his mind to finish replaying the memories it had started earlier.

Asa finished his address, but nobody moved. Daniel patted his hufflud, and it immediately raced forward.

"To the palace, my friend."

The hufflud pulled its four legs close to its body, making it look more like an eel than a lizard. It slithered through the water with not only grace but tremendous power. There was no time to waste. The swarm would soon arrive.

Horo resided too deep in the sea to be reached by sunlight, however light was readily available. A small fish no larger than an Aquati's hand and no thicker than three fingers provided this light. Minites, as the fish were called, traveled in massive schools that sometimes numbered in the tens of millions. They feasted on the insects that flew close to the sea's surface every morning and the algae that rested there. While feeding, their scales absorbed the sunlight, allowing them to glow, and their bodies were able to retain the energy for roughly a day. After they had their fill, the minites dove to the depths and swam through Horo. As they passed through, the Aquatis captured enough to light the city, and when their lights dimmed the next morning, they were released and fresh ones were caught. This was the daily ritual.

Daniel and his pet sped past and weaved around the other Aquatis in Sky Lane. Some were riding dolphins, others huffluds, and a few were atop large bass. At the speed they were moving, it didn't take long before they were at the city's limits and treading outside an extravagant castle.

Asa's castle, like the other buildings in Horo, had numerous openings that served as both entrances and exits. Each section of the castle was elevated a little higher than the last, causing it to vaguely resemble a steep mountain. Daniel had always marveled at the beautiful architecture, from the coral columns holding up domed roofs to the high towers that looked over the city.

While he gawked at the castle, Daniel failed to notice that five members of the Royal Guard armed with long spears had surrounded him and his hufflud. One of them floated down and faced Daniel. The man had a long scar running diagonally across his chest. His name was Thomas Consor. He had saved Daniel and a number of others from certain death at the hands of Gideon, receiving that scar in the process. He was powerfully built by Aquati standards, and his hufflud skin leggings clung tightly to his muscular legs.

"State your business," he ordered with his spear aimed at Daniel's throat.

Daniel raised his hands. *"Captain Thomas, my*

name is Daniel. I served under you in the war. I am a friend of Asa."

With his spear still trained on him, the captain nodded and stared at one of the Aquatis behind Daniel. Daniel knew they were having a discussion he was not privy to, so he did all he could to patiently wait until they finished. Finally, the captain's eyes were again on him.

"Follow me." He lowered his spear and swam toward the top of the castle.

Daniel nudged his hufflud and they followed, flanked by the rest of the Guard. Daniel doubted that the captain even remembered him from the war.

They arrived at the highest tower of the castle. Asa was there waiting for them. The tower overlooked the entire city. Besides the Guardian, there was nothing in there. The tower's roof was held up by coral columns that encircled them.

The Royal Guard treaded outside of the columns while Daniel and his pet ventured inside. Daniel dismounted his hufflud, who then rested on the floor of the room, and approached the Guardian.

"Yes, Daniel..." Asa said with his back to him as he gazed out at Horo.

"Sir, what are you doing? Do you really think this is wise?"

"It's time that we open our doors to the rest of Aela.

We have been living alone far too long."

"Our women and children have never seen the surface world. Should we really expose them to that? You, me, and the rest of the men have all seen the kind of destruction that occurs up there. Do you really think we are ready for this!?"

Asa turned around, his arms folded across his scrawny chest, his feet treading gracefully under him and his face stern. His eyes locked with Daniel's.

"Daniel, I understand Phoebe was your sister, and I mourn her passing too, but do not forget your place. Do not forget who you're talking to. I may be your friend, but I am first and foremost your leader, and the decision has already been made. As I said, construction will begin immediately following the swarm."

"I'm sorry, Asa, and I suppose you're right—maybe it's for the best. I just don't want to see another war," Daniel admitted.

Asa turned his back and swam to the edge of the room, treading between two columns. *"You're dismissed, Daniel."*

A weight pressed down on Daniel's shoulder. A meaty hand dug into his flesh and twisted him around. The captain released his grip and nodded toward one of the exits. Daniel understood.

"Let's go," Daniel said to his hufflud. His pet immediately raced toward him. Without missing a beat,

110

Daniel stretched out his hand as his pet was flying by, grabbed onto the reptile's scaly skin, and was whisked away from the castle.

As they swam back to the city, Daniel witnessed the lights throughout Horo dimming. He looked toward the surface and in the distance could make out a long streak of brilliant silver fluidly cutting through the water that was heading directly toward Horo.

As it approached, Daniel was able to identify the individual fish that made up the massive school. They snaked down into Horo, weaving through the houses and streets. Aquatis held up nets of all sizes to capture as many of the minites as they could and at the same time released those that had been caught the day before.

Daniel watched as the brilliant silver streak lost some of its luster and even developed dark splotches as the dimming minites rejoined the school. The silver streak then sped past Asa's castle and beyond. The Aquatis closed their nets and tied them to the sides of the buildings, allowing them to float and illuminate Horo.

"Hello, Daniel," said a smooth, beautiful voice.

His heart skipped a beat. It was her. *"Maria?"*

He again looked toward the surface, and from where the minites had come moments ago were hundreds of people swimming down to him.

"How is this possible?" Daniel asked.

"Asa has linked us and all the Aquatis together so we're able to communicate during the project," Maria responded.

"I understand that. I'm talking about how are all of you able to make it this deep without air?"

Maria didn't need to answer. She was now treading in front of him, and he saw exactly how she was able to breathe. A large bubble of air covered the bottom of her neck and stretched up to her nostrils. Goggles also covered her eyes; small war hammers were etched on the side. He glanced at the rest of the group and saw she was not the only one. He also saw they were all dressed in hufflud suits.

"A little something I have been working on," Uri said, swimming next to Maria. *"It will only last about half a day, but that should be plenty. Daniel, can you direct us to your town square?"*

"Of course, Uri."

Uri turned and motioned for someone. A hulking man swam from the middle of the crowd.

"Hey, Danny!" Cyrus boomed as he drew near. He torpedoed right past Maria and Uri and right into Daniel—wrapping him in a smothering embrace.

Daniel kicked his hufflud in the side, signaling him to leave him. Daniel hugged Cyrus back, and they both kicked desperately to stay afloat in Sky Lane, which was quite difficult without their arms. Cyrus released him and joined the other two Guardians.

"We should start to head down, Asa is expecting you," Daniel said and looked to Uri for confirmation. He nodded, and Daniel led the descent to Town Square.

Maria swam beside him. *"I've missed you, Daniel, how have you been?"* she asked on a private channel they had established years ago. However, her close proximity and body language made it clear to anyone looking that they were conversing.

Unlike the Aquatis, the surface dwellers demanded eye contact when they communicated. This idea was lost on the Aquati—there was no use for it in their form of communication. Giving eye contact had been a major adjustment for them when they initially interacted with the other races during the war.

"Drop back a little bit and don't look at me, you're making it obvious," Daniel answered, and Maria obliged. *"I've missed you too,"* he continued. *"I've been getting by okay. I still miss Phoebe, but I'm starting to readjust. How's Candace?"*

"I never got a chance to tell you how sorry I am about your sister's passing," she replied. *"And Candace is great, but I wish she could see her father..."*

"You know that can't happen."

"We'll see. The hope is that this project will unite

us all and reduce the chances of another war. But what I'm hoping for is that it might allow me and her to see you more often. I know it's best that you two don't formally meet, but if all goes well, I might be able to arrange something where you can live in Beliel, and you'll at least be in the same city as us."

"Thank you—and that would be amazing. Watching her from a distance is better than not seeing her at all." Daniel felt the soothing warmth of hope overcoming him.

Daniel and Maria touched ground first, followed by Uri, Cyrus, and the hundreds behind them. They set down in Town Square near the gathering of all able-bodied Aquati men between ages fourteen to fifty, and it suddenly occurred to Daniel that they were all standing on the sea floor. He understood how the Aquatis were able to do this. By taking short, quick breaths, they were able to keep their lungs, which acted like flotation devices, from fully expanding, thus making their bodies heavy enough to fall to the bottom. What Daniel did not understand was how the surface dwellers were able to do the same.

Movement by his feet caught his attention. Chunks of the sea floor snaked around the ankles of the visitors, effectively weighing them down. Daniel glanced at a smiling, glazing Cyrus and nodded.

"Welcome, my friends!" Asa proclaimed.

He swam over the heads of the Aquati crowd, followed by the Royal Guard. He landed gracefully in the middle of the two masses and stood next to his fellow Guardians. He nodded at Daniel, who understood and took his place among the Aquati citizens.

The Royal Guard fell in line and stood near the Guardians. The four Guardians stood stoically in the middle of both groups. It was Asa's city, so he took charge.

"This day will mark the beginning of a united front on Aela. Within the next season, Horo will open its doors to all citizens. There will be a tunnel connecting to every capital: Tesa, Beliel, Ira, Rolte, and a new extension of Horo that will rest above us. For three seasons, Horo will be dry, allowing for visitors to come, trade, and experience our great city. For one season, it will be submerged, and life will be as it is now. Uri, if you would..."

The Windwalker Guardian's eyes glazed a dazzling green. He held his hands in front of him as if he were holding a small ball, and a dull-green sphere formed between them. A small bubble broke away from the air supply around his mouth and drifted slowly toward the green sphere. Once the bubble made contact with the sphere, it shone a blinding green.

Uri let the sphere go and allowed it to drift upward several feet. He then spread his arms wide, and the sphere expanded exponentially. As it expanded, it pushed the seawater farther and farther out. The sphere quickly enveloped all of them, and instead of water, there was air.

It continued to grow, racing down the streets and wrapping around the buildings. It stopped growing once it reached the city limits. There was a stunned silence as the gathering of people took in what was occurring. Everyone but the Guardians shared the same expression of amazement.

Uri, still glazing, wiped away the air bubbles that were wrapped around all the surface dwellers' faces. There was a collective gasp as the visitors desperately reached for their mouths, but it took only seconds for them to realize they were now able to breathe without assistance. They then removed their goggles.

Daniel stood in awe. A mile or two above him where the bubble reached its peak, he saw fish, huffluds, and other animals swimming on the outside. It was magnificent. Horo was somehow even more beautiful to Daniel without water. The colors that made up the coral buildings were even more vibrant without being submerged in the dark-blue sea.

"This is the future of Horo!" Asa exclaimed. *"We will use this air bubble as a guide and build around it using the specially designed metal sheets that are being forged in Rolte as I speak. The first batch is on its way*

to Horo now. The age of peace and the dawn of a united Aela begins today!"

BEEEEEEHHH!...BEEEEEEEEHHH!...BEE EEEEEEEEHHHHHH!

Daniel was jolted back to the present; the train had arrived. It docked at the Horo-Beliel station. Daniel watched the little boy and his mother walk up the aisle to the train door. He unstrapped his harness and followed.

While he walked down the aisle, his heart quickened and his stomach dropped. He hadn't been home in a long time. When he reached the train door, he paused and tried to gain control of himself. He had to manage his emotions. He was here to get Azriel and nothing more. He walked out of the train door.

The instant he caught a glimpse of Horo, tears freely ran down his cheeks, and he could no longer suppress his emotions. Even under the unfortunate circumstances of his return, he was powerless to contain his happiness. It was good to be home.

REUEL (IV)

Sophia observed the pupils, each on their own stone block, cleared her throat, and continued her address.

"I am the bridge between you and your potential," Sophia explained. "During classification, I opened your minds and bodies in order to assess your hidden potential, and by doing so I have given you the opportunity to achieve that potential. We will start with meditation. This will calm you and allow you to begin the search for your individual chests. Each of your abilities were naturally suppressed at birth until your bodies were able to handle them. They will manifest themselves in your minds as locked chests, and now that you are of age, you will be able to reach and unlock them through meditation. All I require is your patience. I will walk you through the process."

Reuel looked over at Eve. "What do you think it's going to be like?"

"I don' know, but we' about to find out."

"Well, that was helpful…"

"That's the best I got for you, Slim, just wait, we' both know soon enough."

"Quiet!" Sophia shouted while she paced. "There must be complete silence, and my directions must be followed precisely for you to successfully locate your chest. Now, everyone close your eyes and focus solely on regulating your breathing, until you're taking long, slow breaths."

Reuel closed his eyes and began to slow his breathing. He heard his heart pounding and anxiously waited for something to occur. His mind was filled with the possibilities, each one more fantastic than the last. Then Reuel heard Sophia again, but she sounded farther away.

"Do not open your eyes," she said sternly. "Continue to focus only on your breathing, until all your thoughts have cleared and you are alone in the darkness of your mind."

Sophia sounded so far away that Reuel had to fight the urge to open his eyes and check if she was still in the room. He forced himself to continue onward, and his mind eased. His thoughts were less frantic and chaotic. Soon, there was nothing, only him, sitting alone in darkness. He again heard Sophia's voice. This time, it was not much more than a whisper.

"Do not be afraid of the darkness. Embrace it. It is your mind, your spirit, you have complete control. There is no turning back now. You will only return once you have located your chest. This is as far as I can take you. How long it takes is your decision. Good luck."

There was nothing more. Reuel got to his feet and began to walk. The darkness was as unsettling, as it was dense and even seemed to weigh him down. He was reminded of his nightmare but clung to Sophia's words: "You have complete control."

He mustered all the courage he could and shambled forward. He walked and walked and walked, and the longer he walked the more hopeless he felt. He had no sense of time, and for all he knew he had been in his head for hours. When all seemed lost and he had come to the conclusion he would be trapped in his own mind forever, he saw a small white dot in the distance. A wave of relief washed over him, and he sprinted toward the dot, but no matter how fast he ran, he didn't seem to gain any ground. It just sat on the horizon, teasing him.

Reuel continued to sprint on; there was no turning around now. He had failed too many times already today. Eventually, the white dot expanded, and as he closed in on it, it morphed into a chest.

He arrived in front of a strange chest that rested on

a pedestal. Carved into the top of the chest was a web of intricate designs, while the bottom was solid gold. On each side of the chest were two small gold handles. The Windwalker emblem served as the latch of the chest. The soaring hawk was embossed.

He reached for the chest, but his progress was halted by what appeared to be a force field of some kind. It was invisible until it was touched, which was when it vibrated and became opaque. Each of his attempts to grab the chest became more and more ferocious until he was banging on it savagely, but it did not give. Reuel backed up and then charged.

"Ahhhh!" he screamed as he ran. He threw all his weight into the force field and it gave slightly, but then it recoiled and sent him flying. He flew from the chest's presence and continued to fly backward at a tremendous pace, his feet never touching the ground, his arms flailing, until he hit a wall and opened his eyes.

Reuel was staring at the ceiling, lying flat on his back. He had been thrown from his stone block. Eve and Sophia were kneeling next to him. Many of the children had gathered around, mouths agape.

"Child, are you okay?" Sophia asked in a tender voice.

"I think so—there was a—"

Sophia placed a finger on his lips and shook her head. "Not now…"

Her eyes revealed there was more she wanted to say, they were almost pleading for him to pry but before he could, Sophia rose to her feet.

"Congratulations, you are all full-fledged Auxiliaries!" she declared to the children.

Reuel heard a few claps and a couple of cheers, but nobody took their eyes off of him.

"You are all dismissed, there is nothing more to see," Sophia continued. "I will see you all again at the Ascension Ceremony for the Elites and Premiers next season. I wish you all the best."

Reuel sat up and rubbed his eyes. Eve placed her hand on his shoulder and leaned in close to his ear.

"You sure know how to put on a show, Slim," she whispered.

The other children began to file out, stealing glances as they passed.

"Why is everyone staring at me?" he asked.

"Well, you were the last one still tryin' to ascen'. So we were all watchin' and waitin' for you to wake up, when all of a sudden you flew from your seat and land' on your back," Eve explained. "It was a sight to see."

Reuel once again had more questions than answers. Eve pulled him to his feet, helped brush off the dirt from his pants, and led him toward the line of children exiting the chamber. He suddenly stopped walking, grabbed Eve's elbow, and pulled her close to him. The children behind them let out a collective annoyed sigh and walked around.

"I couldn't reach my chest," Reuel whispered to Eve. "It was surrounded by a force field I couldn't break."

"Tell me everythin'," Eve said.

Reuel described what happened in excruciating detail, and to his surprise, Eve did not mock or disregard him but genuinely listened, her eyes never leaving his.

After he finished, he waited intently for her answer. She nodded her head. "The same thin' happen' to me. I couldn' get to my chest either."

"If you didn't ascend either, then why isn't everyone looking at you, too?"

"When I woke up, I saw the others ascen'in', it was actually quite beautiful, all their eyes glazin' simultaneously. So I just start' glazin' too so no one woul' suspect anythin'. I also wasn' the last one in meditation, and I ain't I fly off my block."

Reuel rubbed his head. She had a point. "Yeah, I guess you're right. But we *didn't* ascend. I didn't know that was possible."

"Me either, and does it even matter? We're Auxiliaries. There isn't much lock'-away potential anyway. Plus, who' gonna believe us?"

Reuel then remembered the look in Sophia's eyes and anxiously scanned the room for her.

She knows what happened. I know she does, Reuel

thought. But Sophia was nowhere to be seen. The chamber was nearly empty. Only he, Eve, and a few other stragglers remained.

"Who are you lookin' for?" Eve asked.

"Sophia. I think she might know what's going on."

Eve looked around. "Well, she ain't here anymore."

"Yeah, I know," Reuel answered. "Come on, I think I know someone else who might be able to help." Reuel grabbed Eve's forearm and led her through the door of the chamber into Assembly Hall.

The shouts and grunts from the Elite and Premier pupils echoed from the other doorway. A part of Reuel was curious, but he didn't take the initiative to check it out. Instead, he tightened his grip around Eve's forearm and pulled her toward the entrance of the Institute. There were more pressing matters at hand.

The last bits of sunshine danced on the Institute's steps, and long shadows played at the bottom. Evening-light had arrived. There were a handful of people walking through the Institute's courtyard, their faces cloaked by shadows. Reuel reasoned they were just passing through on their way home, but there was one silhouette that caught his eye. It was tall and bulky, and its long arms swung powerfully by its side. The silhouette was heading toward Old Ira. Reuel knew exactly who it was, and the fact that he was walking by the Institute at this exact moment didn't surprise him. The way this day was going, not much could.

"That's him, let's go," Reuel said.

Eve jerked her arm from Reuel's grip. "Who is that? And why are you pullin' me? I' more than capable of walkin' on my own."

"It's a friend, and if you want to figure out what's going on, you'll follow me," Reuel said as he began to leap down the stairs.

"Fine—wait up!" Eve yelled, chasing after him.

Once Reuel's feet hit the bottom of the stairs, he was sprinting toward the large silhouette. The distance between him and the figure had grown, but Reuel refused to lose him. He concentrated, and his eyes glazed a vibrant green. He felt his legs strengthen, and each stride became more powerful. His vision had become tunneled. Everything that had been clear in his peripherals just moments ago was nothing but a blur, and he quickly gained on the figure.

He took a deep breath and shouted. "Elon!"

The figure turned around, and Reuel could just make out the curious expression on his friend's face in the fading sunlight. Reuel beamed at the sight of the Grindbler as if they were lifelong friends. Elon showed similar excitement, his grin revealing all of his teeth.

The excitement caused Reuel to lose focus. He concentrated on slowing down and his eyes returned to their normal color, but he still didn't have complete control over his speed, and in a desperate attempt to lose momentum, he brought both feet together, which caused him to go rocketing into Elon's chest.

If Reuel didn't know better, he would have sworn he had run into the side of a building. He was sent sprawling across the ground, and his right shoulder throbbed. He laughed at himself. Elon wasn't the first person or thing he had run into while glazing. Reuel held out his hand, and Elon lifted him to his feet.

"Sorry about that," said Reuel.

"Don't worry about it, I've been hit much harder," Elon replied. They both chuckled at this, but their laughter soon died, and Reuel's smile faded.

"Well, it looks like I'll be getting that stand right next to you, my friend," Reuel said.

"I'm sorry to hear that," Elon replied.

This was followed by silence, and then both boys erupted in hysterical laughter. Eve trotted up to the two of them, gasping for breath.

"You—really—are—fast," she said between gasps.

"This is Eve Demas," Reuel said. "She's an Auxiliary too."

Eve hesitated before she held out her arm. Her eyes gazed admiringly at Elon and traveled up and down his body. Elon reached out and grasped her forearm, returning her gaze with an equally affectionate one.

Reuel stood to the side witnessing it all, feeling increasingly uncomfortable.

"'I' from Beliel. I met Slim here on the way to Instruction this mornin'."

"My name is Elon Warring, and same here. I mean—not on the way to Instruction—but this morning in the market, he helped set up my stand," Elon said, clearly flustered.

"Well," Elon continued, "I'm on my way home. Am I right to guess that you live in the mountains too?"

"I live nearby," Eve replied, grinning.

"You're more than welcome to walk with me if you wish."

"That would be nice," Eve responded in a sweet tone that Reuel had not heard from her all day.

Reuel watched Eve's already red cheeks turn scarlet. "I'm sorry to intrude, but there is something important I wanted to ask you, Elon," Reuel said.

"Of course, we can talk about it on the way home," Elon responded without taking his eyes off Eve.

Reuel shook his head and began to walk toward Old Ira. It took a while before Elon and Eve even realized he had left them, but when they did, they quickly jostled through the crowd until they were next to Reuel.

Darius's Way was packed. The majority of the

Zurielians were heading toward Old Ira, while the bulk of the Angelics in the crowd were heading in the opposite direction to New Ira.

"Funny how even in the new 'united' Ira, the Angelics still live on the other side of the city," Elon quipped.

"Abel said that they will never accept living with us," Eve added.

"Who's Abel?" Elon asked.

"My caretaker," Eve said.

"Where are your parents?" Elon asked.

"Good question," she replied.

They walked a while in awkward silence. It was Reuel who broke it.

"My parents told me that most of the other cities are the same way. The Shimmers in Beliel are not all that welcoming of outsiders," Reuel explained.

"And how exactly do you know that? Have you ever been to Beliel? Have your parents been there?" Eve's voice grew more aggressive with each question.

"No I haven't, and I didn't ask, but I don't think they would say something like that unless they had some kind of firsthand experience," Reuel answered.

"I live' there my whole life. I live' next to a family of Windwalkers and near a pair of Grindbler brothers," Eve said. "We may not have been open to outsiders in the past, but we live among and with them now."

"Let's calm down," Elon said. "I know *this* is not what you wanted to talk about, Reuel."

"You're right, but there are too many people around," Reuel said.

"Follow me," Eve replied. She pointed to 22nd Street, which was coming up on their right.

They followed closely behind Eve as the street bent and curved around houses. Reuel wondered who would ever think it was a good idea to build such a winding road. While he was contemplating the purpose for such a street, he realized that Eve had stopped walking.

They were standing in the outskirts of the city. There was plenty of space between the base of the mountain and the houses on the side streets. Reuel had never been in this area before, and until this moment he had thought the houses touched the mountain wall. They had been looking for seclusion, and Eve had delivered.

"All the even the streets of Old Ira empty into the outskirts," Eve explained.

There were makeshift huts that ran along the base of the mountain. There weren't many, and there was enough space for countless more.

"Who lives out here?" Reuel asked.

"People who can' afford the homes in the mountain," Eve answered.

"How do you know about this place?" Elon asked.

"Me and Abel stay in there," Eve answered, pointing at a small hut made of mud bricks. There was a small space between the bricks around five feet off the ground that Reuel guessed served as a window. The roof of the hut was a sheet of discarded metal from the loading docks.

There was another long, awkward silence while Elon and Reuel looked around. "I had no idea," Reuel managed to say.

"How coul' you? I just met you this mornin'," Eve replied. "Anyway, I don' need your sympathy. Abel didn' think it was necessary for us to buy a home in the mountain when we woul' only be here for a season."

Elon and Reuel nodded in unison; it was the best they could do. Neither of them knew the appropriate thing to say.

"Well, this is as secluded a place as any. What did you need to tell me?" Elon said, smoothly changing the subject.

Reuel cleared his throat and began to describe the pale man with the dragon tattoo he and Eve had seen in their dreams. He told Elon about the force field they had encountered while they had tried to ascend, and how it had flung Reuel from his seat.

Elon listened patiently and allowed Reuel to get every part of his story out. When Reuel had finally finished, Elon took a moment before he answered. Eve and Reuel stared at him, anxiously awaiting his response.

He took a deep breath and said, "Same thing happened to me."

Reuel nodded. "I thought so."

"So do you know why this is happenin'?" Eve asked.

"No, but I've been seeing the man with the tattoo almost every night for the past year. And I also couldn't break through that force field." He paused. "But what does it mean?"

"I' not sure if it means anythin', it coul' easily be a coincidence," Eve stated.

"I guess, but that's a little bit of a stretch, isn't it? All three of us meeting today and having the same experiences—Elon's Instruction incident happening a year ago. This doesn't just happen," Reuel explained.

"Thin's like this happen," Eve said. "Strange thin's happen, we live in a worl' where Grindblers can lift mountains and Windwalkers can run on water. Amazin' thin's, so what is so spectacular about this?"

"She has a point," Elon said.

"I suppose, but I still think it's a big coincidence," Reuel said. "I mean, how many people go to Instruction and don't ascend?"

No one answered the question. "Well, you two can keep discussin' this, but I' goin' home," Eve said, then

131

turned toward the makeshift shack.

"See you around!?" Elon blurted out.

Eve turned her head and smiled. "Yeah, more than likely." She continued walking but then stopped, turned her head again, and said, "Later, Slim."

"Bye," Reuel said.

They watched Eve enter her shack before they headed back into the city.

The feeling that they were part of something bigger continued to nip at Reuel's mind, like a lobit pecking at its paralyzed prey. However, Elon made it clear he sided with Eve and had tried to convince Reuel to do the same. His reasoning fell on deaf ears. Reuel was convinced something was going on. He felt it in the pit of his stomach. They said their goodbyes and parted ways a couple of landings up the mountain stairs.

The sun had set by the time Reuel reached home, and it was now night. He paused before he went through the curtain and looked out at Ira. He observed Auxiliaries lighting lamppost after lamppost—illuminating the city. His eyes fell on the Institute, and his stomach dropped as he was reminded of his classification.

His eyes burned. He curled his hands into tight fists as tears rolled down his green cheeks. The pain, anger, and disappointment he had been holding in all day had finally reached its tipping point. His chest heaved as he tried to keep his cries as soft as possible. He was disgusted with himself, revolted by his actions.

Stop crying, you're not a child… You're a man now, deal with this as such, he thought. He took a deep breath and exhaled slowly, releasing his tension. He wiped his eyes, took another moment to compose himself, and then walked through the curtain into his home.

Reuel was puzzled by what he saw when he walked in. Sitting at the table with his parents was Sophia. His parents sat across from each other while Sophia sat in the middle, facing him.

A single candle was lit in the middle of the table. They were leaning over it, talking in hushed whispers. The light from the candle danced along their faces.

Reuel stood completely still in the darkness—they had not noticed him yet. This did not last long. Sophia glanced up and locked eyes with the young Windwalker. She held her hand up and nodded in his direction. His parents fell silent, and all attention was on him. The light from the candle allowed Reuel to make out the wet trails left from tears running down his mother's face. His father was expressionless.

Sophia stood. "Hello, Reuel, please sit down." She motioned toward the empty chair in front of her.

Reuel stepped forward. He had never seen his parents like this. He had never been so uneasy around them. They had always given off an air of protection, but that was gone tonight. In its place was overwhelming anxiety and fear. Reuel sat down timidly, looking from his mother to his father, hoping for some sign of reassurance. None came.

"Why are you here?" Reuel asked Sophia.

"I've known you and your family for a long time, Reuel. Snaretooth and I were there when you were born."

That's why he licked me, Reuel thought randomly.

Sophia, too, sat down. "I know you've had a rough day. I know you have a lot of questions, but before we can explain, you have to understand all this was done to protect you."

Reuel had a feeling where this was going, and he was relieved. The anger he had toward his parents at the Institute had dissipated. All he wanted was to understand what was going on, and he could sense answers were finally on the way.

"Protect me from what?"

"Abaddon," Abigail said.

"Isn't he dead?" Reuel asked, puzzled, remembering one of the few facts of the Civil War he knew.

"No, we thought he'd been killed, but we were wrong," Hazael answered. "The Guardians have been missing for more than a year. We fear he murdered them all."

"Murdered…" Reuel repeated. "How can you be sure?"

"I'll take it from here," Sophia said. "A short while after Asa disappeared, Uri found his body. This news, of course, was never made public. The High Council met and decided your family and the Grindbler royal family should go into hiding. So Maria erased your family and their family's royal lineage from the minds of all the citizens of Aela. We then planted other royal families in Tesa and Rolte."

"Huh? Why…she can do that?!"

"I'll get to why later, but yes. What you must understand is that your and Elon's safety was of the utmost importance, so we had to move both of you to one place where we could watch over you. You were instructed to never speak of your royal lives because we couldn't risk you jogging anyone's memory," Sophia explained.

"But why?" Reuel asked.

"We have no idea who else can be in cahoots with Abaddon. We had to hide you."

"But why is Abaddon looking for *me*?"

"You see, as long as the Guardians were alive, there could be no others. But once they passed away, a new generation would rise up to replace them. There is a man named Aden Lambton, a Grindbler scientist, one half of the original pair that discovered the Guardians. He speculated that the Guardians possessed an unusually large portion of Zuriel's soul."

"His soul? I thought that was just a story," Reuel said, rubbing his throbbing temples. "Can we please slow down?"

"I'm sorry, there's not a lot of time and we have to catch you up," Sophia answered. "Yes, his soul. It's not just a story. It is said when Zuriel created his four races out of rock, water, wind, and fire, he had to use part of his soul to do so, which gave us the abilities we have. However, Aden believed the Guardians had a more concentrated amount of Zuriel's life energy within them that gave them their longevity and their fantastic abilities, like manipulating and generating the element of their people's origin. Their longevity is similar to the Angelics. Gideon didn't have to infuse his soul into four races, only one. With so much of his life energy, the Angelics developed long lifespans and an amazing intellect."

"What does all this mean?" Reuel said.

"Life cannot be told how to evolve or grow. It does so however it sees fit. That is the basis behind Aden's theory. Somewhere along the way, as generations passed, Zuriel's life energy or soul was stockpiled through certain family lines, and it produced the

Guardians. This surplus of dormant energy happened to blossom in the individuals we knew as the Guardians. It amplified their natural abilities to the point that they were able to manipulate the elements themselves. Aden also believed that the Guardians were not a one-time phenomenon and that their abilities would be passed down. They would lay dormant within their successor until they died. But of course, all of this is only a theory."

The room was silent. Reuel's hands massaged his forehead while his mind slowly put all the pieces together. It was clear to him now where all of this was heading. The conclusion filled his heart with dread, but at the same time caused it to flutter.

"Pass down," he whispered. "I'm related to Uri?"

"He's my father," Hazael answered.

"Your father!"

"Yes, your grandfather."

"Why didn't you tell me this?"

"Only a select few know of Uri and Cyrus's families," Sophia explained. "Unlike Maria and Asa, they decided they didn't want to rule over their people and wanted distance between them and those they cared about."

"So what does this mean? Am I supposed to replace Uri?"

"I believe so," Sophia said plainly. "A year ago, during my annual trip to Horo for the Aquati classification, a trip I must take since most of them refuse to have it done in Ira, I came across something quite interesting. During the classification process, I sensed a great power in one of the queen's sons, Azriel, who according to Aden's theory would be a candidate to become a Guardian. Before my trip, Asa had recently disappeared, and Uri instructed me to be on the lookout for anything unusual. Clearly, that fit the description. Azriel had an immense power deep within, a power I had never sensed before, but I couldn't tap into it to fully assess it. And *that* has never happened before. If I can't assess it, I have no choice but to classify the pupil as an Auxiliary."

Reuel was beyond confused, but he continued to prod. "Then what happened?"

"A travesty would be putting it mildly. The queen's youngest son, groomed to be the General of Horo's army, was an Auxiliary. The festivities were canceled. She refused to even look in his direction—"

"I don't understand how this applies to me," Reuel interrupted.

"I'm not done. As I helped Azriel ascend, we ran into another problem. He told me there had been a force field that prevented him from reaching his chest. He couldn't penetrate it. Based on your incident today, I'm assuming something similar happened to you."

"Yes," Reuel answered.

Sophia nodded. "You and Eve were the last two. I sensed the same power within you two and within Prince Elon," she said. "I believe that none of you will be able to ascend until you're all together. Again, this is not a certainty, but we have to believe it…we have nothing else without you four. According to a good friend, Azriel will arrive in Ira in late summer, but until he arrives, I will train the three of you in secret every night, starting tomorrow."

Suddenly, Reuel remembered something from earlier. "What about Asher Ruskit, what happened when you accessed him?"

Sophia looked at him curiously. "I didn't think anyone noticed."

"I did. What happened?" Reuel asked again. "Is he a Guardian too?"

"No, there's never been an Angelic Guardian. Honestly, I don't know what he is."

With that, Sophia rose to her feet and headed toward the door. "Get some rest, Reuel, you'll need it."

ASHER (I)

Asher, shrouded in darkness, stared out of his bedroom window overlooking the Kingdom of Ira. He watched as a couple of Angelic soldiers returned to the palace carrying a large, black sack.

Another harvest tonight. The thought excited him. His room was in the top of the tower adjacent to the Institute, providing him an excellent view of New Ira.

Since that strange man had arrived at the palace, the soldiers ventured out every few nights. They used the darkness to hide their actions and returned carrying black, lumpy sacks. He hoped one day to join them.

His bedroom view allowed him to see not only the soldiers but the citizens from the safety of his room, concealed by the dark. He had grown fond of the darkness that surrounded him. He would even go as far as to consider it a companion of sorts, and because of this, he seldom lit candles. Not only did the light chase away his accomplice, but it would alert people that there was someone up there, someone watching. And that would spoil the fun. He reveled in being an unknown observer. But on this particular night, he was unable to take pleasure in this pastime.

His mind was too busy replaying the incident from the Institute. He hated how that old hag had stared at him. Like she knew. It had bothered him so deeply that he had not gone to visit his hideaway in the forest in fear that she would be there waiting for him. The feeling disgusted him. He had originally planned on going to his hideaway after leaving the Institute. It was not a far journey, just outside the kingdom's walls and a short walk into the Dead Forest.

Asher had long been fascinated by one of his people's more morbid abilities, harvesting hearts. Their vast intellects interested him, but it was their ability to absorb Zurielians that mesmerized him. It wasn't temporary absorption, either. That was nothing more than a tease. It was permanent absorption that had a strangle hold on his imagination.

His family didn't understand. They couldn't. It was his grandfather and father, after all, who had stood behind the Guardians' decision to outlaw permanent absorption. They couldn't comprehend his thirst. The need to harvest a heart consumed his every fiber, invaded his every thought.

He had come to the conclusion that in order to fully indulge his hidden pleasure he needed more privacy than his father's palace could provide. He needed his own sanctuary, and the only place that could provide such privacy was the Dead Forest. Its animals and legends were enough to keep away prying eyes. He, however, had no *fear* of the place. That word meant nothing to him. Only the weak felt fear.

Roughly two years prior, around his twelfth birthday, Asher executed his plan. He steadily began spending more and more time by the gates of the city interacting with the gate guards, slowly gaining their trust and affection. He would run errands for them and even bring them food from time to time. He spent both early and late winter steadily building a rapport. When early summer arrived, he made his move.

He asked the guards for a small favor: use of the side door. That door was a fortified, average-sized door built into the wall next to the gate. The guards used it to go on patrol outside the walls. It was the only way through the city wall besides the main gate.

At first, they balked at the request. None of them wanted to be responsible for allowing the king's son to venture outside the gates without permission. This was nothing but a bump in the road. If Asher wanted something, he got it. In order to resolve this small problem, he turned his attention to the lieutenant in charge of the gate.

Asher had known the lieutenant long before he had hatched his plan. His name was James. Asher neither remembered nor cared what his last name was. James had started as a palace guard. He was silent and watchful, great attributes for any guard, but Asher believed him to be too observant for his own good.

During his time at the palace, Asher was unable to escape his prying eyes. James seemed to be around every corner, ever vigilant. Most of the palace guards left Asher alone. They knew he had his father's ear and didn't dare wrong him.

James was unlike the others. He took a certain pride in his job and put the wellbeing of the royal family above all else. Some small part of Asher admired James for this, so instead of having him tossed from the Guard altogether, he had his father promote him. He was put in charge of the gate. Asher's privacy was restored, and James owed him a debt that he would now collect.

Asher approached the lieutenant at his post on top of the wall next to the east gate door. James was staring off in the direction of the Dead Forest when Asher loudly cleared his throat to announce his presence. James whirled around and faced the prince.

"I heard you were looking to use the side door," James said. "I knew you were up to something. I'm not like the rest of these fools. I know you're always plotting. I was stationed at the palace for years and never once saw you even attempt to help anyone but yourself."

"Well, then, this should be a short meeting, Lieutenant."

"You're not using the door, Asher. I may no longer be at the palace, but my primary duty is still to ensure your safety."

Asher smiled. James stood in front of him in full armor. On top of his head, he wore an officer-issued Angelic helmet. It was plain in design except for a large, five-pointed star embossed on the forehead. His sleek iron breastplate reflected the sun into Asher's eyes, but he didn't blink.

Around James's waist were two belts. One was attached to long, thick pieces of leather that hung down to his knees, resembling a skirt. The other held his sword. Underneath the skirt were his harem pants, and on his shins he wore sheets of iron.

Asher deduced that James's promotion had not only come with finer armor but a new sense of confidence.

"James, I have come to collect on your debt." Asher's eyes were intense and trained on the lieutenant. James locked eyes with him and immediately redirected his gaze to the ground. This act of submission sealed his fate.

"What debt?" James asked, now staring at the ground. "I owe you nothing, and if you continue to insist on such foolishness, I will inform your father that you have been bothering my men."

Asher's smile widened. James's words sounded tough but lacked the gusto of before.

"Haven't you ever questioned why you were suddenly promoted and sent to the gates?"

James hesitated before he answered. "No. The king rewarded me for my excellent service, simple as that." James raised his gaze.

Asher laughed. "You're only here because I want you here. I had my father promote you to get rid of you. Have you been enjoying this promotion, James? Or do you want it to end?"

James dropped his head in defeat and stared at his sandals. His crushed spirit filled Asher with pride.

"What do you want?" James mumbled.

"I need access to the side door. I wish to come and go as I please."

"Where are you going to go?"

Asher had heard his question but felt no obligation to muster a response. He turned and descended the wall's stairs.

Asher used the side door for the first time the following day. He was up with the sun that morning. Even though he was eager, he didn't allow his enthusiasm to rush him. He enjoyed every step from his bedroom in the tower to Ira's gate. He wanted to savor his liberation.

The guards again became nameless soldiers to him. They had served their purpose. He paid them no attention as he approached the door. He grabbed the door's handle and pushed. He tentatively inched forward and outside of it.

He heard the door latch behind him and a guard's voice along with it. "Knock when you return."

Asher picked up his pace, as he was no longer able to contain his excitement. He was finally alone. He reached the forest's edge. His eyes strained to see the top of its towering trees. He could see no light ahead of him, only the darkness of the forest. A smile spread across his face. He was home.

Asher wasted no time and was able to put together a makeshift enclosure. He cleared out a small area just inside the forest. He was not foolish enough to travel too far into its depths, at least not on his first day.

Once the zip tunnels were built, only Shimmers continued to use the trail through the Dead Forest because of Beliel's relatively close proximity to Ira. But a large entourage was required for safe travel. Asher kept that in mind.

He used fallen branches to create a fence and a small shelter for himself. He utilized the thick, large leaves that the forest used to blot out the sun as his roof. When he had finally finished, he sat outside his shabby shack and waited. It wasn't long before what he was waiting for came trotting along.

The Dead Forest was home to a variety of creatures, many of which had yet to be discovered. However, there was one animal in particular that Asher was looking for. It was known as a whipskat, a purple-and-black-striped feline with whiskers that hung down to its knees. It didn't grow much bigger than the average Angelic child and was known for its ferocity, which was only matched by its bloodlust. It was believed to have been the cause of many child disappearances before the building of the gate.

Asher's eyes adjusted to the darkness just in time to make out the approaching animal. The whipskat sauntered toward the enclosure, every step powerful yet graceful. Its long tail dragged behind it, displacing dirt and small leaves as it approached. The silver whiskers that hung from its mouth glowed slightly in the dark. It momentarily inspected the fence that separated it from Asher then effortlessly leapt over it.

Asher rose to his feet, his eyes never leaving the whipskat's bright-yellow ones. Asher's right arm slowly reached behind his back and grasped the handle of his dagger.

The whipskat crouched, its muscles coiled, ready to pounce. Asher's heart thrashed about in his chest, his fingers tingled, and adrenaline freely flowed throughout his body. He had never felt such a thrill. He withdrew his dagger, slowly rocked back and forth, and then he charged. The whipskat roared and followed suit.

It pounced, paws outstretched and its claws unsheathed. Asher saw there was just enough space between the cat and the ground to give him hope his plan might actually work. He immediately dove at the ground underneath the flying cat.

In one motion, as he flew through the air, he twisted his body so his back was to the ground. He plunged his knife into the underbelly of the feline. The blade sliced through the flesh with minimal resistance. He ripped the blade toward him as the animal's momentum pulled it in the opposite direction. Blood showered Asher's face and bare chest.

The cat landed a few feet from him, dead on impact. A swelling sense of pride rose in Asher. He wiped the blood from his face with the back of his hand and licked the remaining droplets from his lips. A smile broke across his face as he examined his kill. He knelt down beside the cat and prepared for his first harvest.

Asher cut away the flesh covering the cat's chest, revealing a small, still heart. He was careful not to puncture it as he removed it. The heart sat perfectly intact in his palm. He marveled at its beauty and was in awe of what it meant; he had taken a life.

Finally, he placed it in the shack. The heart was not Zurielian, so he could not absorb it. It would hold only sentimental value.

By the time of his first day of Instruction, Asher had filled his shack with hearts from all sorts of animals of the Dead Forest. He kept these hearts in chests and jars of various sizes. It was his prized collection. He wouldn't hesitate to kill to protect it, especially that filthy Zurielian hag. His sister and father were expandable as well if need be. They could never appreciate what he had done. They were scared of the harvest. They failed to realize that they were superior beings. The Zurielians were their crop, but he watched them treat their livestock as beings deserving respect. Disgusting.

Asher's eyes were suddenly heavy from the long day. He glanced out his window once more. He knew the guards were long gone by now, but he looked anyway. There was nothing. He reasoned the harvest had already happened. He climbed into bed and found comfort in his final thought of the day.

I will be a part of the next one.

REUEL (V)

Sleep was the last thing on Reuel's mind after Sophia left. He found it hard to entertain the idea of sleep knowing that the fate of his family, friends, and all the people of Aela was now resting on his scrawny shoulders. He was fourteen. He still hadn't figured out how to fit into the world, let alone save it.

His parents didn't say much once Sophia left. They tried, but it was a waste of all their time. He couldn't stand the sight of them. So he left. He wandered around the kingdom until he found a bench near 14th Street across from the fountain. It was a wide basin of water with a beautiful sculpture of a dragon in its center. From the dragon's mouth flowed a jet of water that kept the basin in constant motion. The sculpture's beauty was the only reason it had not been torn down after the Civil War.

Reuel's brain ached from the information overload. It seemed to have stalled, unsure how to process it all. His parents had no right. There was no excuse for keeping this from him. He had a right to know about the world outside of Tesa and to have some understanding of how things worked.

Save the world?! he thought. *I don't know anything about it!*

His hands cradled his head while his fingers tugged on his hair as if trying to pull out the solution he was so desperately seeking. Suddenly, Reuel felt something on his leg and nearly jumped from the bench in fright. There was a slender white hand resting there. It was attached to a wrist sporting a gold dragon bracelet. The clasp was a dragon's head biting its own tail.

"I didn't think you would actually show up," Ruth said.

"Huh? What are you talking about?" Reuel asked, staring forward, not looking at her.

"Remember, I told you I like to people-watch by the fountain in the mornings. I invited you to join me."

Reuel stared at the fountain and shook his head in disbelief. "Of course."

"Is something wrong?"

"I didn't even mean to come here." He shook his head again. "I've lost control of my life—but besides that, everything's great."

"Did you ever really have control to begin with?"

"What do you mean?"

"I mean did you have control over when you were born, or to whom?"

Reuel thought for a moment and surrendered a small smile. "No, I didn't."

"If you've never had control, then how can you be so surprised that you don't have it now?"

"I don't know. I feel like I'm not even in charge of my *own* actions. It's like something is deciding everything for me."

Ruth nodded. "Well, if everything seems predetermined, then maybe you should stop fighting it and just let it run its course."

Reuel looked at her. "But what if I'm scared? What if I can't be who they want me to be?" He said nothing for a while. "If you're so wise, answer that."

Reuel continued before Ruth could respond. "My whole life, I've lived in my own world, and things were good there. But today, I learned that my world wasn't real. *This* is the real world, and I don't know if I can handle it."

She gently nudged him with her shoulder. "You're stronger than you think. I bet the people pushing you wouldn't expect so much if they didn't think so too."

He nodded. "Maybe you're right. But still...Why can't things be how they used to be? You know what I mean?"

Ruth sighed. "Before my mom died, we used to spend time as a family—me, my mom, my dad, and Asher. Those were the best times. But now my father is always too busy, and my brother is constantly off by himself, doing who knows what. So I wander around by myself in the middle of the night until the wee hours of the morning. I sit here *by myself* and watch others interact at the fountain. So yes, I think I know the feeling. The thing is, you can't be selfish with the great moments of the past. You love them, cherish them, hold them tight, and remember them. But you have to allow them to be memories so you can allow yourself to experience even better ones. They weren't meant to last forever, just for that moment."

Her eyes expressed an understanding that he couldn't quite explain, a caring that shouldn't have been there. Her hair fell almost perfectly around her face, but there were a few strands slightly out of place resting on the inside of her right eye. He couldn't stop himself from reaching out and brushing the stray strands away and over her ear.

That was the trigger. He could no longer hold in any more secrets, he couldn't carry this burden alone anymore. He told her everything, from his own royal lineage to the revelation that he was a Guardian. She took it all in, hanging onto every detail. She didn't interrupt him, never once asking for clarification or offering suggestions. She just listened.

When he finished, she interlocked her fingers with his and simply said, "We have each other now. We'll never be alone again."

They sat on the bench talking until the sun peaked over the kingdom's gates and showered Ira in light.

The quiet evaporated as the sun rose. The city was again alive. Reuel leaned in and gently planted a kiss on her cheek. "Thank you," he said. "Will I see you later?"

"I'm sure you will," she answered and walked away toward New Ira.

On his way home, Reuel thought of nothing but Ruth. There was something special about her, something marvelous. She had somehow reduced his burden to nearly nothing. He didn't know what it was about her, but he loved how she made him feel.

He arrived at the mountain staircase and realized that he was still not ready to go home. He turned around and headed toward Elon's stand. He remembered that Sophia had mentioned him, too.

He's probably going through the same things as me. He'll need someone to talk to, too, Reuel reasoned.

By the time Elon's stand was in view, Darius's Way was bustling. There was a decent-sized crowd in front of Elon's stand. Reuel maneuvered his way through the crowd until he was only a few people away from the counter. He was tall enough to peer over them and see that Elon was busy packing fruits into a basket for a stubby Grindbler woman.

"Elon!" Reuel shouted, but Elon didn't flinch. Even at this distance, it was still too loud for Elon to hear him.

Elon handed the woman her basket and pointed into the crowd for the next customer. Reuel continued to shout and wave his arms frantically. Elon finally spotted him, and Reuel watched as his face lit up with a brilliant smile. Elon was ecstatic. He turned and waved to somebody behind him, and a boy a little smaller than himself came into view. There was a scar that stretched from the boy's right ear down to his lips.

While the boy took on the plethora of customers, Elon came from behind the stand and embraced Reuel. He lifted him off the ground and spun him around. This garnered many annoyed looks from those around them.

"Put me down," Reuel laughed.

Elon released him and scratched the back of his head in embarrassment. "I'm sorry. I'm just so excited. Aren't you? I knew I was more than just another Auxiliary. And why didn't you tell me you're a prince too?"

"Not so loud," Reuel hissed. "My parents told me

155

not to. Aren't you nervous about all this? I mean, do you understand what's ahead of us?"

"Do *you* understand what's ahead of us!?" Elon asked, then dropped his voice before he continued. "We're Guardians. We. Can. Do. Anything. We're gods!"

"We shouldn't talk about this here," Reuel said, looking around nervously. "Can we go somewhere?"

"Sure. I have to go to the loading docks to pick up an order. We can talk on the way there."

Elon led the way back onto Darius's Way and toward New Ira where the loading docks were located. They had a ways to go but moved quickly enough through the crowd. They passed the Institute and turned onto 55th Street. The traffic on this street was greatly reduced. There were only a handful of people around them. Reuel had been silent the whole trip, wondering how one broached a topic of such magnitude.

Maybe it won't be so bad, he thought. *Elon doesn't seem worried.*

This thought only soothed him until he remembered that they were only Guardians because Abaddon had hunted down and murdered the previous ones. Reuel was certain that Abaddon was not going to treat them any differently.

"You realize that the Guardians are dead. That's

the only reason we're in this position," Reuel stated.

"I do," Elon said solemnly. "But that doesn't mean this is not a blessing. This happened for a reason. Sophia said a war is coming, and when it comes I want to be able to do something. I want to be able to protect those I love. That would've been impossible as an Auxiliary. I wouldn't have lasted long on the front lines against Elites or Premiers, and especially not against Abaddon. But now I can make a difference. *We* can make a difference."

He was right. They were now in a position to do something. "Aren't you mad that our parents kept this from us?" Reuel asked. "I don't know about you, but I knew *nothing*."

"I didn't either. My mother never even mentioned that her father was Cyrus. I was a prince, just like you, who didn't know much beyond the palace and city. I don't understand why they did it, but I assume they did it to protect us."

"Protect us? They might have killed us. We have no real training. We really have no idea what we're even going up against!"

Elon stopped walking and turned to Reuel, his expression stern, all traces of excitement gone. The sight of him not wearing a smile troubled Reuel.

"They're our parents and they did their best. They didn't expect the Guardians to be murdered. They weren't planning to have to train us to save the world. We don't have the luxury of being mad at them or holding grudges anymore. That's what kids do, and after last night, we're not kids anymore. Yes, they might have messed up, but we need their help, and we have to forgive them. We're the only hope Aela has, and we have to embrace it for everyone's sake."

Reuel searched Elon's eyes to see if he truly believed what he was saying. Elon stared back confidently without faltering. "You're right," Reuel finally said.

"All we have is each other: you, me, Eve, Azriel, Sophia, our parents, and the rest of our families. We don't need to be fighting in the family."

"I guess I didn't see it that way," Reuel said. "You think we're going to be able to do it?"

"I don't know. But we have to try, right?"

"We do."

"Come on, we still have to get to the docks." Elon started walking again.

The street eventually opened up, and they had arrived at the loading docks. Like the market in Old Ira, the docks were crowded and in constant motion. Similar to how all the even-numbered streets in Old Ira led to the outskirts, all the odd-numbered streets in New Ira led to the loading docks.

There were Giant Hawks swooping in overhead

hauling large boxes full of wheat, grain, and corn. Horses trudged along, pulling crates of apples and cabbages. Fathers and their sons wore baskets on their backs, filled to the brim with fresh meats. There were men pulling out jugs of what looked like water and bundles of fish tied together with thick pieces of rope.

From what Reuel saw, there was actually some kind of order to the chaos. The docks were built around Ira's zip tunnel. The tunnel station was positioned in the middle of all the commotion. The imports were separated into sections labeled with large picket signs. Elon led them toward a sign that read "Horo's Freshest Fish and Water."

Elon approached an old, sickly looking Angelic man who stood near the sign. His hair was thinning, even missing in places. A silver chain dangled from his thin neck, and when he saw Elon, he dug through a pile of fish and pulled out a bundle along with a large jug of water.

"Elon!" the old man exclaimed. "Good to see you this morning."

"Good to see you too, Samuel, how are the fish today?" Elon asked.

The old man pointed at his picket sign. "The freshest in the market, maybe one of the best batches we've had in a while."

"Great!" Elon smiled. "And this is my friend Reuel.

He's new to Ira…"

"I don't mean to be rude," Reuel interrupted. "But how old *are* you?"

Samuel chuckled. "It's nice to meet you, too, and welcome to our great city. And I'll have you know I'm in great health for my age. I recently turned two hundred and seventy-three years old, but my body isn't a day over a hundred and five. Why do you ask?"

"I've never seen someone so old," Reuel answered. "You look too old to be…out and about. Again, I don't mean to be rude," he added hastily.

Samuel laughed long and hard. "It's fine. I only have a few years left in me, and I've learned to laugh when I can." But then the smile vanished, and Samuel became deathly serious. "I used to have a few friends who were Elites. Now, they had seen many things in their time. They had some stories."

"What happened to them?" Reuel asked.

"The Guardians."

"What do you mean?"

"They felt they had lived long enough."

Reuel's next question was on the edge of his tongue when Elon gave him a firm elbow to the side, and he was silent.

"Thank you again, Samuel. See you tomorrow." Elon picked up the bundle of fish and the jug of water.

"You are more than welcome!" Samuel smiled

widely, as if his previously solemn demeanor had never occurred.

As they turned to leave, Samuel grabbed Elon's arm. "You boys be careful, I heard more children went missing last night. Be vigilant when you're out here at night. No one's safety is guaranteed, even Grindbler children have vanished."

"Don't worry, Samuel, we'll stick together," Elon said.

Samuel released his arm. "Make sure you do."

The boys pivoted and reentered the hectic loading dock crowd. Elon again led the way. People bounced off of him as he walked, making a clear path for Reuel to follow.

"What do you think he meant by the Guardians 'felt his friends had lived long enough'? You think they killed them?" Reuel asked.

"Who knows," Elon responded over his shoulder. "He's an old man, you can only imagine all the things he's seen in his life. I think it's done something to his head. I doubt everything's together up there."

"You're probably right, and it was war anyway, people die." Reuel stopped walking and grabbed Elon's shoulder. "We're going to have to kill some people too, besides Abaddon—aren't we?"

"I suppose so..."

They continued onward, but neither of them said

another word. When they reached 55th Street, they saw
a man dressed in Angelic armor hammering a "Miss-
ing Person" sign onto a light post on the side of the
street. Reuel started toward the light post and nudged
Elon to follow. The soldier was walking away as they
got there. The boys quickly read the sign. The parch-
ment was encased in a wooden frame and covered by
glass. There was a detailed sketch of a young girl. Under the sketch read:

Race: Shimmer

Last Seen: Mountain Housing

Age: 16

Reuel recognized the girl. She had played the trick
on the little boy on the landing yesterday.

"I've seen her before," Reuel said quietly.

"Did you know her?" Elon asked.

"No. I saw her playing yesterday…You think any
of the kids are going to turn up?"

"I don't know, but I doubt it."

The boys were unable to pry themselves away from
the sign.

"We have to do something," Reuel said flatly.

"I know," Elon answered.

"This is why," Reuel said. "This is why we have to
be brave. We have to fight for those who can't fight

for themselves. If we don't, these signs will cover all the light posts in Ira. If evil people have to die for the innocent to live, then so be it."

Elon nodded.

But what if...we have to kill some of the innocent? The thought flashed across Reuel's mind. *Can that be justified?* He had no answer for himself.

"We have to get back," Elon said. "I can't leave my brother at the stand by himself for too long."

They arrived at the stand at high-day, and the mid-day crowd that had surrounded the stand earlier had dwindled. Elon's brother wore a tired and mildly aggravated expression, but it was washed away and replaced with a triumphant smile when Elon expressed how proud of him he was.

"Now take this home," Elon said and handed his brother the bundle of fish and water.

"Yes, sir," he answered obediently. But before he left, he stretched out his hand to Reuel. "Aaron Warring."

"Reuel Haldane." Reuel tried to avoid staring at the scar running down the boy's face, but it was futile.

"Don't worry about it. It gets a lot of attention. I tripped and fell on my knife a few years ago. I won't run with it unsheathed again, that's for certain. Well, at least until my skin is as strong as Elon's."

"It'll get there, Aaron, you're only ten," Elon chimed in.

163

"Ten? Wow, you're big for ten," Reuel said in awe.

Elon laughed and puffed out his chest. "He's still got a lot of growing to do. Hurry up and get that home so Mother can salt it," Elon ordered.

Aaron said nothing more. He grabbed the goods and sprinted off toward the mountain homes. They watched him until he was too far to make out. They were so focused on him that they didn't notice Eve had arrived at the stand.

She shook her head. "I' been lookin' for y'all all day. I spent my mornin' walkin' up and down Darius's Way. Sophia said Elon's parents own' this stan' but I didn' see him when I got here."

"We just got back," Reuel explained. "We went down to the loading docks for a while."

"Hey, Eve," Elon said with a goofy smile.

She smiled but didn't take her eyes off Reuel. She seemed all about business at the moment.

"How did it go when Sophia came to see you?" Reuel asked.

"Abel cried when he hear' the news. He tri' to comfort me, but I think I was really comfortin' him. I did fin' out that Maria was my mother."

"That's amazing!" Elon exclaimed.

"Yeah, I guess this is a bigger deal than I thought. You were right, Reuel."

Reuel nodded.

"It is…" Elon touched Eve's shoulder. "But we're in this together. From here on out, we look out for each other."

"I agree," Reuel added.

"Me too. So, what do we do now?" Eve asked. She shook her shoulder slightly, freeing it from Elon's hand.

"Get ready to train tonight," Reuel responded.

"Sophia said we should wait 'til it's night before we meet her behind the Institute," Elon said, staring at the ground, seemingly embarrassed by Eve's subtle rejection.

"I think we should stay together," Reuel said. "But I don't want to go home."

"We can stay here," Elon offered. "I have to close the stand at evening-light anyway."

While they waited for evening-light to arrive, they gradually began to open up to one another. They discussed people and things they missed from their homelands. Eve educated them on some of the many things they were unaware of about the rest of Aela, and they laughed together at their ignorance. It was in these moments that their collective bond grew stronger. As dusk approached, Elon pulled down the curtains of the stand, closing it.

They walked in the direction of the Institute, and with each step, it seemed to grow darker. By the time they arrived, night had taken its hold on Ira. Even with the candlelight from the light posts, it was hard to make out the things in front of them. They arrived at the Institute and walked around back, passing the palace along the way.

Reuel had a sudden urge to gaze up at the tower closest to them. There was a large window near the top, and he wondered if anyone ever used it.

It was nearly pitch-black when they reached the back of the Institute. The building blocked the little light that the light posts provided. The only light came from the white sun above them. It didn't provide heat like its yellow counterpart, but it did provide a ghastly light. It was just enough for Elon to make out a couple of silhouettes leaning against the Institute's wall.

He pointed in their direction and whispered, "Over there."

They shuffled toward the figures but came to a halt when one of the figures started to walk toward them. The figures were clothed in long, hooded black robes. Reuel counted five of them in all. The one that had approached them pulled their hood down, revealing an old, red face.

Sophia looked at each of them, nodded, and spoke, "We've been waiting for you. Follow me."

She led them back to the other robed figures. They said nothing, nor did they remove their hoods. They remained motionless against the wall. Sophia and the children stood facing them. She took a step forward and they spread apart, leaving a patch of wall bare. She approached the wall and placed her hand on one of the stones and pushed. The wall rose, revealing nothing but more darkness. Sophia bent down and picked something up off the ground. She then dragged it against the inside of the opening, creating a spark.

Reuel watched as the spark lit a torch on the wall and a trail of fire ran along the wall to the next torch, and then to the next, until a stairwell was visible. Sophia began descending the stairs, and the others in robes followed closely behind her.

Reuel squeezed both Elon's and Eve's forearms and then followed. Elon stuck close to Reuel, and Eve took up the rear. The opening closed behind her.

ASHER (II)

Asher sat in darkness, enjoying his view of the city. Earlier that evening, he had once again watched the palace soldiers venture off into the kingdom. His only wish was that they returned with a black sack. If they did, then tonight would be *the* night. His body tingled with excitement, but there was something nagging him.

Not long after the guards had left, he saw three children walk around the Institute and never emerge. Naturally, he was intrigued. They clearly weren't Angelics, and at this time of night, there was nothing for them in New Ira.

It was an unwritten but understood rule that Zurielians were not to be in New Ira after dark. One of them even had the audacity to look up at his window, and in that moment, Asher had been afraid. In the depths of the Dead Forest, he had stared down and killed beasts that few had ever seen, but that boy's glance had somehow struck him with fear. Asher couldn't make any sense of it, and part of him didn't want to.

His eyes didn't leave the Institute until he spotted the soldiers returning to the palace. He quickly scanned their persons and saw they were in fact carrying a large black sack.

He jumped to his feet and leaped at his door. He flung it open and took three, four, then five steps at a time until he was on the ground floor. He then raced through a well-lit corridor. The statues that stood along its walls were just blurs in his peripheral vision. At the end of the corridor, he hid behind a column and looked into the palace lobby.

The three soldiers had dropped the sack in the middle of the lobby and gathered around it, but they made no moves toward it, as if they were waiting for something.

Or someone...the stranger, he thought. The lobby walls were lined with gold leaves, and large marble columns were spread throughout, which held the domed roof in place. The inside of the dome roof was a purportedly beautiful mosaic that Asher didn't much care for.

The guards suddenly stood erect and focused their attention on the corridor that led to his father's quarters. Asher heard the rhythmic pattern of footsteps coming from the corridor. With the aid of the torches that lined the corridor's walls, he was able to see the outline of a mountainous figure approaching. It took long brisk strides and was standing in the lobby within moments.

Him...

The figure was covered in a hooded black cloak. The hood concealed his face, but the cloak fell awkwardly around the figure's body. It bulged strangely around the figure's shoulders and back. The cloak was split down the front, revealing a muscular abdomen and core. His legs were covered by black silk harem pants. The figure was only slightly taller than the guards but dwarfed them in girth. Large, pasty hands hung by his side.

The soldiers knelt in his presence, heads bowed. Asher had only seen the stranger a few times since he first arrived at the palace. He isolated himself, rarely leaving the guest room located next to his father's quarters.

Asher knew only a few things for certain about him: he never left his room during the day, he didn't allow anyone to look at his face, and everyone in the palace feared him—especially his father.

However, the man evoked no fear in Asher, only inspiration. Asher envied the fear the man struck in the others. His father wasn't the bravest man by any stretch of the imagination, but he was a proud king. And no proud king allowed a stranger to come into his palace and take charge. Yet that was exactly what the stranger had done.

The stranger strolled past the soldiers. Asher noticed his eyes were glazing a dull yellow. He easily picked up the sack that the three soldiers had struggled to drag in. He juggled it in his hands and then looked inside of it. This was the moment. Asher stepped from behind the column.

The stranger's glazing yellow eyes left the contents of the sack and focused on him. Asher wasn't sure what to do next, so he waited for the stranger to make the first move.

The stranger raised one of his large hands and motioned for Asher to come closer. Asher didn't hesitate. He fearlessly walked toward the stranger. He stood in front of him and stared up at the looming man.

At this distance, he was able to see how misshapen the man's body was. The cloak struggled to hide the strange lumps, and Asher could only imagine what he looked like without it.

The figure dropped the sack, and Asher heard muffled cries as it hit the ground. The stranger reached toward his head and pulled back his hood. Asher stood unfazed. He didn't flinch at the sight of the man's ghostly white face. It looked thin and sickly but at the same time radiated strength.

His sunken eyes were locked with Asher's. They were no longer glazing. One of the soldiers made the mistake of raising his head, hoping to catch a glimpse. The stranger's eyes remained locked with Asher's, but they began to glaze again, this time a dull red.

The stranger stretched his hand out toward the soldier. Sweat suddenly dripped from Asher's face. The stranger's hand was emitting intense heat.

A stream of fire erupted from the stranger's hand and engulfed the misguided soldier. The soldier shrieked as his body burned. After a few moments, the stream of fire ceased and the charred corpse of the soldier lay face down on the ground. Asher kept eye contact with the stranger, catching the action only in his peripheral vision. The stranger smiled, revealing dirty, ruddy teeth. He nodded toward the soldier's body.

Asher took the hint and glanced at the soldier's remains. His skin was black and peeling. One of his arms had been completely melted off. Asher looked back at the stranger, who was still smiling.

"Come," he said coldly. He pulled his hood over his head, picked up the sack, and turned to head back down the corridor from which he came.

"Clean up the body," he said to the two remaining soldiers. "And bring the girl to me."

Asher was confused by the latter statement until he heard a gasp from behind one of the columns near the entrance of the lobby. His sister sprinted from behind a column and out of the palace. The soldiers started after her.

"Now, if you wish to harvest these hearts, then follow me."

The stranger slung the sack over his back and walked down the corridor. The bag's contents moaned and squirmed. Asher followed anxiously behind the stranger. He didn't give his sister a second thought.

REUEL (VI)

Reuel and the others sat cross-legged on the floor of an underground room. Sophia stood in front of them, with Reuel and Elon's parents on either side. They had taken off their hoods and stood expressionless. Reuel's parents, Abigail and Hazael, stood to one side of Sophia while Elon's parents, Moriah and Jonas, resided on the other.

This was the first time Reuel had seen Elon's parents, and he immediately noted that Elon took after his father, sporting the same strong jaw, skin tone, and large build. Elon's mother was much smaller by comparison, and her skin was a little lighter. Her robe covered her body, but Reuel saw the strength in her eyes. Reuel's father cleared his throat, and all eyes were on him.

"We will be the new High Council," Hazael said. "The five of us will train you three to fight, and you in return will lead us. We will be the resistance. The war on the horizon will not be like the last. The loser will not be imprisoned and allowed to live as Gideon was. The winner will control Aela. Either Abaddon and Gideon die, or we die. Cohabitation is not an option."

"What happen' to Zuriel?" Eve asked. "Couldn' he help us? Didn' he fight with you last time?"

"He did," Abigail answered. "But nobody has seen or heard from him since the end of the war. He disappeared…"

"He left us," Sophia interrupted. "Zuriel no longer believed in interfering with our lives, so he exiled himself after we won the war."

"Why would he do that, knowing that Gideon wasn't dead?" Reuel asked.

"He sealed Gideon away. Only the Guardians knew of the location and how to release him. Zuriel knew that the Guardians were the only ones with this information and that they had sworn to protect Aela. So he decided he'd leave everything in their hands. I'm sure he didn't know Abaddon had survived. No one did," Sophia explained.

"Then he'll come back now since Gideon could possibly be released, right?" Reuel asked.

"I don't know," Sophia responded. "We have to prepare as if he won't, and until Azriel arrives, we will train you in all aspects of combat."

Hazael took off his robe, revealing a slim, muscular build. "Hand-to-hand combat training starts today," he said.

His green torso was bare. He wore only black harem pants and sandals. He cracked his neck, loosened his shoulders, and looked Reuel dead in the eyes.

"I know you're mad at me, son, but this is what you wanted, after all, isn't it? Me training you."

"Hazael, he's not ready…" Abigail protested.

"There is no more time to debate this. They haven't ascended. They are not yet Guardians," Hazael answered. "They have to learn how to defend themselves."

"Hazael is right," Moriah interjected.

"Moriah, they are children," Abigail said. "Our children."

"Exactly. It's time. No more lies. No more postponing the inevitable," Moriah continued. "I will not lose my son. Go ahead, Hazael."

Abigail sighed. "I understand."

"Reuel will be first. Everybody give us space," Hazael said.

Elon and Eve didn't leave Reuel's side until he nodded in agreement. They got up and stood several paces behind him, opposite of the Council members who stood behind Hazael. Reuel and his father stood alone in the center of the room.

Reuel glared at his father and allowed himself to remember the depth of his deception. The anger swelled like a bubble on the precipice of bursting. His scrawny chest heaved with frustration, and a surge of adrenaline flooded his system as he began to glaze.

Everything around him blurred. He felt nearly weightless. He charged at his father. Hazael was ready, his knees slightly bent, his fists clenched, and his eyes glazing a vibrant green. With his right arm, Reuel threw a wide punch at his father's face. It was fast, but Hazael dodged it easily. He ducked under the arm and shoved a flat hand against his son's chest, sending him across the room.

Reuel got to his feet and again raced at his father. This time, he faked high and threw a powerful left fist at his father's stomach. He hit nothing but air. His father sidestepped the jab and sent an elbow crashing into Reuel's face. He dropped to the floor. Blood shot from his nose.

Hazael's eyes returned to normal. "How did I beat you?"

"You're faster—stronger," Reuel stuttered.

"Yes, but that's not all. You're fast, especially for an Auxiliary. But you're reckless, you can't control your speed, and you're predictable. You have to learn how to channel your anger and use it constructively. And I will teach you." Hazael reached out his hand.

Reuel wiped the blood from his face with the back of his forearm and grabbed his father's outstretched hand. "Yes, sir."

Hazael faced Elon and Eve. "What did you guys see?"

"Not much," Elon answered.

"Yeah, you guys were mostly blurs," Eve added.

"I expected as much, but in time you will be able to follow our movements," Hazel explained. "The rest of the Council I'm sure were able to follow along."

"The war trained us all to follow the movements of even glazing Elite Windwalkers," Jonas, Elon's father, said.

Hazael nodded his head. "Elon, you're next."

Reuel took Elon's place next to Eve while Elon stepped into the center of the room with Hazael. Elon wasted no time. His eyes glazed immediately. Hazael smirked and was then a blur.

Reuel's previous training in Tesa helped him to follow his father's movements. Elon, however, scanned the room frantically, trying to catch a glimpse of the speedster.

He swung widely at Hazael; at least what he thought was Hazael. From the effort put into each punch, Reuel safely assumed that they would have done devastating damage if any landed, but none did. At last, Hazael planted a powerful punch of his own into Elon's unflexed stomach, causing the Grindbler to crumple.

Hazael stood over him. "You're strong, but you can't hit what you can't catch. You have to learn to use your head before you can effectively use your strength."

Elon, still struggling to catch his breath, only shook his head.

"Eve," Hazael said.

Elon stumbled over and sat next to the bloodied Reuel. Eve stepped forward for her turn in the ring with Hazael. He again became a blur. He moved swiftly around the Shimmer, but she only stood there, perfectly still.

Hazael went in for the finishing blow. He raised his right fist and threw a punch at Eve's head. In a fluid motion, she dropped to the ground and swept his feet with her leg. Hazael went sprawling across the floor. A collective gasp came from Reuel and Elon. The Council members clapped and smiled.

Hazael sprang to his feet. "How did you know where I was?" he asked.

"I couldn' see you, but I' hear you." She pointed at his sandals and smiled. "I didn' have a lot of room for error, but the soun' of your sandals against this floor gave me a rough idea of where you were. You' really fast. I almost miss' you."

Hazael smiled too. "I expected nothing less from a Shimmer. You live up to your reputation."

Eve's smile grew wider. "Thank you, sir."

Reuel and Elon embraced Eve, and they all held each other for a moment before Sophia interrupted.

"That's all we have time for tonight. We'll continue with your lessons tomorrow. We will have to leave here separately. You three will leave first, and we will follow soon after. We can't risk all of us being seen together."

"Yes, ma'am," Reuel said. He then looked to his parents. "I'll see you at home."

Hazael nodded as Abigail helped him put his robe back on. Sophia led the children up the stairs and pressed on a panel on the wall, which raised the entrance.

"Be quiet, and stick to the shadows. No need to have any Angelics seeing you in this part of the kingdom this late," Sophia whispered.

They nodded in agreement and walked into the night.

Reuel didn't hear his parents come in behind him that night. The instant his body hit his cot, he fell into a deep sleep. He woke up the next morning perplexed. He laid in his bed trying to interpret his latest dream.

It wasn't a nightmare, but instead, he had dreamt of Ruth.

He had been outside of his body, watching himself, but he could still *feel* what was going on. He and Ruth stood side by side. Her beauty mesmerized him, even in his dreams, but she was much older here. Her blonde hair was tied up in a bun on top of her head. Reuel noticed that he, too, looked older and that his hair was cut short.

They stood atop a mountain, holding hands. He didn't know where they were, but it felt like a real place. He felt the wind brush against his cheeks; it was warm to the touch.

Ruth's right hand gripped his left tightly, and they both clutched swords in their free hands. They were dressed in armor. She wore a dull silver chest plate decorated with deep gouges. Her legs were covered by a skirt made up of thick pieces of leather, and silver plates protected her shins. He was dressed in a shiny silver chest plate. The Windwalker crest was embossed on it. His armor lacked the gouges and scratches, but it was adorned with red splotches. He had on black harem pants and steel boots.

He could feel the weight of a second sword that was attached to a scabbard on his back. He felt relieved, happy even. The reason for this happiness was unclear, but he and Ruth stared off into the horizon wearing matching weary smiles. Then he woke up.

Like all his dreams lately, Reuel wasn't sure what it meant, but it was a welcomed change from the nightmare that had plagued him. After spending sufficient time analyzing the now fading dream, he got up from his bed. He walked out of his room and into the empty living room. He picked up the apple that was waiting for him on the table without breaking stride and headed out the front door.

He didn't want to run into his parents until it was absolutely necessary at the Institute later. The searing anger he had harbored just yesterday was gone, but he still had no urge to talk to them at the moment. He wanted to see Elon and Eve. He craved their presence. His parents could sympathize, but they didn't truly understand.

Where's Ruth... he suddenly thought.

He couldn't keep her out of his head. She had somehow burrowed her way into the deepest recesses of his being. Her presence had even managed to rid him of his reoccurring nightmare, at least for a night. The thought of her calmed his mind and bathed his heart in pleasure. She provided balance, and that was something he couldn't do without.

Reuel was just ahead of the morning rush and was one of the first people on Darius's Way. He briskly walked among the growing number of patrons. He could see Elon in the distance pulling up the curtain of his family's stand and opening it for the day, but something else caught his attention.

Something was redirecting the sunlight straight into his left eye. His eye twitched uncontrollably in response. He scanned the stands and houses to his left for the culprit. From out of the shadows of 7th Street protruded a hand wearing a gold bracelet. The bracelet was aimed at him and gleamed in the morning sun.

As Reuel started toward 7th, the hand disappeared. He lengthened his stride and his pace quickened. He arrived at an empty street, bewildered. He was willing to bet he knew the owner of that bracelet. But where was she?

This particular street was narrow, and the houses were built almost too close together. Even in the morning, this alley was dark. The roofs of the houses blocked most of the sunlight, and it had few street lamps.

Reuel moved cautiously down the alley. "Ruth…" he whispered. There was no response. "Ruth…" Still no response.

Reuel waited a little longer then turned around to head to Elon's stand. But before he reached Darius's Way, a hand wrapped around his mouth and pulled him back into the shadows. He whirled around, his eyes already glazing, ready to defend himself.

Ruth stood before him in a dirt-stained tunic. Her hair was messy, and her face was filthy. Nonetheless, Reuel admired how even in all this grime, she was still stunning. He relaxed and his eyes reverted to their normal state, but the bags under Ruth's eyes highlighted the fear they held, and Reuel was again on edge.

"What's going on?" he asked.

She shifted uncomfortably. "Things are bad…"

Her anxiety was unsettling. Her usual upbeat demeanor was nowhere to be found. "Explain," Reuel prodded.

Her eyes anxiously darted from side to side. "I'm in trouble, Reuel. I saw something I wasn't supposed to see."

"What was it?"

"I don't have time to explain. They're looking for me." Her head was on a swivel, and she had yet to sustain meaningful eye contact with him.

"I can help you, but you have to tell me what's going on."

"No…you can't. You need to get out of here. You and your family need to leave NOW!" she screamed. Her hands raced to her mouth, and the fear in her eyes was nearly palpable.

Reuel grabbed her by the shoulders, pulled her into his chest, and wrapped his arms around her. He felt her tears run down his bare chest, and her body heaved and shook violently as she wept.

"I got you. Nothing's going to happen."

She clung tightly to him and cried for a while. The heaving slowed, and she pushed him away softly, shaking her head.

"I can't ask that from you. You don't understand what's happening. Things are going to get bad…really bad. You need to get as far away from Ira as you can. I'm leaving now."

A familiar anger rose up in him. "Where are you going? Why won't you tell me what's happening?"

"There's not enough time, and I don't want to put you in any more danger. I've already spent too much time talking to you right now. I just wanted to see you before I left."

"How are you going to get out of the city? The tunnels are shut down for the season."

"I was planning on getting a ride from one of the hawk riders at the dock." She rose up on her tiptoes. Her mouth hovered just slightly away from Reuel's lips. She leaned forward, pressed her hands against his chest for support, and kissed him deeply. For a moment, Reuel was at peace, but then Ruth withdrew and started to turn away.

"You said we would never be alone again," Reuel whispered. "That we have each other."

"I don't want to leave, but…I know too much…I'm not safe here!" She was nearly hysterical.

"I'm a Guardian, I can protect you."

"Not against this."

"But you're the *Princess* of Ira. They will look for you."

"That's precisely my problem now. I have to go."

It was clear he wasn't going to convince her otherwise. Whatever she had seen had scared her too much, but before Ruth completely turned to leave, he grabbed her hand and swung her around so that she faced him one more time. He held her face and stared at her until her eyes focused on his.

"This is not the end. I will see you again."

"…I hope so."

He kissed her again, this time planting it on her forehead. She backed away slowly, maintaining eye contact, then turned and sprinted down the street.

Reuel stared into the darkness of the narrow street, unable to move. His chest ached as if his heart had just exploded, leaving only a pulpy mess. Helplessness had become an all too familiar feeling, but this time from it a realization was birthed—it was both swift and poignant. He was going to keep his promise.

This would not be the end. The thought was firmly cemented in his subconscious.

In the midst of this declaration, Reuel found himself wondering if what he was feeling for Ruth was love—the type of love that his father had for his mother. The type of love that could make a Windwalker move mountains. They all needed him to be a man: his parents, Aela, and now Ruth. He wouldn't fail her.

Reuel emerged from the side street and headed toward Elon's stand. From a distance, he saw that Elon and Aaron were finishing the final preparations for the morning rush. It was then that Reuel noticed Eve was also about to arrive. No one had noticed him yet, and he knew that Elon was itching to get some time alone with Eve, so he glazed and sprinted a few stands down from Elon's. He was just within earshot.

When Eve arrived at the stand, Elon lightly nudged his brother, who took the hint and went to the back to organize the empty crates. Eve had her hair tied up in a bun on the top of her head, leaving her face completely exposed. It shone in the morninglight's sun, and even Reuel had to admit she was radiant.

"Have you eaten yet?" Elon asked.

"No, not yet. I was hopin' to maybe get somethin' here?"

"Well, you're in luck. We just finished unpacking the apples, if you're interested."

"That's fine."

Elon plucked a juicy red apple from the display and handed it to her. "A beautiful red apple for a beautifully red girl," he said in his most charming voice. Reuel chuckled from his hiding spot.

"Thanks." She took a bite. "Where's Reuel?"

"He's probably on his way." Elon sounded slightly disappointed.

She nodded. "I really do appreciate the apple, Elon."

"You're welcome..." Elon smiled, and it looked as if he was going to say something more, but a Windwalker woman came to the stand asking for a basket of apples. She was the beginning of the morning rush, and with that, his alone time with Eve was no more.

Elon grabbed Aaron for help as the number of customers grew. Reuel waited until the mob of customers thinned momentarily and then headed to the stand.

"Here he comes," Eve said.

Reuel navigated his way through the dwindling crowd until he was standing next to Eve.

"Reuel—great timing." Elon rolled his eyes.

Reuel chuckled. "Believe me, I took my time."

Elon didn't laugh. Instead, his eyes intently scanned Reuel's face for a few moments.

"What happened?" he asked.

Reuel looked from him to Eve, then to the ground. "Nothing. It's not important right now. We have bigger things to focus on."

"Just tell us," Eve demanded.

Reuel again looked from Elon to Eve. "I was on my way here…"

He was interrupted by a violent tremor. The tremor soon morphed into a full-blown earthquake. The stand jostled uncontrollably back and forth as if it were ready to collapse. Elon took hold and held it steady.

The ground rumbled and groaned like a large Grindbler's starving stomach. The earth tore and cracked—rising and falling in random places. Buildings rocked back and forth, and just as suddenly as the earthquake had arrived, it was gone. But it had left its mark. Darius's Way was in ruins, but from what Reuel could tell from his immediate surroundings, no one was seriously injured.

"What was that?" Reuel asked.

"I have no idea," Elon answered while straightening the stand.

"All citizens report immediately to the palace. The king has an urgent announcement," a voice said.

The puzzled looks on the faces of the surrounding citizens revealed they, too, had heard it.

"Was that the captain?" Reuel asked.

"I don't know," Elon answered.

The ground had steadied itself, but Reuel's legs continued to wobble. From his initial survey of the aftermath, he hadn't seen much devastation, but a closer look revealed the truth. A slew of stands had collapsed, along with multiple houses and buildings behind them. Some had crumbled while others tilted slightly, and a few had sunk into the ground altogether.

Eve was the one to refocus the group. "Let's go. Somethin' ain't right."

The three of them, plus Aaron, joined the mass exodus toward the king's palace. A look of confusion was all too common among the citizens of Ira. Reuel could see that the sudden earthquake had taken its toll on the masses. There was little to no conversation among them, and only the smallest children mumbled to each other. Everyone else marched on in silence.

With so many people moving in the same direction, progress was slow, so Reuel focused on the only thing that brought him peace lately: Ruth. He imagined her flying on the back of a Giant Hawk over the Baron Sea, with the wind in her hair and her face radiating in the sunlight. The corners of his mouth turned upward at the thought.

Eventually, all progress halted just outside the heart of the city. There was no way for them to get any closer. All attention was on the newly erected walls around the palace that now connected the four towers and the new wall that stood behind the Institute that stretched the width of the city, effectively separating Old and New Ira.

"This isn't good," Eve mumbled.

Reuel watched people climb the sides of buildings to get a better view; some hung out of the windows of their homes. Standing in a straight line in front of the wall that now separated the cities were armored soldiers. Through the doorway in the center of the wall, Reuel saw the Angelic citizens, lumped in a mass like their Zurielian counterparts. Reuel turned his attention to the top of the wall where two men stood.

There was a man who wore a modest gold crown, and next to him was the captain, his eyes glazing dark blue.

"Today is a day of change. As you are all aware, during the last season, citizens, children included, have gone missing. None have returned, and the worst can be assumed. My heart weeps for the grieving families and parents," the king said.

Reuel looked to Eve, confused. "Jadon must be broadcastin' his message."

"The loss of a child brings forth an unimaginable pain that I wouldn't wish even on Gideon. It was because of these disappearances that the Guardians visited me last night. They informed me that changes must be made in Ira to ensure the safety of all citizens.

191

The earthquake that shook our kingdom was not nat-
ural but was brought on by Cyrus building the very
wall I am standing on and those that now surround my
palace. The threat has escalated to the point where the
Guardians believe my family and I are also in danger,
and in response, they have re-erected the walls around
my palace as a precaution.

"In order to protect our kingdom, we must separate
our kingdom. Which is why Cyrus raised this wall that
now separates Old and New Ira. It has become clear
that Zurielians have been targeted in these kidnap-
pings. The Guardians and I have decided that
Zurielians, for their own protection, will no longer be
permitted beyond the palace and into New Ira. New
Ira will be exclusively for Angelics. Angelics will only
be allowed into Old Ira from sunrise to midday in or-
der to buy the day's food and drink."

Reuel assessed the masses and was surprised to see
that instead of looks of disapproval, he saw nods of
agreement. He turned his head to Eve and whispered
in disbelief, "They can't believe this?"

"Wouldn' you? Why shoul' they have any doubts?
No one but Cyrus coul' do somethin' like this in such
a short amount of time." She nodded at the wall.

The king continued his speech. *"This separation*
will allow both Angelics and Zurielians to sleep
soundly at night knowing they are safely among their

own. I have no doubt that this is what is best for our kingdom. The Angelic Guard will enforce this new order."

The king gave a single wave, turned, and descended from view, followed by Jadon, who was no longer glazing. Once they were out of sight, everyone was in motion. The Zurielians headed back to Old Ira in surprisingly good spirits.

Reuel overheard a Grindbler man talking. "Finally, we only have to put up with those arrogant pale-heads once a day."

A Windwalker patted the man on the back and laughed.

"Indeed, and it's good to know the Guardians have returned," the Windwalker said.

Reuel shook his head. "Darius didn't talk to the Guardians."

"We know," said Elon. "Go home, Aaron, I'll see you there."

Once Aaron left, Elon and Eve huddled close to Reuel so their conversation would not be overheard.

"Who built the walls, then?" Reuel asked.

"I don' know, but it wasn' Cyrus. And if he's lyin' about that, then there has to be more to this separation idea," Eve said.

"But what will he get out of separating everyone?" Reuel asked.

193

Eve exhaled, and Reuel watched her face sag. The bags under her eyes were pronounced.

"I don' know, Reuel. I don' have all the answers. I might have a couple more than you two, but nowhere near the amount we need."

"The Council will know what's going on, we can ask them tonight. I'm sure they'll have something to tell us," Elon offered.

"If any of us needed any confirmation that this is really happening, I guess this is it," Reuel said.

On their way home, they were careful to step over the cracks and avoid potholes. Nonetheless, Reuel still managed to trip over a rather large piece of debris. As he fell, he looked up in time to see a pair of Giant Hawks as they climbed into the sky. From the ground, he followed their progress until they crossed in front of the sun and he was forced to look away. He hoped that Ruth was on the back of one of those hawks, on her way to safety and away from this mess.

They didn't have to wait long for an explanation. Sophia began talking as they were sitting down. Again, the Council stood before them, with Sophia at the head.

"We were right to assume that we don't have a lot of time to prepare. Abaddon has already put his plan into motion. I think he's going to use the separation of the cities to galvanize his troops and spread his propaganda."

"But how did Abaddon raise the walls?" Elon asked.

The Council members all shared a worried expression. "If what we believe is true and Abaddon has, in fact, killed the Guardians, then it's safe to assume that he permanently absorbed them as well," Hazael said.

"How is that possible?" Eve asked. "They were Guardians. Their abilities outclass even Elites. And Angelics can only absorb Zurielians from their class or below."

"True," Moriah said. "But Abaddon clearly found a way around that. There is no other way to explain it. The reason Angelics only permanently absorb from their class or lower is because their bodies can't handle the strain. I can only assume that he somehow managed to train his body to harness all that energy."

"Abaddon was an Elite," Sophia explained. "So containing the power of one Guardian would be a remarkable feat. Harnessing the power of all four Guardians would be an unimaginable strain. When we face him, I doubt we'll recognize him. His body will be far too distorted."

"If he has all the abilities of the Guardians, then what are we supposed to do?" Reuel asked. "He could erase our minds like Maria, right?"

"Doubtful," Sophia answered. "My ability to classify and unlock a child's potential is the same ability the great Phoebe possessed. She and Aden Lambton were the team that found the original Guardians. Our ability to classify is similar to Maria's ability to erase minds. It's rare and unique, something that I believe cannot be absorbed. I don't think Abaddon has more than their basic abilities and their elemental powers, which alone are more than enough to seize control of Aela. But I think this solved one mystery. I had wondered why Maria didn't simply erase Abaddon's mind during their confrontation—eliminating the threat altogether. But after absorbing Asa, Abaddon must have become too powerful for such trickery."

It was suddenly clear to Reuel. "Abaddon is the pale man…" he whispered.

"What?" Sophia asked.

"Nothing," Reuel answered. "But what if you're wrong? What if all of your theories are wrong?"

"I'm not."

"How can you be so sure?"

"You just have to trust me, Reuel. You have to have some faith," Sophia said firmly. "We don't have the luxury of sitting down and feeling sorry for ourselves, or the time to debate theories and ideas. We only have time to prepare. You can begin, Jonas."

Reuel nodded and was silent. Jonas stepped forward holding a long wooden rod in each hand.

"Weapons training," he declared.

Jonas tossed one of the rods at the feet of the children and twirled the other around, showing off his dexterity.

"Who's first?"

DANIEL (IV)

On his way to Horo, Daniel had one task: retrieve Azriel. However, once Daniel had actually arrived in the underwater utopia, he convinced himself he had more than enough time to do what he needed to do. The zip tunnels were closed until the end of the season, and unless they were going to swim to Ira, there was no leaving Horo.

For the most part, Daniel considered himself responsible and task-oriented, but the urgency of his mission was washed away when Horo was re-flooded. The steel box that surrounded Horo during the dry season retracted, and the wet season began. With the flood of water came the overwhelming nostalgia that even Daniel's war-weary heart failed to overcome. He soon fell into his old habits as if he had never left.

There were five gates used to create the steel box that transformed Horo from an underwater sanctuary to a hospitable place for all citizens of Aela. Four gates surrounded the city. The walls of the steel box extended from these gates. A fifth gate rested overhead and was connected to a tunnel that pumped in the air that filled the box during the dry season.

Horo had expanded onto an island that Cyrus had formed above the city. The island city, Kiro, had been constructed around the air tunnel. Kiro allowed for the other capitals to continue to trade with Horo during the wet season. Exports were delivered from Horo to Kiro on the backs of huffluds and dolphins. The goods were then sent out to the other capitals with the help of the Tesa Air Service.

Daniel had to admit, the tunnels had done exactly what Asa had predicted. They made Horo a vital part of Aela.

Daniel spent the majority of his season in Horo traveling through the city. He especially enjoyed the Horo racetracks, where he spent his time gambling on hufflud races. Old habits die hard. He saved visiting his childhood home for his last day.

He treaded water outside the coral home for a while. It was now inhabited by another family, both his parents having passed years ago. The mere sight of the house stirred up countless memories, but of all of them, one fought to the top. The day his sister Phoebe had come into his life. She had appeared a few seasons before the war officially began and caused quite a stir. A Shimmer visiting Horo was unheard of at the time.

She had been a beautiful young woman in her early twenties, a few years Daniel's senior. Daniel remembered thinking she almost seemed too delicate for her Shimmer heritage, but he smiled when he remembered how quickly that notion was wiped from his mind. It was her eyes that did it. They told a far different story than her physical appearance. They were sharp and fierce.

Daniel was the first to meet her. He had been riding his hufflud when he spotted a large crowd gathered near his house.

He tapped his pet, and they dove. They set down in front of his home, and at first he didn't know how to process what he was seeing. He had never seen a Shimmer in person before. She was wearing a hufflud body suit that covered her body from the neck down, and only her red face, hands, and feet were showing. Her long hair was tied in a ponytail. She had soft features and round black eyes. She didn't seem to have any trouble breathing and looked at ease.

She stood in the doorway, staring out at the crowd, just waiting. At last, Daniel climbed off his hufflud and held out his hand. She took it, and their personal mental link was established.

"I'm Daniel Talbit, this is my home. Are you waiting for someone?" he asked.

She smiled. *"My name is Phoebe. I came here looking for my father."*

Daniel wrinkled his brow. *"I'm sorry, you must be mistaken. No Shimmers live here, or in Horo, for that matter. I'm not even sure how you're still breathing at these depths. And by the looks of it, I'm not the only one."* He gestured to the crowd.

Her eyes didn't leave his. *"My father is not a Shimmer, he's an Aquati named Joseph Talbit. I'm your sister."*

Daniel's jaw hung open, and he was powerless to do anything about it. All of his brain activity was focused on making sense of the absurdity he was hearing. It didn't add up. Bearing children of mixed race was just not done. His father of all people knew this particularly well since he was a captain in the Aquati army. One of his many duties was to uphold this unwritten law within the Aquati Empire.

"What makes you sure that you have the right man?"

"I'm sure. I've been asking around all day, and there is only one Captain Joseph Talbit in Horo, and he lives here."

"Why should I believe anything you say?"

"My mother was on her deathbed when she confided in me. She had no reason to lie."

"Then you're *the liar,"* he shot back. *"Shimmers and Aquatis don't mix. My father couldn't have been with your mother. You have no business here!"*

Her smile faded and in its place was a stern, emotionless face. *"I am not leaving until I talk to my father."*

"Well, that is going to be a problem, because your father does not live here!" Daniel shouted.

She did not flinch nor waver in her stance. She merely repeated herself. *"I am not leaving until I talk to my father."*

Daniel couldn't believe it. More accurately, he wouldn't *allow* himself to believe it. The thought of his father having a child with another woman bothered him, but the idea that it was with a woman who wasn't an Aquati infuriated him. Their law had been drilled into him since he was a child. It had been preached especially fervently with the impending war on the horizon. With all the races working so closely together, the potential for mixing was high. As much as he didn't want to believe her, he wasn't left with many options. The only way she could survive at these depths was if there was some Aquati in her blood.

"FATHER!" he shouted in a personal link.

"Son—what's wrong?"

"There's a problem at home."

"I'm on my way."

"We will get to the bottom of this soon enough," Daniel said to Pheobe.

It wasn't long before a lean man and woman swam up beside Daniel. All three of them stared at the red girl standing in front of their home.

"Son?" Joseph asked.

"She's here for you."

"There is nothing more to see here," Joseph broadcasted to the spectators. *"Clear from my home!"*

The gathered Aquatis scattered, following the captain's orders. Joseph held out his hand and Phoebe took it, establishing a personal mental link.

"My son tells me that you are looking for me?" Joseph broadcasted so Daniel and his mother could hear.

Daniel watched as the girl's hard demeanor began to crack. Her chest heaved, which broke her controlled breathing, and she began to rise toward the surface. Daniel grabbed her arm and anchored her until she could regain control. If he didn't know any better, he would've thought she was trying to cry underwater.

"My mother was Delilah Capis, a Premier Shimmer. She was a high-ranking member of The Link." She steadied her breathing and once again fell to the ocean

floor. *"She sent me here to find you. She said it was time I met my father."*

As the words poured into Daniel's head, he studied every part of his father's face, gauging his reaction. His father had his eyes trained on Phoebe, absorbing every word. And it was his father's own wide eyes and thin smile that told the story. Phoebe was not lying.

"Everyone inside," Joseph ordered.

He ushered them all into the coral home. Daniel swam in and stood in the middle of the room. They joined him. His mother stood to his right, Phoebe to his left, and his father was facing him. Daniel glanced at his mother. Her eyes were emotionless, vacant, and her lips were pressed tightly together, reducing their natural fullness to a thin strip.

The sight of his mother reignited the raging anger he was holding at bay. *"Are you going to explain yourself?"*

His father had been holding Phoebe's gaze. However, after Daniel's outburst, he slowly took his eyes off his daughter and glared at him. *"Do not forget I am your father, boy. I owe you no explanation. But for the sake of your mother, and in the hopes that we can all live together, I will explain."* Joseph grabbed his wife's hand. *"Jescha, my love, Phoebe is my daughter."*

She shook her head. *"How could you?"*

"I have no excuse for my actions. I met Delilah

years ago while I was stationed in Beliel. We were set to meet with The Link about the Angelics' military advances. She had been sent to our camp to meet with our captain. It was around the time I had just been promoted, so I, too, was in attendance at that meeting. It had been almost two years since I had been home. I was lonely, Jescah. In my loneliness and weakness, I fell in love with her."

"You loved her?!" Jescah exploded. *"She was a Shimmer, Joseph!"*

"I know...but if I learned anything while preparing for this war, it's that not only is the separation of Angelics and Zurielians wrong, but our own self-imposed segregation amongst Zurielians is wrong. Love is love no matter the race, and that love has taken shape in my daughter." He lifted Phoebe's hand to his mouth and kissed it lightly.

"She's an abomination!" Jescah ripped her hand away from his and swam out of the house. Daniel was set to follow.

"Stay here," his father ordered. *"I will handle your mother."*

Joseph swam from the house in pursuit. Daniel and Phoebe were left alone again.

"You see the problems you have brought to my family?" Daniel sneered.

"He's my father too," Phoebe said plainly. *"You had*

him all this time. Now I've come for my turn."

"It's not right. You are not one of us, you're not my sister."

"Why is it so wrong? Did Zuriel not create us all?"

Daniel had to pause at this. *"He did...but he made four different races. We were not meant to mix."*

"Our separation is not an order from him but was created by our kings and queens. The war that is coming could have easily been avoided if Gideon would see that we are not so different. But some people will forever carry hardened hearts. That is why I'm here today."

"What do you mean?"

"My mother felt it was necessary for me to meet my father in case I don't survive my journey."

"Where are you going?"

"Zuriel is sending me and a Grindbler scientist to find what he feels will save us when the Angelics finally attack. He told me that I was the only one who could locate it because I'm not only a Shimmer but also an Aquati. Mixing does not dilute, but reinvents."

Daniel didn't say anything for a long while. *"It may take me a while to get used to this, but if you're really my father's daughter, then we are family. You have my support. For the sake of Aela, I hope you find what you're looking for."*

All these years later, Daniel could only laugh at the irony. Just like his father, he had fallen in love and fathered children with a Shimmer—a Guardian, at that. He was still amazed at how Phoebe had come to mean so much to him in such a short amount of time. His mother, however, never did accept her. But that didn't stop Phoebe from staying with them for a couple of seasons. She spent part of her days with Daniel, then the rest with her father, searching Horo for whatever she was looking for.

She never explained to Daniel exactly what Zuriel had her searching for, but looking back, it was clear. It wasn't something, but *someone*. The day Phoebe left Horo, she took a young man named Asa back to the surface with her.

I guess it's my turn now, Phoebe, Daniel thought. He turned from his old home and started swimming toward the palace.

He arrived at the palace and was met by the Royal Guard. Unlike when he came looking for Asa years before, the Guard was not trying to keep him out but waiting to accompany him. He had known Queen Joanna long before she became a queen, their private mental link having been established when she was just a little girl. When he had first arrived in Horo, he had alerted her of his visit.

The Guard led him into the palace. They swam

through the magnificent atrium, through corridors covered in a special kind of coral that glowed different colors depending on the season. Since it was early summer, the halls gleamed a radiant yellow. After traveling through a maze of yellow corridors, they finally reached a great hall.

There was a long stone table that sat in the middle of the room surrounded by chairs. Daniel assumed it was probably well decorated during the dry season. There had been large amounts of tables, chairs, and other accessories imported to Horo after completion of the zip tunnels. During his apprenticeship as a blacksmith, he had watched the carpenters and stone-masons in Beliel churn out tables and chairs by the hundreds.

They stopped at one end of the table. The queen was at the other with a look of dismay painted on her face. She waved the guard off and swam toward Daniel. A long cape was attached to her hufflud body suit. Her hair was short, and in dry conditions it would have fallen just under her ears. She wasn't remarkably beautiful, but she was attractive. Alone in the great hall, she gave him a hug.

"What took you so long to get here, Daniel? The season is over tomorrow, and this is the first time I'm seeing you."

Daniel bowed his head. *"I'm sorry, my queen, I was*

sidetracked. As you know, this is my first time back since the tunnels were built."

She nodded. *"I understand. So you're here to take one of my children, correct?"*

"Yes, my queen. Allow me first to offer my condolences. Your father was a great man."

"Thank you. He was, and I'm proud that one of my children will have the chance to take his place. So, which one will it be?"

"Zuriel told me to take Azriel."

An interesting expression crossed the queen's face. It was one of intrigue and confusion.

"Zuriel?" she asked. *"He's alive? You've seen him?"*

"Yes and no. He contacted me using our mental link."

Again, she nodded. *"Well, that's good news! We're going to need him again. I can only imagine how bad things are getting up there without my father and the others. I'm shutting down the tunnels after this coming season. I can't risk the inevitable chaos reaching Horo."*

"But my queen, you will fight, won't you?"

"Of course, but we will fight as we did before, on land. I will not allow it to reach my city," the queen answered. *"But Daniel, I think Zuriel may have been mistaken. Azriel is no Guardian. He's an Auxiliary."*

"What?" Daniel responded, shocked.

"Yes. Sophia classified him a year ago. He's nothing special. He was supposed to be my next general. You can imagine my disappointment."

Daniel rubbed his head. "That doesn't make any sense."

"Maybe he meant one of my other children?"

"No. He said Azriel, and that is who I have to take to Ira."

"Daniel, I don't know...but if Zuriel asked for him, what can I really do? I'll call for him."

A boy no older than fifteen swam into the great hall. At first glance, he was nothing remarkable. He looked like an average Aquati. But there was something in his presence. It was not that of an uncertain fifteen-year-old but of a sure-minded adult. His body was still a work in progress, but he was handsome. He had a rounded face with a button nose. His skin was a dark, rich blue, and his black hair flowed above his head as he treaded.

"This is Daniel," the queen broadcasted so Daniel could hear.

Azriel reached out his hand to Daniel and established their personal mental link. "Nice to meet you, sir," Azriel said.

"I'm here to take you to Ira to meet with the other Guardians," Daniel said.

"I'm ready."

Daniel looked at the queen with a bewildered expression. *"Ready? How did you know, Azriel?"*

"I knew I wasn't just an Auxiliary. I knew I had to be more than that. I felt it in my soul, sir. So, after my classification, I continued to train and prepare. I knew someone would come for me eventually."

The queen smiled. *"Maybe Zuriel was right after all."* She hugged her son and held him close. *"Be safe, Azriel. Make us proud."*

"I will, Mother. Before I leave, I wish to say goodbye to everyone."

"Of course, I'll call for them."

The rest of the royal family swam into the great hall. There were two older boys—based on their physical stature, they were closer to men—and there was a young woman maybe a few years older than Azriel. He hugged and spoke to each privately. When he was finished, he swam back to Daniel.

"I'm ready, sir."

"Let's go. You will stay with me until the tunnels open in the morning," Daniel said. *"Farewell, my queen, I pray that the next time we meet, it will be under much better circumstances."*

"So do I, Daniel."

Daniel led Azriel out of the palace and toward the Zip Station. *"Don't worry, Azriel, you will see them again,"* Daniel said.

"Hopefully, sir." They continued for a moment in silence. *"But I said what I needed to, just in case I don't."*

Daniel and Azriel waited patiently outside the Horo-Ira Zip Station. The station was nearly identical to the one in Beliel. Daniel stood near the small gate on the platform that separated it from the train. The platform itself was positioned in front of an enormous rectangular steel wall, which stretched the length of the platform and extended far above the city. A circular hole in the middle of the wall, which was currently sealed, provided an entrance for the train. A few other Aquatis had made their way to the station and settled in behind Daniel.

Daniel and Azriel stayed there all night. Daniel refused to be sidetracked again. He spent the better part of the night observing Azriel. Once they had arrived at the station, Azriel took to his own corner of the platform and sat cross-legged, looking back at Horo. He hadn't moved the entire night.

Talkative one, Daniel thought, chuckling in his head.

The tunnels were set to reopen after the minite swarm. Daniel watched the glowing silver wave of minites cut through the depths of the sea and weave through the city streets. There were a couple of Aquatis in the streets catching them, but they didn't collect as many since the ones caught before the dry season would not be released. Their light would be used until the candles and torches were lit.

"It's almost time, Azriel," Daniel said.

"Yes, sir," he said and swam toward Daniel. *"My mother should be declaring the beginning of the dry season at any moment."*

As Azriel was finishing his sentence, an Aquati soldier swam toward their small group and motioned for them to move.

"Back up!" the soldier broadcasted to them.

It was then that the queen's stern broadcast came crashing into Daniel's head. *"Citizens of Horo, the dry season is upon us. Prepare accordingly. Travel only if you must. This will be the last dry season for the foreseeable future."*

When her voice faded, Daniel heard a loud humming coming from the wall. The wheels and gears inside of the gigantic wall began to churn. Long metal plates emerged from both sides of the gate and stretched out beyond the platform. They continued to grow longer and longer until they reached the Horo-Tesa and Horo-Beliel gates, respectively.

The Horo-Tesa and Horo-Beliel gates stretched out and connected with the Horo-Rolte gate, encapsulating Horo in a steel square. A more aggressive churning sound came from the Horo-Kiro gate above them. This gate wasn't a zip tunnel but an air tunnel. The tunnel in the middle of the gate went to Kiro and provided air for Horo during the dry season.

The Horo-Kiro gate stretched out just like the others and covered the top of the box.

As the box around Horo was completed, Daniel heard a whizzing noise behind him. He turned to see that the circular hole in the gate had opened just enough to allow some water to escape. It was only open momentarily, allowing water to escape so that air could take its place. Once this was done, the tunnel from Kiro began to pump in air. The water level slowly dropped, and the water was pushed out of the numerous one-way filters in the steel walls and into the sea. After a while, all the water had been cleared and Horo was dry again. The station's circular gate opened, releasing the water it had drained onto the floor.

"I still can't believe we managed to pull this off," Daniel said, admiring the technological miracle.

"It never gets old, either," Azriel responded. *"Just imagine what we could do if we sincerely all united. The possibilities are endless. The Angelics' intelligence and the Grindbler's strength and mechanical expertise. The thought is scary."*

Daniel could only smile at the boy's naivety. If only it was that simple. *"Keep that idea in mind. When this is all over, maybe you and the other Guardians can work on that."*

The zip train eased through the gate and hovered in the large space between the platform and the gate. The ground in-between the two acted as a large magnet, repelling the magnets that lined the train and allowing it to hover in place. Chains fell from the nose and body of the train. The Aquati soldiers at the gate used the chains to rotate the train so that the body was horizontal to the platform, allowing entry. The doors of the passenger cars opened, and planks were extended onto the platform.

"When we arrive in Ira, what's our plan?" Azriel asked.

"We locate Sophia and the other Guardians and pray it's not too late."

Daniel strolled through the small gate and onto the train, followed by Azriel. They sat in the back by themselves. Daniel again took the window seat, Azriel settled in next to him. Like his trip to Horo, the train was nearly empty. Only a few Aquatis trickled through the door and found seats.

"Are there always so few on the train for the ceremony?" Daniel asked. *"It's a really big deal up there."*

Azriel gave him a puzzled look. *"Of course, as long as Jadon is director of the Institute, Horo will not support it."*

Daniel looked out the window. *"I understand. I haven't attended one either since Jadon became the director. But it wasn't just that that kept me out of Ira. I couldn't go back after what they did to Phoebe."*

Azriel put his hand on his shoulder. *"What happened to her?"*

Daniel said nothing. He rarely talked about Phoebe's death, but Azriel needed to know the monster he was on his way to confront.

"No one knows the specifics..." Daniel started. *"My account is secondhand and is based on what Maria told me. She and the other Guardians found the body of my sister, or what was left of it. In the final days of the war, they had gone to visit her as they routinely did. She was staying at her hidden home outside of Ira, a little past the Dead Forest."* Daniel stopped. It had been a long time since he had allowed himself to think of this story, let alone tell it.

Azriel tightened his grip on his shoulder. *"Go on..."*

"It was a horrific sight when they arrived. The grass outside her home was saturated with her blood. Locks of her hair and pieces of her flesh lay everywhere. In the distance, they saw Abaddon and his dragon returning to Ira."

"Why would he kill her?"

"Isn't it clear? The Guardians had turned the tide of the war in a few short years, and it was only a matter of time before all the Angelic forces were defeated. It was a known fact that Phoebe was like a mother to the Guardians. She held a special place in their hearts. In order to protect her, they hid her and placed her in a fortress of their own creation, checking in every opportunity they got. So Abaddon, hoping to cripple them, went after their heart. But by doing so, he actually quickened the Angelics' demise."

"Why didn't they chase down Abaddon when they saw him retreating that day?"

"They would've, but he was too far ahead, and Ira was still a stronghold at the time. Its defenses gave even the Guardians pause. It eventually took the combined might of the Guardians, fueled by the anger of Phoebe's death, and all the Zurielian armies to get past the dragons and through the kingdom's mighty walls."

"The Battle of Ira, the final day of the war..." Azriel said.

Daniel gave Azriel a side glance and nodded. *"Indeed. Abaddon took my sister and then Maria from me. I will be the one who kills that monster."*

"We will get you that opportunity. He doesn't know about us. He has no idea we're coming for him. If we make our move fast enough, there won't be a war, Daniel. We can end it before it begins."

217

"Don't underestimate him. Look where that got your grandfather. We have to assume he knows about you and the others, and that war is inevitable. If we don't do that, he has the upper hand."

"We can stop him before it gets to that point."

"I hope you're right, Azriel, but don't forget what I said. This isn't a training exercise. The stakes are real. This is life or death, don't ever forget that."

Azriel's hand fell from Daniel's shoulder and he sank into his chair, retreating within himself again. Daniel watched out the window as the Aquati soldiers grabbed the chains from the train and dragged them until the nose of the train was facing the tunnel. A steel plate rose behind the train, protecting the platform from the engine flames. Daniel felt a slight rumbling as the workers in the caboose began to shovel the coal into the engine. The train slowly inched forward and then rocketed off into the tunnel toward Ira.

REUEL (VII)

Reuel woke up in a small shack in the outskirts of Ira. The shack had one room that he and his parents shared. There were three wooden cots pushed together against one of the walls. His mother slept in the middle, his father in the cot against the wall, and Reuel on the other side. Reuel sat up in his bed and rubbed his eyes. He hadn't slept well since they were kicked out of their home in the mountain.

The Angelic Guard had rounded up all Zurielian Auxiliaries and forced them to the outskirts.

He stared at his parents, motionless as they slept. As Elites, they had the option to remain in the mountain but chose to leave with him. He slipped into his harem pants and sandals and mentally prepared for the day's work.

He walked toward the shack's entrance, but the roar of his starving stomach forced him to pause. He looked into the apple basket by the door and saw only a single apple. He glanced at his parents and left the apple untouched, even though he knew his parents would not accept it and would leave it for his dinner. It was their daily back-and-forth.

He grabbed his wooden bucket beside the door that contained a brush made of horse hair and walked out into the sunrise. He headed to a nearby shack. There were so many shacks in the outskirts now that they were almost on top of each other.

He wasn't sure how it had come to this. It had started as an attempt to protect the Zurielians from becoming victims of the kidnappings, but things had escalated. Their relationship with the Angelics continued to deteriorate until this point.

Reuel stood in front of a shack and knocked on its wall. He heard rustling coming from inside, and soon enough, Elon came through the door.

"Another great morning in Ira," Elon said sarcastically.

"Did you see your brother yesterday?" Reuel asked.

"I couldn't. The guards wouldn't let me get into the city." He paused and looked around before he continued. "If I didn't see my parents at the Institute every night, I wouldn't be seeing them, either."

"You'll see your brother soon enough."

"When? We are no closer to knowing what's going

on now than when we started. It's been a whole season, and things have continued to get worse. We've been doing all this training for what?"

"Elon, calm down," Reuel said and reached out in an attempt to comfort him.

"Don't touch me!" Elon knocked Reuel's hand away and stormed back into his shack. The ground around them shook gently with each of his steps.

Reuel took a deep breath and followed his friend inside. Elon was on his knees, his hands curled into fists, and his back trembled as he sobbed quietly. Reuel stood behind him with his hand firmly gripping Elon's large shoulder.

"I need you, Elon. I can't do this without you. Sophia said it would be hard. All we can do is prepare and wait for Azriel."

"Reuel don't you see...We need to move now. These new laws are absurd, banishing the Auxiliaries to the outskirts and then forcing us to *serve* the Elite Angelics. We're slaves. My family didn't come here with me like yours. They didn't want my brother living here, and I don't blame them." He slammed his fist against the ground, shaking the shack violently.

"Sophia said we must be patient."

"Sophia is wrong! We're ready. We need to make a move now before it gets any worse."

"Stop," Reuel said firmly. "The last thing I need is

for you to lose faith. You once told me that we should embrace the fact that we're Guardians because we can make a difference. It was never going to be easy. You are the strongest among us, and if you crumble, we might as well hand Aela over to Abaddon now. Stay strong, my friend. Sophia and the rest of the Council have done nothing but prepare and protect us. The least we can do is have faith and be patient."

"Yeah." He smiled at Reuel. "You're starting to sound like me now. But I guess you're right. I mean, Eve is no longer the only one who can fight."

"My point exactly. When the time comes, we will be ready. We can't even ascend until Azriel arrives, and if we don't have access to our Guardian abilities, we stand no chance against Abaddon anyway. We have no choice but to wait. So get up."

Elon got to his feet and faced Reuel. "Let's go, then."

As they headed toward the door, Elon picked up his own bucket and horse hair brush. They again stepped out into the outskirts.

Morning-light was upon them, and the outskirts began to teem with life. Unlike the bustling of Darius's Way in the morning hours, the Auxiliaries in the outskirts lacked any hustle in their step, enthusiasm having left them long ago.

"What took y'all so long?" Eve asked, leaning up

against the side of the shack, her own bucket at her feet. "If we don' hurry up, we' be last in line for water."

"Just talking," Reuel responded. "You're in high spirits today."

"The tunnels open tomorrow," she said, grinning. "Azriel will be here soon, and I can' wait to face Abaddon when he arrives. What is there not to be happy about?"

A couple of soldiers of the Angelic Guard strolled by and banged on the walls of shacks. Reuel shot her a sharp look.

"I' sorry. I didn' mean to say it so loud."

"Get moving, scrabs!" one of the soldiers yelled. "Those homes don't clean themselves!"

Reuel nodded in the direction of the growing line heading out of the outskirts and toward Ira's fountain. They fell into line and trudged forward toward another day's work. His current occupation of scrubbing dirty floors was a far cry from his life as a prince.

He had wanted to join Elon in his complaining. He, too, was tired of waiting. He was tired of watching everyone he cared for suffer. His heart was regularly heavy with sorrow, especially when he noticed how accustomed he had become to seeing the tired and dejected faces around him. They had become as common as smiles had once been. Fortunately, he had no time to wallow in his despair. His time to complain had passed long ago. He had to keep them together. He had to lead them.

Reuel passed one of the many posted wooden framed scrolls that littered the outskirts, declaring the new laws of the land.

The Guardians' Decree:

Zurielians shall not address Angelics unless addressed first OR unless an Angelic's life is in danger.

Auxiliary Zurielians are to reside in the outskirts at all times. Auxiliary Zurielians are only to be permitted into Old *OR* New Ira while serving Angelic patrons.

Elite and Premier Zurielians may continue to reside in Old Ira and/or New Ira.

It had happened so quickly, yet it had been a gradual process. Days after the earthquake, things began to change. The Angelics became increasingly more hostile toward the Zurielians. They took the *supposed* Guardians' decree to heart and refused to shop during the same time as them. The more days passed, the bolder they became. They even started to declare their own prices on items.

Coincidently, the less interaction the Zurielians and Angelics had, the more kidnappings occurred. It wasn't long before Darius announced the Guardians' declaration that in order to further protect both Angelics and Zurielians, Auxiliary Zurielians must be separated from the rest of the city. They were, as he put it, "a plague," and said that their lethargic tendencies bred "horrific behaviors such as kidnapping and murder."

The fear of being ostracized as well kept the Elite and Premier Zurielians from taking much of a stand.

Thirty days after the earthquake, the Angelic Guard made their move at dusk. They went to each mountain home with census scrolls in tow in order to round up all Auxiliaries. Reuel had been sitting at his family's dining table when two Angelic soldiers came to the door. They barged in, throwing the crates and table aside and doing their best to make as much of a mess as possible. They seized Reuel by the collarbone and examined him for a moment.

His parents had been in their bedroom at the time. They came rushing in after the ruckus. His mother's eyes glazed the instant she saw the Angelic's hands on Reuel. She moved swiftly and far too quickly for the Angelics to catch her movements. The knife she used to cut apples and meat in the mornings was firmly in her grip. She was mere moments away from plunging it into one of the Angelics' jugular when his father caught her arm, his eyes glazing just as furiously. He twisted it firmly, and the knife dropped harmlessly to the floor. He wrapped his arm around her waist and pulled her away from the situation.

This scene went unseen by the Angelics. Reuel was the lone witness of the events. At most, Reuel assumed the Angelics had only seen his parents come into the room, and by the time they had blinked their eyes, his father was holding his mother tightly by the waist and a knife was at their feet.

The Angelics gave his parents the option of joining him or staying in their home. They decided to come along. The same events unfolded to various degrees throughout all of the mountain homes. There had been many injuries, but no casualties.

Reuel understood why there hadn't been any meaningful resistance. Even though the Zurielians didn't agree with the actions taken against them, they were the result of orders given by their saviors, the Guardians. That was more than enough for them to go along rather peacefully.

After Darius had successfully separated the Auxiliaries from the rest of the Zurielians, it was easy to deny them their previous jobs as vendors. By denying them access to their shops and stands, they had no way to support themselves or their families. The only way for them to earn anything they could live on was to serve Angelics in New Ira.

It wasn't until their exile to the outskirts that Reuel's parents shared with him that they had been living off the gold they'd smuggled from Tesa, which had recently run out. Their noble gesture of coming with him meant that he would have to work to support them. They didn't own a stand, and Reuel wouldn't allow the former King and Queen of Tesa to serve any Angelic. So, within a season, Reuel and the other Zurielian Auxiliaries of Aela had become servants for hire.

Reuel and the others finally reached the fountain. It was the closest most of the Zurielians got to their former homes.

The soldiers stationed at the fountain waved for Reuel to come forward and collect his water. They took his bucket, filled it halfway, handed it back to him, and then waved for Elon.

Reuel waited over to the side until Elon and Eve had received their share. They trudged toward him, dismay and aggravation painted on their faces.

"I'll see you both at training tonight," Reuel said. "Stay calm, be patient. It'll be over soon."

Elon and Eve nodded and disappeared into the crowd heading to New Ira. Reuel waited until he could no longer see them before he made his way toward the home of the Yetes.

The Yetes were one of the few Angelic families that still lived in Old Ira. The patriarch of the family, Jerimiah Yetes, had inherited his current home from his father, who had inherited it from his father, who had originally built it. It had been constructed before the current layout of the city, during a time when Ira was home to only Angelics.

When the Zurielians began to move in and took up residence near the mountain, many of the Angelic families migrated to what is now New Ira. However, the Yetes family remained.

Like the Yetes men before him, Jerimiah, a Premier Angelic, did not concern himself with the propaganda that many of the Angelics bought into. He prided himself on the fact that he did not judge a person by what they looked like but on their actions and character.

His wife, Margret, an Elite Angelic, didn't share his idealistic view. She was a large woman who loved to indulge in the finer things Ira had to offer. Her vast intelligence was only surpassed by her girth. One of her favorite pastimes, besides beating Reuel for his disobedience, was monologuing about her supposed supremacy. She had decided long ago that since she aged much slower than everyone she knew—except for other Elite Angelics—she could live however she wished now in Old Ira. As she outlived the people she knew, she would reinvent herself into a more acceptable version and move to New Ira. Why waste her youth doing the right thing when she could do that in old age?

Margret loved her husband but at times believed he lived in a much different world than she. And the world he lived in simply did not exist. Her parents had been wary of their marriage but permitted it since the Yetes name carried weight in the Angelic community. They were not fond of his beliefs but tolerated them since tolerance was the status quo.

Margret believed she saw things as they were. She was superior to the Zurielians, especially Auxiliaries. Their lack of any significant abilities relegated them to sad, mundane lives that disgusted her.

"You should be glad your life has meaning now, scrab," was one of her favorite sayings to Reuel. In Margret's world, a scrab's sole purpose was figuring out ways in which to make life more manageable for her and her family.

Her favorite story to tell Reuel was how she selected him to serve her household. When news of change had reached Margret, she had expected there to be a plethora of eager scrabs ready to clean her floors, set her table, and buy her daily goods—but to her surprise, there were no scrabs coming to her door. She chalked this up to their lazy nature.

She learned from a childhood friend, Jezebel Terrek, who had already hired scrabs of her own, that she could get her pick of the litter if she waited by the city fountain at sunrise. So Margret did just that. She found a comfortable spot in the shade of a building near the well and watched as the scrabs handed their pails to the soldiers on duty to get their water for the day. None of them caught her eye. In fact, she wasn't sure exactly what she was looking for, but she was confident she would know when she finally saw it.

As the line dwindled, her eyes fell on a tall green boy. Tall even for Windwalker standards, she noted.

"There was nothing particularly spectacular about you, except for your height," Margret would say as she watched him dust the towering vases in her home. "The moment I saw you, I knew you would be perfect for the job."

She waited until he received his water before she approached. He had started to head toward New Ira when she reached out and firmly squeezed his right bicep, signaling him to turn around. He turned slowly and stared down at her. His expression seemed better fit for a man than an adolescent child. She stood there, lost in his weary gaze, holding his right bicep. She pulled herself from this dreamlike state and released his arm.

"Looking for work?" she asked him.

"Yes, I am."

"I can pay you two gold coins for a day's work."

"I can do better in New Ira," the boy said and turned to leave.

Margret again grabbed his arm, but this time she spun him around herself. "Don't turn your back to me, scrab! You don't leave until I dismiss you. I'll give you five coins for a day's work. That's more than generous."

He looked down at her arm, then back at her. He opened his mouth as if to say something but then slammed it shut. His lips pressed firmly against each other, and the muscles in his arm coiled. She quickly glanced over to the fountain to make sure the soldiers were still there. They were, and she again felt she was in complete control of the situation.

"What's your name, scrab?" she demanded.

He had seen her look to the soldiers, and his arm was again limp. "Reuel Haldane," he said.

"Reuel, you start today."

Reuel had worked for her for almost the entire season and had received his fair share of beatings for not following the rules of the house. The beatings she administered had been just short of savage. He now worked efficiently, was quiet, and kept to himself while in the house.

That last part Margret especially seemed to like, since her son Zachariah was fond of Reuel and, according to her, children his age were quite impressionable. She already had to deal with his father filling his head with nonsense of equality. She didn't need it coming from a scrab, too.

On this particular morning, while Margret waited for Reuel to arrive, she found herself wrestling with a peculiar idea. She wasn't sure if it was the excitement of the Ascension Ceremony the following day or the fact she hadn't indulged in her midday drink with Jezebel in countless days—or maybe it was a combination of the two that was clouding her judgment—but she had started to become more comfortable with the idea of leaving Zachariah alone for the day with Reuel when she ventured to see Jezebel in New Ira.

Margret was sitting on the bench outside of her tidy two-story home when she saw Reuel turning off Darius's Way and sauntering toward her.

The Yetes house was one of the first homes on 3rd Street. It was nestled between two others, both owned by Zurielians. Margret wasn't thrilled by this, but the house to the right was now vacant since the Auxiliaries who had lived there had been relocated to the outskirts. She was hopeful that the Premiers to her left would eventually suffer a similar fate.

Reuel's bucket knocked against his leg as he approached, splashing water on the ground. Margret held up her hand, and he stopped in front of her.

She rocked her body slightly in order to generate the momentum needed to lift her large mass. She swayed back and forth as she gained her balance.

"Your usual chores are waiting for you. I'll be going to New Ira and won't return until evening-light. Jerimiah has already left for the bakery and will be back at evening-light as well."

She took a step closer and pointed a meaty finger in Reuel's face.

"Zachariah is inside. You are not to say a single word to him. If he asks you anything, you are to remain silent and ignore his existence. You are to do your chores and then sit on that bench until I return to pay you. Is that clear, scrab?"

Reuel found it hard to concentrate with Margret's hot, musty breath assaulting his nostrils, but he knew better than to not respond. She may not have been quick or skilled in combat, but she was smart and big. When she did make contact, it was to a soft spot and did significant damage. He still had faint bruises along his stomach and back from when he had learned this firsthand.

"Yes, ma'am," he answered.

She nodded and picked up her satchel and brushed past Reuel. He watched her as she waddled down 3rd Street toward Darius's Way. He was consistently amazed by how such a large woman was able to walk at all. Once she was out of sight, he turned to the house and pushed the wooden door open.

The Yetes lived lavishly. Their house was furnished with polished wooden furniture, and their floors weren't dirt like many other homes in Old Ira but were covered with marble tiles. Along their walls were beautifully decorated vases and sculptures, and this was where Reuel usually began his day: dusting these expensive decorative art pieces.

He put down his bucket and pulled a long piece of cloth from the waistband of his harem pants and started to carefully remove the thin layer of dust attached to the artwork. As expected, such work was tedious, but a discovery Reuel had made early on allowed him to venture back in time and remember better days.

During his first few days in the Yetes's house, he had thoroughly inspected one of the vases while dusting and was pleasantly surprised to see it had been made by Mark Gulton, who was widely considered the best sculptor on Aela. He was a fellow Windwalker, and Reuel had had the pleasure of meeting him years ago.

Mark had sculpted a splendid statue of his father for one of his birthdays. That day had been one of celebration and joy, one that Reuel thought would be a vibrant memory for the rest of his life, but recent events had caused it to dull and decay. It almost seemed as if it had never occurred at all, just a dream from long ago. That, coupled with the fact he and his family had been wiped from the minds of the people of Tesa and Aela as a whole, only further caused him to question the validity of the memory.

After he finished dusting, he made his way toward the kitchen, which branched off from the living room. The same marble tiles from the living room decorated the floor, and a dome-shaped oven sat near the center of the room under a couple of rows of rectangular slits in the ceiling. The slits allowed for the room to be ventilated during heavy use. The wall behind the oven was dotted with rows of hooks. Frying pans, cauldrons, and knives of all different shapes and sizes hung from them. A long marble counter rested to the right of the oven, red streaks staining its surface. Reuel had spent the better part of the season scrubbing those bloodstains, but they were relentless.

He moved to his right, in the direction of a mound of used cooking utensils. The tiles had been removed, and a small ditch had been dug. The dirty pots and utensils rested in this depression. He squatted down with his bucket of water and sorted everything into smaller, more manageable piles. He had just started washing the pans when he heard the soft tapping of footsteps on the marble tiles. He turned and greeted Zachariah with a wide, welcoming smile.

Unbeknownst to Margret, her son and Reuel were quite well-acquainted and shared a rather unique relationship. Zachariah was a small, chubby boy with short blond hair and pasty skin. He was exceptionally bright, like most Angelic children.

After only days at the Yetes's, Zachariah had taken up the hobby of stalking Reuel as he completed his chores. He peeked from behind walls and crouched behind the larger vases, quickly vanishing when Reuel turned in his direction. At first, Reuel paid little attention to him since Margret had been especially clear that any contact with Zachariah would not be tolerated. Yet fate intervened once again.

One day, at midday, while hiding behind one of the large vases, Zachariah had moved too quickly in an attempt to conceal himself from Reuel and knocked it off balance. The priceless vase rocked and fell to the floor. A look of pure fear flashed across Zachariah's face. Reuel dropped his brush, his eyes glazed, and he was moving.

Over the course of the season, Reuel had gained control of his speed, and his perception of the things around him while he was glazing had changed. Instead of things whizzing by, they slowed down as he sped up.

He quickly covered the ground between himself and the boy. One side of the vase had reached the floor, and cracks from the impact raced along its body. Reuel grabbed the lid and pulled it back to its original upright position.

He had reached the vase before any of the cracks put the vase's integrity into question. Finally, he rotated it so that the cracks faced the wall.

Reuel's eyes returned to black while the little color that naturally painted Angelic faces was slowly injected back into Zachariah's. His small chest heaved as he gulped air. Reuel patted the boy's head and went back to his chores.

Margret eventually noticed the cracks and pummeled Reuel for the deed. He took that one with a smile.

Rather me than the boy, he thought.

From that day onward, Zachariah inched closer and closer until he nearly sat next to Reuel while he worked. Zachariah now sat cross-legged next to Reuel as he scrubbed a small cauldron.

"Why do you clean our house?" Zachariah asked, breaking the silence.

Reuel flinched. The boy had never talked to him before. He glanced up from his pot and studied him. Zachariah's brow was furled as if he were contemplating one of Aela's great mysteries.

"This is what scrabs do," Reuel responded.

"Are you sure? It's not how it used to be. Mother did the cleaning before you came, and she was doing that for a long time."

Still scrubbing, Reuel answered, "Times have changed. This is how things are now."

"Well…it's not much fun. My friends all moved away, and Mother won't let me see them anymore. She says I'll catch their lethargic tendencies. Do you have lethargic tendencies?"

Reuel stopped scrubbing and stared at the boy once again. This time, honest curiosity was the expression he wore. Reuel shook his head. He had allowed himself to forget that Zachariah was not Margret. He had allowed himself to let the wrongs of the few corrupt his view of them all. His stomach turned at the realization. It sickened him to the point of nausea.

Great job, Guardian, he thought.

"I don't have lethargic tendencies, and neither do all Auxiliaries, or scrabs."

"My mother says that scrabs can't help it. It's in

238

their nature to do nothing and take up space. But you don't act like that at all."

It was slowly dawning on Reuel that saving Aela didn't mean only saving Zurielians, but also Angelics. Zachariah rocked back and forth on his bottom, waiting for Reuel to respond. It was clear to Reuel that the war for Aela's future would start in that kitchen. The war for Zachariah's mind had begun.

"Not all people act the same. Do you act the same as your father or mother?"

"My mother's friends say I act like my father."

"Would it be fair for someone who you have never met to claim there is no difference between you, your father, or your mother simply because you're all Angelics?"

"I'm Zach. I can't be my father or mother. They are already themselves." He smiled, revealing two missing front teeth.

"Then how can all scrabs be the same?"

The boy's smile vanished. His rocking came to halt, and his brow again furled. He didn't say anything for a long time. Reuel went back to the dishes while the boy watched in silence.

"That's not fair," Zachariah finally said. "Why does my mother say those things, then?"

"Honestly, I can't tell you. I'm still trying to figure things out myself. I'm not much older than you. What you have to do is form your own opinions. You have to gather your own experiences."

"How do I do that?"

"You can start by continuing to do what you're doing right now: ask questions. Don't take your mother's word as the only truth. You can't form an accurate picture of anything until you analyze it from different angles and perspectives. Learn about someone before you decide to judge them."

Reuel wasn't sure where these words were coming from, but they flowed from his mouth with such ease and grace he didn't question it. It was as if they had been floating in his mind all along but just out of reach, and Zachariah provided the lift needed to grab hold of them.

"Why didn't you tell my mother that I cracked the vase?"

Reuel pointed to the fading bruise on the boy's ribcage. "I thought you would appreciate a break."

Zach shifted uncomfortably. "She says that she does it because she loves me and doesn't want there to be any chance that I become a scrab. I am lazy sometimes, so I understand."

"Don't give her any excuses. What does your father say?"

"Not much."

"Your mother can't determine your class." Reuel

pointed at Zachariah's chest. "It's something that's always been in you and only certified at your classification. I didn't want to be an Auxiliary. I didn't plan on cleaning houses, but here I am. An Auxiliary is who I am, and I've accepted that."

"What if I am an Auxiliary?"

"Then you embrace it, in spite of your mother. All you can do is be who you are."

Without a word, Zachariah rose to his feet and lunged at Reuel. He wrapped his arms around his neck in a tight embrace. Reuel felt the boy's body shake violently as he sobbed on his shoulder. Reuel firmly grasped Zachariah's forearm and gently shook it, reassuring him.

Zachariah's sobs were just loud enough and close enough to Reuel's ears that he had not heard Margret return home. Nor did he hear the dragging of her sandals on the tiles as she approached the kitchen. He did, however, hear the thud of her satchel as it hit the kitchen floor. He turned his head in time to see the massive woman charging at him.

"Let go of my son, you dirty scrab!" Her normally pale face was flushed red. Globs of spit erupted from her mouth as she roared.

Reuel shoved Zachariah out of harm's way. He skidded across the slick tiles and landed safely near the wall dotted with hooks. With Zachariah out of the way, Reuel turned his focus on the charging mad woman.

I won't kill her, he thought. *She may be a foul beast, but she doesn't deserve death. I won't spill innocent blood.*

But Margret clearly had different intentions. Before he could glaze and properly defend himself, she was on top of him. She wound up and planted a savage kick in the middle of his chest, sending him sprawling.

The impact left him dizzy and gasping for air. His mind was too scattered to glaze. His head was throbbing to the point that he was now seeing three of her.

He swung his fists wildly in a vain attempt to protect himself. She caught his forearm while her own eyes glazed dull silver. Reuel went limp as his energy left his body. Margret's eyes slowly shifted from silver to green.

"I told you to leave my son alone," she hissed. "But you refused to listen, and now Ira will have one less scrab to worry about."

Utilizing Reuel's speed, she unleashed a barrage of punches along his chest. Each punch she landed felt stronger than the last and sent a fresh wave of pain through his limp body. One found the soft tissue of his face. It rattled his teeth and sent his head crashing into the marble.

He coughed, and blood sprayed his cheeks. His vision grew dark and he started to drift away, but before the darkness took him, the onslaught abruptly ended.

The last thing Reuel saw before his eyes closed was Zachariah staring down at him.

When Reuel came to, he wasn't sure where he was, but his aching head reminded him where he had been. He sat up, but the seething pain in his chest forced him to lie back down.

He knew he was outside and that he was lying on a bench. He gathered that he was on one of the side streets but wasn't sure where, exactly. He took a deep breath and began to sort out his thoughts. His mind was a fragmented mess. He could only remember bits and pieces of his encounter with Margret, but there was one thing in his mind that was clear: the image of Zachariah staring down at him.

He immediately jolted upright. He grimaced, but for the most part, he could ignore the pain. His head was now on a swivel. He looked up and down the street in search of Zachariah. The sunlight was quickly fading, and the lamps hanging in the doorways had yet to be lit.

Reuel could sense movement a little way down the street to his right. A small figure waddled toward him. As it got closer, he could make out Zachariah swaying back and forth, trying to carry Reuel's water bucket.

He placed the bucket by Reuel's feet and took a seat next to him.

Reuel cupped his hands and plunged them into the water. He splashed the cold water onto his face and wiped away the dry blood.

"The water is cold…" Reuel said, puzzled. "Did you refill it?"

"Yes, I thought you would need some fresh water when you woke up."

"How long was I out?"

"The entire afternoon. I had to drag you here from my house."

Reuel stopped washing his face and turned his full attention to the boy. "What happened, and where are we?"

Zachariah looked down at his hands and twiddled his thumbs. "Mother came home early. She was going to hurt you real bad, so I helped you. I took one of the cauldrons and hit her in the head. Then I put you in my cart and pulled you here." He pointed at a small cart that rested near the bench.

Reuel stared at him, astonished. "Nobody saw you? How did you manage to pull me by yourself?"

"You're not very heavy. I cut between the houses and waited until it was clear before I moved between streets."

"What street are we on?"

"The edge of 8th. The outskirts are down there." Zachariah pointed down the street.

"Thank you." Reuel grabbed Zachariah and hugged him tightly. He stood Zachariah up in front of him, both hands firmly gripping his shoulders. "We have to get you home."

Zachariah shook his shoulders free from Reuel's grip. "No, I'm not going back. There is nothing there for me."

"Your mother and father are there."

"My mother almost beat you to death. My father does nothing when she beats me for no reason." He stared Reuel dead in his eyes. "I hit her in the head with a cauldron. If I go back, she will kill me, and my father will do nothing. I'm going with you."

Reuel nodded. "I understand, but they will come looking for you."

"Even if my mother knew I was in the outskirts, she wouldn't go there. She would rather let me go than be surrounded by Auxiliaries."

"I see there will be no denying you. You're a smart kid, Zachariah. You can come, but we need to leave now. I have somewhere to be." Reuel rose to his feet and nearly collapsed to the ground, but Zachariah stabilized him.

"Thanks. You can stay with me and my parents. There isn't much room, but we can make it work. But if she does come looking for you, we will have to give you to her."

"I know." Zachariah nodded. "Thank you, Reuel."

It took them a while to reach Reuel's shack. They were only able to pick up the pace once Reuel had gotten used to the pain in his chest. The shack was empty when they arrived. Reuel lit the lamp on the floor near his bed, vanquishing the darkness. The lamp was still hot, so he assumed his parents had recently left for the Institute.

"I'll be back soon. There is an apple in the basket in the corner when you get hungry."

"Where do I go if I have to…" Zachariah bowed his head and stared at his feet.

Reuel smiled. "There's a scrab shed right outside. You'll be fine."

With that, Reuel's eyes glazed. He ran out of the shed and toward the Institute.

Even though he was moving at full speed, he was careful to stay near the buildings as he ran. He was fast but was still only an Auxiliary. Any soldiers paying close enough attention would have seen him, and that was the last thing he needed. The day was already bad enough.

He wasn't sure how he was going to explain Zachariah to his parents, but that was something he could deal with when the time came. He pushed the thought of Zachariah, Margret, and his throbbing chest to the side. A much more pressing thought had seized his attention. Azriel was due to arrive in Ira tomorrow at high-day.

The thought made him giddy with joy. The end was near. Reuel sprinted around the Institute and came to a halt at the secret entrance. He pushed the irregularly shaped stone and walked down the stairs with a smile on his face.

ASHER (III)

Asher hurried down one of the palace's corridors toward his father's throne room. The hood of his cloak fell off his head and its tail flapped behind him as he ran. Abaddon had called for a gathering, and Asher didn't want to be the last to arrive. There was no telling what mood Abaddon might be in.

Asher reached the grand doors to the throne room and was pleased to see they were still closed. He was the first one there. He heard the growing sound of scurrying feet coming from the corridor adjacent to the one he had just left. The first to emerge from the corridor was a lean, attractive Angelic woman. Her blonde hair was tied in a tight ponytail that bounced against her back as she walked. Unlike the others behind her, her hood was down.

"Asher," she said without breaking stride. She pushed open the throne room doors and confidently walked in.

"Leah," he muttered.

Like all Angelics, especially Elites, her physical appearance was deceiving. Her youthful, early-twentysomething body was home to a middle-aged mind. She had arrived shortly after Abaddon had erected the walls.

Asher was still unsure of the depths of their relationship, but he could tell Abaddon was fond of her. He had not only seen them walking the corridors alone hand in hand, but she also occupied the most coveted seat in the throne room, the one to Abaddon's right side—directly across from Asher.

She was followed into the throne room by the Legion, a group of Abaddon's most trusted officials. Asher had personally recommended the group's name to Abaddon. He had never felt such a profound sense of accomplishment when Abaddon actually agreed with his recommendation. It was Leah's glare of disapproval after this endorsement that had cemented their mutual hatred for one another.

Asher shoved his way through the Legion and into the throne room. Before Abaddon had arrived, the throne room was used only for special occasions, such as the ball after the Ascension Ceremony. It was now used on a regular basis. A large table had been constructed and placed in the middle of the room. Nearly twenty seats rested along each of its sides. At the head of the table was the throne.

Asher took his seat at the end of the table and to the left of the throne. The rest of the Legion quietly filed in and found their seats. They sat in silence for a while before Abaddon marched proudly into the room, followed closely by King Darius.

Asher couldn't help but notice that there was something different about his father this evening. He, too, walked proudly. He held his head high and he radiated regality, something Asher hadn't seen since Abaddon arrived.

The king settled into the seat next to Asher. Abaddon stood, shrouded in his usual black cloak, at the head of the table and placed his right hand over his heart. The Legion followed suit and bowed their heads.

"Praise Lord Gideon and the Angelic Empire," they said in unison.

It was at this time that the Legion removed their hoods and all their faces were revealed. Asher always found it amusing that the Legion was not made up of solely Angelics. They were the majority, but every other race was represented in the room. It was amazing what fear could drive people to do.

Asher's eyes were drawn to an elderly man, very sickly looking, who sat farther down the table next to Captain Jadon. His name was Samuel Longston, and he worked on the loading docks and was the only member of the Legion who Asher respected besides Abaddon. Samuel was one of the oldest members of the Legion and rarely hesitated to share his disgust of Zurielians.

Asher then glanced across the table to the chair next to Leah. It was again vacant. The seat had yet to have an occupant since it was placed there. Asher had contemplated asking who the chair was for, but frivolous questions were not tolerated. The seat placement alone signified importance, and Asher figured that if he wanted to know, he would just have to be patient.

"Legion!" Abaddon boomed. "Tomorrow is the day Gideon and I have been preparing for since the end of the war. It is the first step to freeing our Lord, and it is of the utmost importance that everything goes according to plan. There cannot be a single detail overlooked. Everything must be perfect."

"My Lord, after you are successful, have you decided what will be done with the ones you take prisoner, especially the children?" Darius asked.

Asher glanced at his father in disgust. It was sentiments such as these that had allowed Asher to take his father's seat at Abaddon's side, forcing the king farther down the table.

"Let the Zurielian children burn!" Samuel snorted in laugher.

There were scattered chuckles throughout the room, mainly from Angelics.

"Yes, Darius." Abaddon pulled what looked like a collar from beneath his cloak. "I have called you all here today to reveal this."

He proudly held the black collar in front of him.

"Once the dust settles and the ones that oppose us are killed, these Absolium collars will be placed around the necks of every prisoner. They will completely suppress their abilities and effectively eliminate all threats. This, my Legion, is the key to the new Angelic Empire."

The Legion applauded and cheered at the declaration. A Grindbler named Paul Iteria sitting near the end of the table cleared his throat. "My Lord, how do we ensure our own families' safety?"

"I advise you to make sure they don't leave home tomorrow. We are at war, Paul. There will be casualties. Safety can never be guaranteed in such circumstances." Abaddon paused for a moment. "And if you interrupt me again, I will personally take care of your family. Then you will no longer need to ask such questions."

Paul's mouth clamped shut, and he sank into his chair. Asher smiled, but it disappeared when his father again opened his mouth to speak.

"My Lord, once you have claimed victory tomorrow, will your search for the new Guardians end? Too many innocent children have died, and I won't—I cannot—sit here silently anymore."

"The more the merrier!" Samuel shouted, now laughing hysterically.

Again, there were chuckles throughout the room, mainly from Angelics.

Abaddon glared at the king. "As some of you may know, I have long suspected the existence of other Guardians."

Hushed whispers broke out amongst the Legion.

"Quiet!" Abaddon roared. All was silent, even Samuel. "I have been collecting children for some time now, for the dual purpose of building my army and searching for the Guardians. The situation is more than taken care of. One of my most trusted advisors is on top of it." He waved at the empty chair next to Leah.

Leah pulled out a dagger and plunged it into the table. "Any other questions will be answered by me. Please finish, my Lord."

Abaddon nodded at Leah, and she smiled smugly at Asher. Asher clenched his teeth and curled his fists tightly under the table.

Darius rose to his feet. All eyes focused on him. There wasn't a sound in the room. Nobody even dared to breathe. Asher could sense his father trembling beneath his cloak.

"I cannot support this any longer, and I am nobody's puppet. You have not only murdered innocent children in my palace, but I allowed you to chase away my daughter. I will be a part of this no more."

Darius marched from the room and disappeared down a corridor. Attention again shifted to Abaddon. The Legion waited to see how he would respond.

Abaddon chuckled. "It looks like he actually has some king in him after all."

The Legion let out a nervous laugh.

"Prepare yourselves. Tomorrow is the beginning of Gideon's reign. You are dismissed," Abaddon declared.

The Legion pulled their hoods over and began to clear the room. Asher rose to leave when he heard Abaddon's voice in his head.

"Sit down."

He fell back into his seat and waited patiently. Abaddon sat on the throne, his right hand massaging his bare chin. After a while, the throne room was clear except for Abaddon, Leah, and Asher. Leah's hand played with her dagger's handle while she glared at Asher.

"The time has come, Asher," Abaddon said. "Your father's presence is no longer required."

Asher nodded his head. "I understand, my Lord."

"My Lord, allow me to handle this," Leah pleaded. "He is still a child."

"No," Abaddon said plainly. "This is a task Asher must do, and do alone."

Leah pulled the dagger out of the table and slid it over to Asher.

"I have my own knife," Asher sneered.

"Absolium blade," Leah replied.

"No need. He doesn't believe in permanent absorption. He has no other abilities. My knife will do just fine."

"As you wish." Leah grabbed her knife and left the throne room.

"Is this task too much for you, Asher?"

"No, My Lord, my father will not survive the night."

Asher left the throne room and nearly sprinted to his father's chamber. He was one step closer to becoming Abaddon's top official. It was only moments before the doors of his father's chamber were in sight. Two guards stood outside of it. He slowed his pace and sauntered toward them. He waved them aside and pushed open the door.

There was a single candle burning on one of the tables against the wall. Most of his father's elegant decorations were shrouded in darkness. The glow from the candle produced just enough light that Asher could make out his father sitting on his bed with his back to him, staring out of the balcony window.

"I was surprised I was allowed to leave the throne room alive," Darius laughed.

"It will be quick, father." Asher gripped the knife resting in his waistband.

"I'd wondered who he would send. I shouldn't be surprised he would choose my own son," the king sighed. "Your sister was right to run away."

Asher took a few steps forward. His heart was pounding. He never cared much for the man, but he was still his father, and that was enough to slow his pace a bit. He would allow him to speak his final thoughts.

"She was weak, Father, like you. I would've had to kill her too if she had stayed."

Darius took a deep breath. "I suppose you're right, my son. I will not fight you. I do not wish to live any longer. I have failed as a king. I failed my people and my family."

Asher was now standing behind his father. His knife was unsheathed and gleamed in the flickering candlelight.

"I will restore honor to your name, Father."

"No. You will only further disgrace me. My only hope is with your sister. She is my greatest achievement." Darius sighed deeply. "I hope your mother is waiting for me."

Asher's grip on the knife tightened. "You foolish old man," he hissed. "You won't have to wait long for your family reunion. I'll arrange it myself!"

Asher pulled his father's head back and slid the knife's blade across his throat. His father hitched, jerked, and was then still.

"Give Mother my regards." Asher smiled and licked the blood from the knife as he left the room.

DANIEL (V)

Daniel felt the zip train slow, and the darkness of the tunnel gave way to beams of light. They would arrive in Ira soon. He looked to Azriel, who hadn't spoken a word the entire trip.

"It's time," Daniel said to the young Guardian.

Azriel didn't answer. He only nodded and continued to stare past Daniel and out the window. The train emerged from the tunnel and into the high-day sun.

The first things Daniel noticed were the beautiful homes that adorned the landscape. They were carbon copies of each other, each sporting pristine marble walls and columns supporting beautifully sculpted roofs. Daniel likened their beauty to that of a princess. They were welcoming to the eye, but forbidden to be approached or touched.

The train docked at the station and the side door slid open, allowing the fresh surface air to waft into the cabin. Daniel slung his bag over his shoulder and led Azriel to the door. The city was alive. People of all races were briskly moving around the loading docks. Daniel stood on the platform, scanning the crowd for their escort.

"You can feel the energy in the air," Azriel said. *"The Ascension Ceremony really is a big deal."*

"I suppose so."

"Excuse me, sir, you two have to clear the platform!" an armored guard shouted over the bustling crowd. He stood on the platform steps, waving his arm to usher them along. A slender red hand tapped the guard's shoulder.

"They're with me," Sophia said.

The guard straightened up. "Yes, ma'am. I'm sorry." He dropped his head and disappeared into the crowd.

"Sophia!" Daniel exclaimed gleefully. He wrapped his arms around her and hugged her tightly. "It's been far too long."

She smiled and hugged him back. "It has, indeed, my friend."

Daniel released her and marveled at the elegant black gown she wore. It complemented the intricate tattoos that wrapped around her ruby-colored arms and neck. Her gray hair was wrapped in a beautiful mound on top of her head, and a silver necklace hung from her neck.

"You look beautiful, not a day older than the last time I saw you," Daniel said, still beaming.

Her cheeks grew a few shades darker as she blushed. "Thank you, Daniel, you're kind." Her eyes left Daniel and shifted to Azriel. She stretched out her arm to him. Azriel grabbed hold of her forearm, establishing a personal mental link. Azriel broadcasted their conversation to Daniel.

"Welcome to Ira, young Guardian, we have been waiting for you."

"I'm ready to help in any way I can, ma'am."

"We don't have time to waste. The others are waiting for us at my home. Follow me."

They passed through the loading docks, walked down 83rd Street, and found themselves on Darius's Way. Sophia turned and led them into the crowd.

As they waded through the masses, Daniel took note of the extravagant attire around him. Men wore brilliantly decorated vests to go along with black silk harem pants, and women were draped in breathtaking silk gowns of all styles and colors. The majority of the well-dressed were Angelics. He spotted a handful of Zurielians dressed just as well, but they were few and far between. The majority of the Zurielians he did see were dressed in everyday tunics or harem pants, closely following the Angelics like servants. Some were even carrying the trains of the gowns.

"Has everyone arrived?" Daniel asked Sophia, broadcasting to include Azriel, unbeknownst to her.

"Yes, for the most part. They've been coming in all day. Many have already taken seats in the Institute. Why do you ask?"

"I couldn't help but notice that many of the Zurielians are not as well dressed as you."

Sophia stopped and subtly pointed to her left. Daniel's gaze followed her arm to a large wall that stood in the distance.

"Things are much worse than you know, my friend," Sophia said. *"The separation of New and Old Ira is no longer implied, but enforced."*

"Enforced how?"

Sophia again began walking and shifting through the crowd as she spoke. *"Only Angelics, Elite, and Premier Zurielians live in New Ira. The Zurielian Auxiliaries were forced from their homes and into the outskirts of Old Ira. Their empty homes were offered to Angelic Auxiliaries, and so were their jobs. In order to survive, the Zurielian Auxiliaries have to work for those in New Ira or the Angelic Auxiliaries that can afford them in Old Ira."*

"How did this happen?!"

"Darius claimed that Cyrus had erected the wall

261

and the Guardians were behind the new order."

"Abaddon…"

"Yes."

"The king, queens, and generals from the other capitals won't stand for this when they arrive."

"They won't know, Daniel. They will be ushered by Angelic soldiers to their seats at the Institute the moment they arrive in the city. They will only see what the Angelics allow them to see. The Zurielian Auxiliaries won't be at the ceremony, and the Elite and Premiers won't say anything for fear of ending up like the Auxiliaries. Our hopes lie with the new Guardians."

Daniel glanced over his shoulder at Azriel, whose eyes were fixated on Sophia's back. "If they fail to ascend, the High Council must reveal these travesties at the ceremony."

"If they fail, we will. But if it comes to that, we are already doomed. By now, nothing but the combined might of the Guardians or Zuriel himself could defeat Abaddon." Sophia stopped in front of one of the identical homes.

"We're here," she said, then walked between the columns and led them into her home.

They walked across a thin hallway decorated with vases. From what Daniel could see, the hallway stretched around the house and met at the back wall of the atrium, creating a square. It only took a few steps for them to cross the hallway and into a beautiful atrium. The sun shone down through the roof and glistened off a small pool in the middle. There was a marble bench on each side of the rectangular pool that looked as if they had been erected from the smooth marble floor they rested on. However, it was the people sitting on top of the benches that had Daniel's full attention.

Daniel recognized Hazael and Abigail, who were sitting on the bench to his left, and Jonas and Moriah, who were sitting on the bench to his right. But they held his attention only momentarily. Who held his eye were the three children sitting on the bench directly in front of him.

REUEL (VIII)

Reuel and the others had spent the night at Sophia's. Sophia made it clear at training the night before that there was no room for error. With Azriel finally coming to town, they couldn't afford any mishaps. So in an effort to do just that, Reuel, Elon, Eve, and the High Council shared Sophia's home for the night.

Sleep, however, eluded the young Guardians. Instead, they spent most of the night sitting in silence in the atrium. But before they had settled into their seats they took their time to familiarize themselves with the house. The living quarters were located in the west wing, while the kitchen and dining area were in the east. The atrium sat in the middle of the house. They could walk across the hallway that boxed it in, into either of the wings.

They each took a bench of their own by the pool, but as the night grew older they drew closer until they were all sitting side by side. Each was lost in their private thoughts, but they found comfort in one another's company. Reuel was the first to break the silence when he talked about Zachariah and others like him who called out for help, but their pleas fell on deaf ears. Elon spoke of Aaron and how it was time for him to be the hero his little brother thought he was. Eve mentioned Abel but hoped that her birth parents would be proud. They talked 'til dawn.

The sunlight crept through the skylight in the ceiling and ushered in a new day. They stood, stretched, and exchanged weary smiles. The day had finally arrived. Sophia and the Council joined them in the dining room, where they had apples and a beef stew for breakfast. It was a welcomed treat for all except Sophia, who dined on such delicacies regularly.

Sophia left shortly after breakfast dressed in an immaculate black gown. Reuel and the others again shared a bench while his parents took the bench to their right and Elon's parents sat to their left.

When Sophia returned, Elon was the first to react to the visitors. Sophia remained in the hallway that enclosed the atrium while the two Aquatis approached the pool. One of them was older, with teal skin and graying, shaggy hair that matched the messy gray beard on his face. The other was much younger, closer to Reuel's age, his skin a rich, dark blue, and his hair short and black. They both were wearing hufflud shorts that reminded Reuel of the ones he had once seen in the market.

Before greetings could be exchanged by either party, Elon ran toward the younger one, who Reuel assumed was Azriel. He wrapped his large arms around him and smothered him in a suffocating embrace. As he did, a strange cry came from Elon. Reuel thought it was an odd mixture of sobbing and laughter. Reuel patted Elon on the shoulder, signaling to let Azriel go.

"I'm sorry, we're all a little excited about your arrival," Reuel explained.

Elon released Azriel and wiped his eyes. "It's good to meet you, brother," he said.

"You took long enough," Eve said with a rare smile.

Azriel smiled. "I, too, have longed to meet you all. If it wouldn't trouble you, I would like to establish a personal mental connection with each of you." He held out his arm.

Reuel went first. He took his forearm in a firm grasp. The embrace was short. Elon went next, followed by Eve.

"This is far more comfortable for me." Azriel's smile widened.

"I've never done this myself, it's strange but amazing." Reuel looked around at the others. They all burst

266

out into uncontrollable laughter. The remaining members of the Council rose from their benches and joined in the small celebration. There was no shortage of smiles or laughs.

"It's been far too long, Daniel," Hazael said.

"It has. I haven't seen you since you were a much younger man," Daniel laughed. "And Abigail, you are even more graceful than on your wedding day."

"Thank you, Daniel," Abigail beamed.

"What did you bring with you, Daniel?" Jonas asked, gesturing toward the bag he was carrying.

"Just a few things to help out the young Guardians." Daniel relaxed and dropped his bag to his feet. He looked Jonas and Moriah up and down. "I see you two are still the epitome of physical perfection."

Moriah let out a hearty laugh and flexed her arms. "Nothing but a little hard work and strong heritage."

Daniel turned his attention to Reuel and the others, but his eyes lingered on Eve for a while. "It's good to see you again, Eve," he said gently.

Eve grinned. "Same here, Daniel. Beliel wasn't the same once you left. The new blacksmith wasn' nearly as knowledgeable or fun."

Daniel grinned widely. He then addressed the rest of them. "I heard how bad things have gotten, and hopefully we can get them back to normal soon enough." He held out his arm, as Azriel had done.

They each took a turn and established a personal mental connection with Daniel.

Reuel looked to Sophia, who had yet to move from where they had entered.

"I think we're ready!" he proclaimed. Sophia smiled back, but something about the smile made him uneasy.

"I often wondered what today would be like," Sophia answered. "If I would be engorged with joy or devastated by sorrow. Now that the day has come, I can say it's an odd combination of the two."

"What are you talking about, Sophia?" Hazael asked, his eyes trained on her.

"Isn't it obvious?" She paused. "Well, probably not, since you still haven't put it together." She pointed her right index finger at her face. "It was me. It was always me."

She took a few steps backward so that there was a comfortable amount of space between her and the High Council. From the shadows behind her, a group of Angelic soldiers emerged.

"Explain yourself!" Hazael roared. He took a step forward in front of the children.

"I suppose some part of me wanted to be caught. I practically told you that I was involved the night after classification, but you couldn't see what was right in front of you. I am greater than Phoebe. I'm the bridge to every citizen's locked-away potential. I have never failed to help a pupil ascend. You should've known something was wrong when *I* said I couldn't help. They never needed to be together to ascend, it was just easier to capture them if they were all in one place!"

Hazael's eyes started to glaze, but as they lit up, a deep snarl came from the hallway. Snaretooth walked to his master's side, his teeth fully exposed, eyes focused on Hazael.

"You may be fast enough, but are the children?" Sophia asked.

Hazael hesitated for a moment, then his eyes returned to normal.

"To be honest, I wasn't sure if I would even be able to suppress the Guardian abilities within them. I had never stopped someone from ascending before, let alone Guardians, but surprisingly it wasn't as difficult as you might imagine. Azriel was the first one, and it went better than I ever could've dreamed. I took care of the others as they came to Instruction for classification. It was simple, actually. Instead of connecting their minds to their abilities, I created a barrier, or force field, as you all call it."

"Why?" Abigail said and walked to her husband's side.

"I had my doubts, Abigail. When Abaddon approached me years ago I…"

"Years?" Moriah gasped.

Sophia laughed. "Yes, this has been in the making for a while now. He offered me a position that I would have been a fool to refuse: a place in Gideon's new kingdom as a queen of one of the soon-to-be conquered capitals."

Daniel opened his mouth to say something. Sophia raised her hand to him. "Daniel, don't you see? Abaddon killed *the* Guardians. The ones that had defeated Gideon! And you expect me to put my faith in these *children*?" Sophia shook her head in amazement.

"After Uri fell, it was clear I had made the correct decision. Gideon will rise again, and this time Zuriel and the Guardians won't be here."

Jonas and Moriah stepped in line with Hazael and Abigail, further providing a buffer for Reuel and the others.

Daniel made a move to come forward but stopped suddenly. He glanced at Reuel, then Hazael. Reuel wasn't sure why.

"You didn't even give them a fighting chance. Who knows what they could have done," Moriah said.

"I was not prepared to take that risk. I have a great life here." Sophia spread her arms wide over her head. "As you can see, I do very well for a Premier Shimmer, and I will not risk it all on *them*. As long as I live, they will never ascend."

She signaled to one of the guards behind her. He

came forward holding a sack. Its contents clanged together as it swung in his hand. He opened it, and she withdrew a black collar.

"You should be happy. There won't be a war. These will end any chance of that."

"What are those supposed to be?" Hazael demanded.

"Absolium collars. They will replace your ascension chains. They will suppress all your glazing abilities. You will be the first on Aela to receive them."

Suddenly, Daniel's voice was in Reuel's head. *"Reuel, I'm linking you to your parents, per their request."*

Reuel nodded, and his father's voice boomed in his head. *"Son, I need you to be strong,"* his father began. *"It's time for you to lead them. Your mother and I cannot go with you any further. I hope you will be able to forgive us for keeping the truth from you for so long. I don't know if we did the right thing, but we did what we thought was best. We love you, and will always love you."*

"We're so proud of you, son," his mother said. *"I know you will save Aela."*

Reuel fought the tears welling up in his eyes. He couldn't allow Sophia to suspect a thing. *"I love you too."*

"This will be over quickly, and it'll be much easier

if you don't resist. No one has to die yet." Sophia turned to the soldiers behind her and held the sack out to them. "Make sure each one of them gets one."

Hazael took advantage of the moment. His eyes glazed, and he was off. Reuel watched in awe. His father was moving so fast he could barely keep up. Everyone else's movements were slow and heavy in comparison.

Snaretooth lunged the moment his father's eyes lit up, but Hazael was far too quick. He easily sidestepped the wolf and planted a powerful fist into its exposed side. The wolf cringed and fell to the ground.

He made a move toward Sophia, but to Reuel's surprise, a soldier was charging at his father, and his movements were not slowed but as fluid as his. The soldier's eyes were glazing dull green, and it dawned on Reuel that these soldiers had taken part in the highest of offenses, permanent absorption.

His father threw a tight uppercut at the soldier's chin, but the soldier dodged it and planted two quick jabs into Hazael's abdomen. Hazael crumpled, and before he could recover, the soldier had slipped a collar around his neck.

Hazael fell to his knees. He seemed no longer capable of supporting his own body weight. His eyes lost all traces of green and were black again.

In response to Hazael's capture, the rest of the

High Council attacked. Abigail picked up where Hazael left off. She charged Sophia.

Elon's parents went to Hazael's aid. The soldier had stopped moving long enough when fastening the collar on Hazael for Jonas to grab hold of him. He effortlessly twisted and snapped the soldier's neck. His body sank to the floor.

Abagail had reached Sophia, who was still in the midst of turning back around. Abigail pulled a dagger from the holster on her leg and thrust it forward, but before the blade could reach Sophia's back, a soldier had grabbed Abigail's arm. His eyes, too, glazed green. He savagely twisted her arm, making her drop the knife. He then twisted her body around and kicked the back of her knee, forcing her to the ground. He slipped a collar around her neck and she went limp.

Daniel ushered the children to the back of the atrium.

"We have to go now!" He led them to the back wall. "Elon, make us an exit."

Elon looked back in time to see his parents surrounded by a large group of soldiers, some whose eyes glazed a dull red, others a dull yellow.

"Projections…" Eve said.

"They harvested Grindbler hearts as well…" Elon muttered.

"We don't have time for this. Elon, knock the wall down!" Reuel roared.

They all looked at him for a moment, Daniel included. Elon nodded and glazed. He clobbered the wall with a barrage of heavy punches. It shook, caved, and then burst, revealing 98th Street.

"Go!" Reuel ordered.

All of them but Reuel sprinted through the hole in the wall and down 98th.

Sophia finally turned around. She glanced at Abigail at her feet and Hazael kneeling to her right. Her gaze then traveled to where Jonas and Moriah were fighting side by side against a couple of soldiers whose eyes glazed yellow.

Five unconscious or dead soldiers were at their feet. They traded hit after hit, neither side yielding. The tide of the battle changed when Elon's parents were surrounded by a small platoon of projected soldiers. The sheer number was too much for the mighty duo, and collars were fastened around their necks.

Sophia then looked to the back wall and locked eyes with Reuel, who was standing alone by the large hole. Two green-eyed soldiers looked at her for orders.

She shook her head and pointed at the fallen Council members. "No need, they will come to us." She said it loud enough for Reuel to hear. "When everyone is off the streets and at the ceremony, bring the bodies to the Institute."

Reuel quickly weighed the odds of him successfully saving his parents at that moment. They were not in his favor. He was again helpless. He sighed, jumped through the hole, and raced after the others.

REUEL (IX)

They found refuge on 100th Street. They were anxious to get out of sight, so they broke into the nearest building. Its wooden shutters were no deterrent. Elon smashed them, and they crawled through the window to safety. It turned out that the building was a bakery. They had crawled through one of the windows in the kitchen that was used as an exhaust vent.

Reuel paced back and forth with his hands plastered atop his head. He tilted his head to the sky. He refused to allow the tears to fall. The others leaned against the stone ovens, their eyes on him, waiting to hear his plan.

Daniel spoke first. "We have to tell everyone at the ceremony that things are not as they appear."

"Why would they believe us?" Elon said. "We're children, Auxiliaries at that. You're the only one whose words carry any weight, and you've lived in solitude for years."

"We have to do something," Daniel responded.

"If we march into the Institute, they will kill or capture us on sight," Eve said. "If we' goin' in there, we have to do it the right way."

"Which is?" Elon asked.

"I don' know." Eve looked to Reuel, who continued to pace in silence.

"We have to kill Sophia," Azriel said.

Reuel stopped pacing. Azriel had all their attention.

"She said that as long as *she lived* we wouldn't be able to ascend. The answer is simple. If we want to be of any use, we have to kill her."

"He's right," Reuel agreed. "But how do we do that? How can we get close enough?"

His eyes traveled amongst them, searching for answers. No one said anything. Just then, something fell through the window from which they had entered. A cloaked figure lay on the floor.

Reuel's eyes were already glazing. He was on top of the intruder before anyone else had a chance to move. One of his hands was firmly around the intruder's thin neck, and his other pulled off the hood.

Blonde locks fell from the hood and down the intruder's back. Reuel jumped back. His eyes were again black, his mouth hung open.

"Ruth?" he whispered. "Why?—How?"

Ruth got to her feet and dusted off her robe. "The details aren't important, but I was sent back here, by a friend, to help you. I arrived this morning on one of the hawks from Tesa. I've been looking for you all day. I was beginning to question if I would find you in time when I caught a glimpse of one of your legs slipping into that window."

"In time for what? Who sent you? Did anyone else see?" Reuel rattled off questions.

"We'll get to that later," Ruth said. "And no, there aren't too many people still on the streets. I was lucky to see you guys when I did."

"Who are you?" Daniel asked.

"Ruth Rukist, daughter of Darius and Princess of Ira. I heard your problem outside the window, and I can help. I know how we can get into the ceremony and kill Sophia."

"It's nice to see you, Ruth, but how do you plan on us doin' that?" Eve asked.

"Before I arrived…"

"Who sent you!?!" Reuel demanded, cutting her off. His heart was thrashing in his chest. The girl he loved and had lost was now standing before him, and he wasn't sure what to make of it. He wanted to reach out, grab her, kiss her, but restrained himself. She had left him, after all.

Ruth stepped to him so that she was nearly pressed against his chest. She looked up into his face, and Reuel noticed her eyes were harder now. They no longer carried the jubilant spark they had before. She was different.

But weren't they all?

"I'm sorry I left," she said. "I couldn't handle it."

"We promised we would be there for each other, but you still left me when I needed you most." Reuel felt the all too familiar feeling of his rage building, soon to reach its tipping point.

Ruth placed a hand on his chest, stood on her toes, and kissed him firmly on the lips. "You're right, I failed you, and nothing I can say will make it right. But know that you will never again look to your side and not see me there."

"With all due respect, this is clearly a very touching reunion and I'm sure everything said was meaningful to you both, but can I remind you that we have been *betrayed.*" Elon exclaimed. "My parents were captured or worse, killed, and we still don't know what we're going to do about it!"

Reuel gently pushed Ruth away and nodded. "You said you had a plan?"

She turned and faced the rest of the group. "This is the key." She tugged at her cloak. "This is what all the ascending Premier and Elites will be wearing at tonight's ceremony. I was able to sneak into the palace and retrieve it."

"And what do you plan to do with it?" Daniel asked.

"I'm going to the ceremony."

"They will kill you when you take off that hood," Reuel said.

"Not if we're there to help," Azriel answered.

"Precisely. Any of you who have attended the ceremony in the past know that when it begins, all attention will be on the arena floor. There will be few if any guards at the entrance of the Institute. Most will be placed throughout the arena. This is when you guys make your move. The soldiers that are posted shouldn't be a problem for you. Once you're past them..."

"Small problem," Elon interrupted, pressing his thumb and index finger together to emphasize his point. "We haven't ascended, and if the soldiers at Sophia's were any indication, it's clear the Angelics have been quite busy. It's safe to say we know what happened to the missing children and citizens."

"I see you guys figured it out..." Ruth said lightly.

"Yes. No thanks to you," Reuel said. "You could've warned us..."

"Reuel, we don't have time for this," Daniel interrupted. "The important thing is she's here now. Some of us have lost loved ones that aren't coming back. Let's focus."

Reuel closed his eyes and took a deep breath. He could again feel all their eyes on him, analyzing his every move, looking for him to set the example, to lead.

"You're right, Daniel. Go on, Ruth," Reuel said.

"Elon has a point. The Angelic soldiers have been permanently absorbing Zurielians, and without your Guardian abilities or even weapons, you'll be marching to your death. So we do have a problem."

"Not necessarily," Daniel said. He picked up his bag and rolled it out on the floor, revealing a small arsenal of weapons. "I've been waiting for the right time to give these to you."

Laid out on the floor were two swords, a bow and a bushel of arrows, two ring blades, a large black war hammer head, two rods, and an assortment of daggers.

"Uri had me make these before his death. He intended for you to use them." Daniel handed the swords to Reuel. The bow, bushel of arrows, and a dagger, he gave to Azriel. The ring blades, he gave to Eve. Daniel took a moment to attach the two rods, making them a staff, and then attached the staff to the hammer head and gave it to Elon.

"The blades are made of Absolium along with the hammer, staff, and arrow heads—practically indestructible."

"Practically?" Elon asked.

"Well, the only things I know that can break down Absolium are dragon digestion fluid and magma, and neither is in high supply here," Daniel responded.

"Good enough for me." Eve swiped the air with her blades.

"These will do just fine," Azriel said. He pulled the string of his bow and slipped the dagger into his waistband.

"Yeah, this is what we needed!" Elon swung his hammer back and forth.

"Daniel, how did you carry all this?" Reuel asked. He slung two scabbards over his shoulders, onto his back, and slid the twin swords into them.

"It was my duty," Daniel replied.

Reuel nodded and then looked to Ruth. "This is all we have, so let's make it work. Tell us the rest of your plan."

ABADDON (I)

Had death come during the war, Abaddon would have welcomed it with open arms—but as fate would have it, his life had been spared, and he was again claiming the lives of others.

He withdrew one end of his spear from the body of the Grindbler Guardian and smiled. He stood defiantly over the corpse, arms outstretched. His bald head rolled back and he unleashed a deep, primal roar. He lowered his arms and allowed himself to savor the moment. Revenge was truly sweet. All the years of waiting and planning had delivered him this enchanting moment, and he was determined to remember every detail.

He allowed his eyes to travel up and down the Guardian's body. The Guardian was on his back, his eyes open, lifelessly staring at the sky. Even in death, his muscles looked as if chiseled from marble. His skin was a dark sandy color, a few shades darker than the rocky ground he was lying on. He had put up a magnificent fight, as expected, but in the end, Abaddon had simply been too much.

Even after the onslaught Abaddon had unleashed, only the Guardian's shoulders were charred, and a skinny slit ran down his abdomen from Abaddon's spear. His injuries were superficial and could have passed off as old battle wounds. If it had not been for the substantial hole in the Guardian's left pectoral, it could have easily been assumed he had died of natural causes.

Abaddon ran his tongue along his teeth. To his dismay, he still felt pieces of the Guardian's heart lodged in there. His long fingers worked diligently to dislodge the strips of flesh, and the instant he swallowed the last of it, his barrel chest heaved and his heart raced feverishly. His dead black eyes widened with excitement and then rolled to the back of his head, revealing only the whites. Every inch of him tingled as his body absorbed the Guardian.

His skin tightened and became exceptionally coarse and durable, almost like armor. He had no words to accurately capture the sensation, but he suddenly felt a strong connection with the ground beneath his feet, as if they had become one. The feeling was familiar. It had happened twice before. After he'd absorbed the

Aquati and Shimmer Guardians, he had felt a fundamental connection with water and fire, respectively. He closed his eyes and stood peacefully. Everything was finally within his and his master's grasp.

With the Guardians finally dead, his thoughts naturally drifted to Phoebe. This was all for her, after all—he owed her that much. The Guardians had been like her children, and she had loved them as such.

But they had a funny way of returning it, Abaddon thought.

Abaddon fancied himself as an ambitious man. His lust for power was innate. Men of such qualities seldom concerned themselves with matters of the heart, but he had loved Phoebe. He had loved her to the fullest capacity of his being. But of all the things love could overcome, death was not one of them. Her Guardians had taken her from him, and as a man of principle, it was only right that he make them pay for their transgressions.

But now that his revenge was complete, the unbearable pain of his loneliness would only subside through the fulfillment of his master Gideon's will. This didn't particularly bother him. Ruling a city in Gideon's new world order was not a horrible way to live out the rest of his days, even if he was alone.

The thoughts of his future kingdom were abruptly interrupted by a fierce gust of wind that knocked him off his feet and into a nearby pillar made of jagged rocks. He collapsed to the ground, stunned. He had crashed into the pillar with such force that it, too, collapsed behind him. Abaddon quickly scooped up his spear, crouched down, and scanned the sky for his attacker.

His battle with the Grindbler Guardian had greatly changed the original terrain. The Guardian had erected several rock pillars of all different sizes, which currently obstructed his view and left him vulnerable. Large chunks of rock were missing from the pillars, which had become projectiles that the Guardian had desperately fired at him. Abaddon had dodged, shattered, or melted many of them, and now rocks of all sizes littered the ground. The Valley of Rolte, which had originally occupied the space, was unrecognizable.

A lifetime ago, he and Phoebe had spent many evenings in the valley. The sky had always been astonishingly clear there. It provided such a breathtaking view of the stars that Abaddon often caught himself wondering how the Creators had crafted something so beautiful. Aela was the Creators' greatest achievement but, as one tends to do, he had grown accustomed to its majesty. The stars allowed his mind to wonder and dream of a place even grander, a place from which the Creators must have come.

"This ends now, Abaddon!" boomed a deep voice from above.

For a moment, Abaddon thought it was Zuriel, and for just a split second, he was scared. His grip on his spear tightened as his mind raced, conjuring ways he might survive this encounter without his master. Abaddon feared nothing Aela had to offer. After absorbing the last Guardian, he had become a god among mortals. Zuriel, however, was a god of gods.

When a giant bird landed on top of the tallest pillar closest to Abaddon, his fear evaporated. He knew who it was. He berated himself for celebrating so early. His work was not yet done.

How could I have possibly forgotten that there were four of them? Abaddon thought. He momentarily admired the Giant Hawk. The species had always fascinated him. He thought the bird had grown even more since the last time he had seen it. He guessed it was roughly fifteen feet tall now. It had a long golden beak and dull red feathers, but when hit by the sun's rays, they glowed like a pulsating fire.

Abaddon watched as a man dismounted the bird. The man leaned over to his pet as if to whisper something in its ear. When the man finished, the bird spread its enormous wings and began to flap busily.

It quickly rose into the sky and disappeared from view. Abaddon watched as the man jumped from the pillar and floated down gracefully to the rocky plain. He now stood ten feet away from him, and several feet away from the dead Guardian.

He was tall and lean, his lanky arms filled with wiry muscles. His face was long and drawn, and his skin was a dark green. He carried no weapons, just like the other Guardians. There was a thin cloth sash that hung from his left shoulder and across his exposed chest.

The gold rings that held his hair in a ponytail caught Abaddon's eye. They shone brilliantly in the sun. A wide gold belt was wrapped tightly around his waist, emphasizing his toned upper and lower body. He wore black harem pants and nothing on his feet.

Abaddon was roughly a head shorter than the Guardian. Like the Guardian, he wore harem pants, but his chest was completely bare. He was also much thicker; his arms were as big as tree trunks. He was a physical wonder, more of a monstrosity than anything. His massive chest, arms, and legs should have made him slow and lumbering, yet he was graceful and agile.

Abaddon's skin was sickly pale, which was made even more evident when compared to the Guardian. On the back of his large bald head was the tattooed head of a dragon. The rest of the dragon's body looped around his shoulders and snaked down to his lower back. His eyes held nothing but contempt.

"Hello, Uri," Abaddon said calmly.

"This will not end well for you," Uri said solemnly.

Abaddon gave a sly smile and asked. "What did you say to your bird up there?"

Uri initially paid no attention to the question. He glanced at his dead brethren, who lay just a few feet away, and shook his head. "What have you done…?"

"What was right. Now tell me, what did you say to your bird?"

"I told her she was free."

"Excellent. At least you had a chance to say your goodbyes. I wasn't as fortunate, but of course, you already knew that. It's funny, I'd forgotten all about you until you threw me into that pillar over there." Abaddon chuckled while gesturing toward the rubble.

"I thought you were dead, Abaddon," Uri said plainly.

"No, just waiting for the right moment to return." Abaddon's smile widened. "I may be wrong, but I'm getting the feeling that you are not thrilled to see me."

Uri glanced once more at the carcass. "Zuriel warned us that the war was not over. That Gideon's forces would rise again. But we didn't believe him. Or maybe we just didn't want to. Now I see that we will pay the highest price for our negligence. Abaddon, believe me, neither Gideon nor the Angelics will ever rule Aela. Aela is free."

Abaddon's smile melted away and was replaced by a nasty scowl. "I see not much has changed. You still take yourself far too seriously. You're nothing more than a puppet and a fool. The fate of Aela is no longer your concern. You took away what was most important to me, and now you will pay with your life!"

"Abaddon…Neither I nor the others ever laid a hand on her. You killed Phoebe."

"Liar!"

With that, Abaddon lunged forward and thrust his spear at Uri's chest, but it hit nothing. Uri was gone. A powerful blast of wind lifted Abaddon into the air and threw him several feet.

He's gotten much faster…I can't even track his movement, Abaddon thought. *How could I have possibly forgotten Uri?*

Uri stood a few feet to the right of where Abaddon had originally been. His right arm was outstretched, his hand spread wide, and it was pointing at Abaddon. Uri's black eyes were now a vibrant green, a few shades lighter than his skin.

As Abaddon rose to one knee, he felt the wind start to pick up at a disturbing rate. Yet despite this, he noticed that Uri's sash and ponytail seemed to move about almost gracefully.

He tried to stand, but a sudden surge of pain shot up his back and he immediately fell again to his right knee. The raging winds that swirled around him had encased him in a dome and gave him only enough space to kneel. The winds were moving so incredibly fast that the dome's walls had become razor-sharp.

Blood oozed down Abaddon's back and pooled around his left leg. Even his new armor-like skin was no match for Uri's power. Adding to his growing list of problems was that the dome was sucking out the little oxygen that was trapped within, forcing Abaddon to take short, shallow breaths.

"I see you have learned a new trick," Abaddon managed to say.

"I learned a lot in your absence," Uri said as he began to walk toward him, his right arm still extended and his eyes still gleaming.

Abaddon chuckled to himself, using up almost all of his air in the process. *Even with all this power, you still never stood a chance,* he thought.

Abaddon placed both of his hands on the ground, his eyes glazed a dull yellow, and he willed it to move. For a split second, Uri's concentration was broken and his eyes returned to their normal black color. The solid earth he had been standing on became quicksand, and his feet slowly sank. Before Uri could regain his concentration, Abaddon was on his feet.

During the seconds Uri's focus was broken, the dome of wind that had trapped Abaddon literally blew away. The mighty winds dispersed and became nothing more than a harmless breeze.

Abaddon held his right hand out to his side; twenty feet away was his spear. The earth it had been resting on rose and raced toward his waiting hand. He grabbed hold of the black handle, which was in the middle of two long blades, and plucked the spear off the levitating piece of earth.

Uri's legs stopped sinking right below the knees as the ground once again became solid. Abaddon plunged one side of his spear into Uri's chest, and his crimson blood erupted from the wound, dousing Abaddon's face. Uri tried to grab hold of Abaddon's arm and retract the spear. Their eyes met as Uri's hands grasped Abaddon's forearm. Uri gave one valiant tug, and the spear began to retreat.

Abaddon looked deep into Uri's eyes, smiled, and whispered, "Goodbye."

His biceps flexed, and Abaddon gave his spear a savage thrust forward. The entire blade passed through Uri, and the spear's black handle rested on his chest. The tip of its blade lightly touched the ground under Uri's back.

Uri uttered a single deep, "Argh…" and fell forever silent. His hands dropped from Abaddon's forearm and hung limply at his side.

Abaddon pulled his spear from the lifeless corpse and dropped it to the ground. If it were not for Uri's feet and shins being submerged in the earth, he would have fallen flat onto his back. Instead, his body just leaned as far back as his current position would allow, bobbing up and down slightly.

The copper smell of Uri's blood drying on Abaddon's face excited him and fueled his bloodlust. He ripped the sash from Uri's shoulder, exposing his chest completely. He extended his right hand. It hovered over Uri's heart. He loved this moment. He loved the harvest. Abaddon shot his arm forward, and his forearm—up to his elbow—was in Uri's chest, his hand protruding out of his back.

A chill ran down his spine as a breeze danced across his fingers, now wet with another Guardian's blood, and in his hand he held the heart of the last one.

He withdrew his arm, causing Uri's body to again bob. He held the heart up to his nose and allowed the aroma to waft into his nostrils. It was intoxicating. He had to taste it. He closed his eyes and savored the scent. Revenge was sweet.

Suddenly, there was a brash voice in his head.

"Finish it!" his master roared.

Abaddon jumped from the vividness of the memory. He was alone in the throne room. It was no surprise that in his solitude the Guardians and Phoebe occupied his thoughts. It had gotten to the point that he didn't remember his life before them.

Gideon had been the one to inform him of the Guardians' plans to murder Phoebe. Their spy in the Zurielian camp, Jadon, had delivered the information. Abaddon had not believed it at first, but Gideon's explanation was sound. The Guardians had learned of Phoebe and his secret romance. Not even her brother knew of their love.

And why should he? He hadn't even known her when they had first met...long before the war...

Abaddon reasoned that the realization must have been brutal. After all the lives he had taken, it must have driven the Guardians mad. Love can only cover so many sins. Even a child's love for its mother has its limits.

Upon receiving Gideon's news, Abaddon raced on the back of Lancaster, his dragon, to inform Phoebe of the impending danger. Her house, more like a fortress, was at the edge of a hidden meadow on the other side of the Dead Forest. It was surrounded by a moat and thick stone walls, the work of the Guardians. He and the Guardians were the only ones privy to the knowledge of its existence.

Sadly, by the time he arrived, the deed had been done. Her body was severely burned and dismembered, no doubt the work of Maria. The sight brought him to his knees and strangled his heart. The agony was beyond comprehension. Tears cascaded down his cheeks and into the blood-soaked grass. He had held her mangled body in his arms and wept.

Abaddon returned to Ira with her remains. Gideon, too, mourned for Phoebe and offered Abaddon a chance at revenge. However, this chance would cost him his will. His life would be forever indebted to Gideon. Abaddon eagerly agreed. He would not hesitate at the chance to avenge his love.

The end of the war was in sight, and it was only a matter of time before Ira fell and Gideon was taken prisoner. So he ordered Abaddon to leave with Lancaster and live in the Terk Mountains until he summoned him again. Abaddon was to keep a strict regimen. He was to train to exhaustion daily and eat only Absolium, no water or meat of any kind.

During his time in Terk, Abaddon was subjected to a level of isolation he never thought possible. To make matters worse, his sole companion, Lancaster, passed away shortly after they arrived. He had finally succumbed to his war wounds.

The first few seasons had been the roughest time of his life. Not only did he have to fend off territorial dragons, but his heart constantly ached and cried out for Phoebe. All the while, his stomach growled for sustenance. It was only his insatiable hunger for revenge that sustained his will to survive and was the only thing that comforted him during the dark and lonely nights.

At first, Abaddon was unsure of how he was supposed to eat Absolium until he watched the dragons feed. The Terk Mountains were rich in the mineral, and deposits were everywhere. When the dragons fed, they would spray a deposit with fire and drink the liquid Absolium. Abaddon would wait until the dragons had their fill and then feed himself. It was bitter and hot, but he found it was best to eat it before it cooled. Amazingly, it did satisfy his hunger and thirst.

In time, Abaddon steadily grew stronger. The dragons ceased to challenge him and instead allowed him to eat with them. They came to respect him and his space. Eventually, his craving for meat and water had completely vanished. The Absolium satisfied all his needs.

Decades passed before he heard from Gideon again, but eventually he did. Gideon was his creator, and his powers were incomprehensible. Even though he had been imprisoned by Zuriel, he was still able to telepathically broadcast messages to Abaddon. Abaddon, however, was unable to respond.

Gideon finally briefed Abaddon on his scheme. First, Abaddon was to recruit a Shimmer named Sophia. Gideon made it clear she was a vital part. When he found Sophia, it hadn't been difficult for him to persuade her. After promising her a life of luxury and leisure as a queen, she was more than willing to play her role. Once she was in the fold, he was to hunt down each of the Guardians, a task Abaddon was more than eager to complete. Yet it was easier said than done.

It was of the utmost importance that he drew them out individually. Confronting them as a unit was certain death. Devising a coherent plan took time, but once implemented it was executed almost flawlessly, except for the minor hiccup with Uri.

The Absolium flowing through his veins made it possible for him to permanently absorb the Guardians' hearts, a feat that would have been impossible before. Their energy would have ripped his body apart, but the Absolium suppressed their abilities to an extent, allowing him to harness their power. His revenge was swift and merciless.

Though the Absolium allowed him to contain the powers of the Guardians, it did nothing for the constant pain. His skin routinely bulged and rippled as the power coursed through his system, searching for an outlet. It was excruciating.

Unfortunately, Abaddon didn't have access to all of the Guardians' abilities, like Maria's mind-wiping capabilities. According to Sophia, that had facilitated the mishap with Uri. But he did have Asa's vast telepathic powers, which he greatly cherished. With them, he was finally able to report freely to his master.

Abaddon smiled. At long last, the night he and his master had anxiously anticipated had finally arrived. After the Ascension Ceremony, he would be one step closer to freeing him.

Suddenly, Abaddon's stroll through his thoughts and memories was interrupted by Leah, who entered the throne room.

"My Lord, it's time."

He gazed affectionately at her. "Of course. Let us go."

Abaddon rose from the throne and approached the doorway. He gave Leah a tender kiss on the forehead before they left.

You would be so proud of her, Phoebe.

He walked down the palace corridor with his daughter.

ASHER (IV)

Asher was at the front of the line. His hood covered his face like the others behind him. They were lined up in the Preparation Room, an appropriately named room where they had spent every day of the last season practicing for the night's events. The name of the ceremony was misleading. They had already ascended on the first day of Instruction. The ceremony was more of a showcase of their abilities.

The Preparation Room was so enormous that it rivaled the Institute's arena. It only lacked the stands for the crowd. It had a sand floor, which was home to numerous hidden traps and snares. After they ascended, the captain had split them into teams, each race represented on every team, another vain attempt to foster unity. They competed in various games and obstacle courses to determine which team would be the first to enter the arena and perform the same tasks in front of the crowd as the class representatives.

Asher's team consisted of ten or fifteen others. He only remembered the names of two: Levi Tolls, a Premier Windwalker, and Gabriel Noles, an Elite Grindbler. They were Zurielians but had managed to make a lasting impression. They had helped him maintain his team's top standing throughout the season, and for that their team would be the first to enter the arena.

Asher stood waiting for the soldier at the door to give him the sign to enter. He heard the others behind him mumbling about what obstacles they might face. Asher looked to the far wall where a few of their old nemeses rested: archer platforms, spike beds, and chains. He shook his head. He knew there would be no real ceremony that night. There was no reason to prepare for *those* obstacles.

The soldier finally waved Asher forward. It was time. Asher's chest pounded with excitement. He marched into the arena, followed by his team and the other teams behind them. The crowd erupted as they trotted proudly across the sand and to the middle of the arena. The noise was deafening. They lined up in twenty rows, each row about ten pupils deep. There were around two hundred of them.

The arena was packed. Asher couldn't see a single

seat that wasn't filled. High walls separated the arena floor from the stands. The stands started at the top of these walls and went to the ceiling.

The ceiling had been removed. It was a task reserved for the Guardians, but Asher knew Abaddon had handled it this year. The Angelics occupied one part of the arena. They were the only group that sat in solidarity. The Zurielians sat together with their own races, but for the most part, they were intermixed.

The sight of the Zurielians made his stomach turn. He couldn't stand the thought of them believing they were of the same ilk. They didn't deserve to sit near his kind. Asher's eyes lingered on the Aquatis sprinkled throughout the crowd. It was always jarring seeing so many in Ira. He assumed they were from Kiro. The ones in Horo never attended.

It was customary for the students to face the Ruler's Box. It was a platform that jutted out of the stands with a canopy that lazily wafted over it. As the name suggested, it was where the rulers of Aela resided.

Asher recognized the occupants easily enough. On the far left of the platform were three Windwalkers: King John and Queen Anna from Tesa, and behind them sat their general, Mikeal Vlask. From Beliel were Queen Candace and her general, Antony. The seats reserved for the Horo representatives were predictably empty. From Rolte was King Malak, and finally, next

301

to him, from Ira was Captain Jadon.

Asher chuckled. *Father won't be attending this year.*

Suddenly, the crowd was again in a frenzy. Asher looked to the entrance and saw the old hag, Sophia, entering the arena. She was followed by a well-dressed Aquati who wore a gold chain around his neck.

"Welcome to this year's Ascension Ceremony!" she broadcasted through the Elite Aquati.

Again, the crowd went nuts, many of them rising to their feet to cheer. She turned in a full circle, waving to every part of the arena. She bowed to the Ruler's Box before she continued.

"Tonight, we officially induct this year's Elite and Premiers to our ranks. They will become full adult members of Aela!"

She beamed and pointed at Asher and the rest. Asher imagined slitting the old woman's throat. The thought soothed him.

She'll be the first one I kill when Abaddon strikes, he thought.

"But before we do that, we must first start this ceremony right!"

She raised both hands above her head, and as she did, the sound of cannons went off. The sky above the arena lit up with light and marvelous designs. The crowd applauded and cheered.

Sky blossoms, Asher thought.

"Let us again thank our Guardians for not only removing the roof so we can enjoy these sky blossoms, but for the peace they have allowed us to enjoy all these years." Sophia raised her hands and applauded. The crowd followed suit.

Sophia tugged at her own silver chain. *"I remember when I received this, in this very building, many years ago. I can speak from experience that this will be a special night for all involved."*

Sophia pointed at the pupils. *"It is customary that tonight, the team with the highest score during Instruction demonstrates their mastery of their abilities before us, and then each of these young men and women receives a gold or silver chain signifying their class. However, this year's ceremony will be a little different. Before we award each of these children with their ascension chains, I would like to introduce an old friend."*

Sophia pointed to the door, and out stepped an uncloaked Abaddon.

The arena fell deathly silent, and at first, Asher, too, was confused. *How does she know?* he thought. The answer was so obvious that Asher couldn't believe he hadn't put it together before. The empty chair in the throne room was Sophia's.

Might not be able to kill her after all…at least not yet, he thought.

Abaddon was followed by a group of soldiers that was dragging a pair of Windwalkers and a pair of Grindblers. Abaddon reached Sophia and waved his hand slightly, signaling her to step aside. Asher had never seen Abaddon without a cloak. His body was massive, unnaturally so, not so much in height but girth. His spine stuck out from his back, each vertebra visible. A dragon tattoo started from his bald head and slithered its way down and around his erected spine. His double-bladed spear clung to its holster on his irregular back. His legs were covered by black silk harem pants, and his large feet were bare on the sandy floor.

"Welcome to the new Aela!" he broadcasted. He raised his fists into the air.

Asher looked to the Ruler's Box in time to see Jadon rise to his feet and jam an Absolium dagger into the jugular of the Grindbler King. He went immediately limp. The others in the Ruler's Box turned to respond, but it was too late. The Angelic soldiers that had been stationed at the box had been the proud recipients of Elite Windwalker hearts. Without the proper training in tracking such fast movements, it would have been impossible to have seen what unfolded.

Asher fortunately had received such training. Following the Grindbler King's death, King John un-sheathed his sword, his eyes glazing green, but before he could move, a spear erupted through his chest. The Angelic soldier, whose eyes too glazed green, twisted his spear and jerked it out savagely.

Another king fell. The queen and general of Tesa were next. The general's head was removed with such vigor that it landed on the arena's floor in front of Asher.

The soldier who had killed King John dropped his spear and snapped the queen's neck before her eyes were able to change color. Jadon quickly dispatched Queen Candace with a fatal chest wound.

Asher watched Angelic soldiers stream into the arena from every entrance. Many of them had glazing red eyes. Each was armed with Absolium-tipped spears and Absolium swords.

The Zurielians were on their feet, and the ones with weapons drew them. But what had happened in the Ruler's Box gave them pause, enough so to give the Angelic soldiers the upper hand. Asher smiled, re-moved his hood, and went to stand next to Abaddon.

"Zurielians...I am Abaddon, general of Lord Gideon's army. The time has come for the façade to end. We are the chosen race of Aela, and you are not fit to live amongst us! You are not fit to even breathe the same air as us! You are to serve and bow before us!"

Abaddon turned to the prisoners behind him. The pair of Windwalkers and Grindblers were chained and on their knees. Absolium collars hung from their necks. Abaddon tugged at the male Windwalker's collar. In an act of defiance, the Windwalker spat on Abaddon's feet. Abaddon slapped him to the ground.

"For all who wish to join the new order, you will be issued an Absolium collar. Those who oppose, like these few here, will suffer a similar fate."

Asher felt the temperature suddenly rise, and he knew what was coming. Abaddon held both hands in front of him as intense streams of fire erupted from his palms and engulfed the four Zurielians. Their screams filled the silent arena. The smell of burning flesh was inescapable. Asher's eyes danced with the flames and the squirming bodies they consumed.

Abaddon lowered his hands. Only charred remains lay before him. The Windwalker bodies were indistinguishable from one another. One of the body's legs clung to its hips by a few remaining tendons. The other was a crumpled mess. There was no telling the head from the feet.

Asher was surprised to see how well the Grindbler bodies held up in comparison. He was even more surprised when the larger one still moved. Abaddon brought his spear down on the Grindbler's neck and twisted. Its head shot from its body like a cork.

306

Abaddon looked around the arena. *"No one is coming to your rescue. The Guardians are no more. Your fate is in your hands. The choice is yours. Drop your weapons if you wish to join us!"*

Asher looked to his peers that had walked in with him. Their hoods were no longer covering their heads. Fear and disgust were the most common expressions. Many of them were bent over, throwing up. The smell of burning flesh was repugnant. Two of his team-mates, Levi Tolls and Gabriel Noles, approached Asher and bowed before him.

I knew I liked them, he thought.

However, before he could properly address them, something else caught his eye. It was a girl. She was sprinting toward them, dagger in hand, but her eyes were not focused on him. They were focused on Sophia.

For a moment, he didn't recognize her. But only for a moment.

"Ruth!" he screamed.

All attention on the arena floor shifted to the sprinting girl. Abaddon flicked his wrist, and a sudden furious gust of wind sent her flying back toward the entrance. She landed hard against the wall and didn't move to get up.

Asher looked in the direction of Sophia and Abaddon. Four arrows came sailing from the stands,

307

all four striking Sophia. One hit her in the head, one pierced her neck, and two landed between her shoulder blades. She collapsed to the ground, motionless.

Asher, Abaddon, and the soldiers on the arena floor scanned the stands to find the archer. Asher wasn't mad over Sophia's death. Quite the opposite, he might even allow the archer to live as a reward, but that would be decided after he was caught. Asher had no plans of being the archer's next victim. Again, his train of thought was interrupted, but this time by a slender, silver-haired Windwalker who stood at the entrance to the arena floor, holding what looked like two swords.

"We will FIGHT!" he shouted.

REUEL (X)

Tears ran freely down Reuel's cheeks. His grip on his swords continued to tighten as he replayed his parents' deaths. He had wanted to move when Abaddon dragged them into the arena, but Daniel had held him back.

"Reuel, you mustn't do anything," Daniel had said.

"Are you insane? He is going to kill them!" Reuel responded.

"And he will kill you, too, if you go out there…Stick to the plan, wait until Sophia is dead."

Daniel was right. He watched and did nothing as his parents burned and screamed, but they never yelled for help. Reuel had already dispatched the guard stationed at the arena's entrance with little effort, and his friends were spread across the arena, all of them waiting for Sophia to fall before they pounced. So there was no one around to see him as he sat alone and cried.

DANIEL (VI)

No one could fathom Daniel's pain. He watched as the man who had killed his sister, Phoebe, and the love of his life and mother of his children, Maria, orchestrate the assassination of his eldest daughter. Candace died never knowing him as her father.

No, no one knew Daniel's pain, and he wouldn't have had it any other way. He wanted no sympathy. He had a job to do. The lives of Eve and the other Guardians were now in his hands. He got up and raced from the Institute.

REUEL (XI)

As Ruth flew through the air toward the wall, Reuel simultaneously said to Azriel, *"Now! While all their attention is on her!"*

He watched as four arrows arched high into the night sky and fell through Sophia's head, neck, and back. As she fell, Reuel rose and entered the arena.

"I know it hurts, but use the pain and anger to push through Sophia's force field! It can no longer hold us!" Azriel broadcasted.

There was no more time for Reuel to be unsure. He would no longer be helpless. With tears streaking down his face, his parents in piles of ash at Abaddon's feet, and all of Ira's Zurielians staring on hopelessly, Reuel shouted.

"We will FIGHT!"

His eyes glazed. He allowed his anger and anguish free rein. They washed over him and pushed him. He was nearing the point where he had never passed, and he burst through.

The feeling was one that his vocabulary couldn't capture. All limitations disappeared. His presence was bigger than his body, as if his body could no longer contain his essence. He was connected to the still air that filled the arena, the light breeze that moved along the streets of Ira, and the gusts of wind that pushed and pulled the Baron Sea.

It was all him. He had ascended.

Reuel charged forward, and the Zurielians in the arena came alive. They raised their weapons and attacked the Angelic soldiers. The soldiers around Abaddon sprinted to meet Reuel, but he was far too fast. Even those whose eyes also glazed green moved in slow motion to him. He easily dogged their blows and sent his swords into their abdomens. He summoned heavy gusts of wind to push their lifeless bodies aside and continued his march toward Abaddon.

From Reuel's perspective, the battle raged sluggishly around him. It was chaos. He saw Eve near the top of the arena—*five* Eves, to be precise—a couple of whom shot jets of fire while others battled with their ring blades. Azriel was near the Ruler's Box, firing an arrow at an Angelic that was being juggled on a geyser of water. Elon was on the opposite side of Eve, also near the top. He was in the midst of bringing his hammer down on the head of a fallen Angelic soldier. Reuel looked for Daniel but to no avail.

Reuel was now passing the pupils who were fighting amongst themselves. Some lay dead already. Many battled with their bare hands. He saw Asher holding the end of a sword that was protruding through the back of a Shimmer girl.

At last, Reuel stood before the pale man from his nightmares, and there was no fear in his heart.

"You have ascended," Abaddon said.

"I have. This ends now."

Abaddon licked his lips. "Interesting, your predecessor said the same thing. It didn't work out particularly well for him, as I remember."

Reuel's fury exploded. "YOU WILL PAY FOR WHAT YOU HAVE DONE!"

He summoned an enormous gale-force wind that rocketed from the open sky above the arena and down to the arena floor. It took even Abaddon by surprise, forcing him to drop his spear. The gale scattered everyone on the arena floor, throwing them every which way. It lifted the massive Angelic and slammed him into the arena wall.

Reuel continued to assault Abaddon with hit after hit, keeping him off balance and pushing him deeper and deeper into the wall. However, Reuel could feel his energy quickly draining.

"You're not used to it, are you? It's quite a toll, isn't!" Abaddon broadcasted. *"You won't last much longer, and then it's my turn!"*

Reuel began to panic. Abaddon was right. He couldn't keep this up for long.

But it was then he heard Daniel's voice in his head. *"Everyone get to the arena floor! I'm on my way."*

"It's all clear for you," Reuel responded, quickly scanning the floor to make sure he was still the only one standing. He saw Asher attempting to get up but fall once again after the next gale passed through the arena and slammed Abaddon even farther into the wall.

"We're on our way," Elon responded.

A loud screech came from overhead. Reuel lifted his gaze to see a Giant Hawk carrying Daniel. It swooped down and landed near him. Daniel jumped off and looked around.

"Impressive, Reuel, very impressive."

"I can't keep it up," Reuel strained to say.

"You won't have to for long," Daniel said.

"We need to go now!" Elon shouted as he jumped down from the wall separating the stands from the floor. He waved his hand over his shoulder, causing a small earthquake and forcing the Angelics and a few Zurielians chasing him to lose balance and fall.

Eve and Azriel sprinted through the entrance to the arena floor. A couple of Eve's projections carried an unconscious Ruth. They were trailed closely by a group of soldiers.

Azriel turned and began waving his hands in front of him as if rubbing a ball. Slowly, a blue orb formed and grew steadily. As the ball increased in size, his hands spread farther apart. Once his arms were fully spread and the orb was roughly the size of his own body, he fired it at the charging soldiers. It morphed into a wave of water and washed the soldiers off their feet.

"Get on top of Gale!" Daniel ordered.

They did as they were told and climbed onto the Giant Hawk. Eve's projections disappeared, and Elon carried Ruth. Reuel stood beside the bird and continued to usher blast after blast of wind through the arena and into Abaddon.

Daniel grabbed Reuel's shoulder. "You have to get on Gale. You won't be able to hold him much longer, and you're in no condition to face him when he comes out of there."

"One more hit," Reuel hissed. He used the last of his energy to summon one more explosive blast, which sent Abaddon into the wall with such force it sent tremors through the entire Institute.

Reuel then squeezed onto the top of Gale. He sat nearest to her head and was followed by Elon, who carried Ruth, Eve, and then Azriel.

"Daniel, where are you going to fit?" Reuel asked, even though he already knew the answer.

"Gale, go!" Daniel shouted.

The Giant Hawk took off and soared out of the arena, leaving Daniel behind on its sandy floor.

ASHER (V)

Asher struggled to his feet. His vision was blurry and his head was throbbing. He could barely make out the outline of the monstrous bird that was flapping overhead. By the time his vision cleared, the bird was gone.

For the most part, things had gone as planned. The minor hiccup caused by his sister and her friends had not disrupted things too much. They suffered a few casualties, including Sophia, but Asher was not going to lose any sleep over that. Their plan had been a success. They had taken complete control of Ira and had killed most of the rulers of Aela. Only the Aquati Queen remained.

The Angelic soldiers were rounding up the last of the resistance in the stands while he, Gabriel, and Levi handled the ones on the arena floor.

Out of the corner of his eye, Asher saw Abaddon emerge from the hole in the arena's wall. Asher wasn't the only one to notice this. An old Aquati man charged Abaddon as soon as he was clear from the wall. Abaddon didn't break stride and sent him sprawling with a flick of his wrist. He strolled to the arena's entrance without saying a word, at least verbally.

"Don't forget to collar that Aquati, Asher." Abaddon left the arena.

Asher wasted no time. He grabbed a collar from off the ground and locked it around the old man's neck.

"You're a brave old man, I'll give you that. But look where that's gotten you."

Asher slapped him across the face with the hilt of his sword. The old man dropped back to the floor, coughing up blood and teeth.

"Good luck healing with that collar around your neck," Asher laughed.

He then planted successively savage kicks into the old man's back, relishing in his screams of agony. At last, he bent down to the old man's ear.

"We're going to have a lot of fun together."

REUEL (XII)

The Guardians soared above the Institute. Reuel watched the Angelics firmly take the upper hand and force the surviving Zurielians into collars. They flew over the flaming outskirts while its residents marched from the burning wreck, escorted by Angelic soldiers who were led by a blonde-haired woman. Reuel's eyes again burned, thinking of Zachariah. From behind him, he heard Elon whisper, "Aaron."

They had all lost loved ones.

Gale flew out of Ira and over the Baron Sea. They flew all night in silence as they mourned the dead and wallowed in their shared failure. As sunrise arrived, Gale landed in the Meadows of Tesa. They dismounted and sat at her feet, allowing themselves to rest for the first time in days.

Reuel took Ruth from Elon and held her. She was breathing faintly. Without saying a word, Azriel scooted next to Reuel and placed his hands on Ruth. His eyes glazed blue as he healed her wounds.

"Thank you," Reuel managed to say.

"Of course," Azriel responded.

"What do we do now?" Eve asked.

"I don't know," Reuel answered, almost whispering it.

"It's just beginning," Ruth answered, opening her eyes. She struggled to get to her feet and then looked out into the distance.

"Beginning?!" Elon exclaimed. "If you didn't notice, we lost. My family's dead. Daniel is gone. We got beat down by everyone but Abaddon, who is supposedly the one we need to worry about."

"We were never going to win," Ruth answered. "You just needed to ascend and make it out of there alive. We did that."

"Explain," Azriel said, irritated.

Ruth pointed at an approaching figure. "I was sent by him to bring you here. Daniel was never coming with us. Gale can only carry so many people at once. He knew how it would end before we attacked the Institute."

No one responded at first. "Who is that?" Reuel finally asked.

"You will see," Ruth said.

They waited as the figure drew closer. It wasn't long before an old man stood before them. He had long white hair and a bushy white beard. Wrinkles ran rampant across his olive-skinned face, but even in his advanced age, he radiated life. He wore a ragged gray robe and leaned on the walking stick in his left hand.

Ruth bowed. "Hello, Zuriel."

The others stared, eyes wide.

"Well done, Ruth," Zuriel answered. He turned his gaze on the Guardians. His eyes were filled with love.

Reuel's heart soared and was enveloped in warmth. Zuriel's stare reminded him of how his parents had looked at him.

"My Guardians, I have failed you and your predecessors. I should have ended this long ago, but now you will have to do it for me. I know of the travesties you have witnessed, and my heart weeps for you, but we cannot change what already is. It pains me to tell you that I fear this will get far worse before it's over. But, my children, do not be discouraged. This war is only in its infancy. Now, follow me. We will begin your training."

Zuriel turned and walked back the way he had come. Reuel rose to his feet without saying a word and followed. The others fell in line. Elon followed next, trailed by Eve, Azriel, and Ruth. With the morning-light's sun in their faces, they crossed the meadow with their creator.

ABOUT THE AUTHOR

R.S. Veira is an author, director, and dreamer. He is currently writing, directing, and dreaming at Dream With Me Productions in Los Angeles, California. To learn more about R.S. Veira and his writing, visit him at rsveira.com.